Adrian Caesar is the author of three books of literary and cultural criticism and an experimental non-fiction novel, *The White,* (Picador) which won the Victorian Premier's Award for non-fiction in 2000 and the ACT Book of the Year, 2000. He has also published six volumes of poetry, the latest of which is *This Cathedral Grief* (Recent Work Press, 2020). His novel, *The Blessing* (Arcadia, 2015), was longlisted for the Voss Literary Award in 2016.

A Winter Sowing

Other books by Adrian Caesar include:

The White, (Picador) winner of the Victorian Premier's Award for non-fiction in 2000 and the ACT Book of the Year, 2000.

The Blessing (Arcadia, 2015), longlisted for the Voss Literary Award in 2016.

This Cathedral Grief (Recent Work Press, 2020).

A Winter Sowing

One man's quest for redemption
through art and love.

ADRIAN CAESAR

ARCADIA

ARCADIA

Published in 2021 by ARCADIA
the international general books' imprint of
Australian Scholarly Publishing Pty Ltd

Australian Scholarly Publishing Ltd
7 Lt Lothian St Nth, North Melbourne, VIC 3051
Tel: 03 9329 6963 / Fax: 03 9329 5452
enquire@scholarly.info / www.scholarly.info

Cataloguing-in-Publication details are available
from the National Library of Australia
www.trove.nla.gov.au

ISBN: 978-1-922454-99-7 (print)
ISBN: 978-1-922669-18-6 (ebook)

Cover design and typesetting, Luke Harris, WorkingType Studio
Text: Ten Oldstyle

For Ellen and Ben

More important than a work of art itself is what it will sow. Art can die, a painting can disappear. What counts is the seed.

Joan Miró

The love of gardening is a seed once sown that never dies.

Gertrude Jeckyll

I

David Young is on his knees in the small bedroom he uses as a makeshift studio. It's the room with the most light in his third-storey housing commission unit on the outskirts of Canberra's city centre—the area known as Civic. Autumnal afternoon sunshine radiates through the windows, making David sweat as he works, but it doesn't bother him. The physical rhythm soothes and absorbs him. The smell of turps and oil paint is intoxicating. It's the scent of his work and his survival. He's priming a new canvas, working the gesso in with a broad brush, creating the blank white rectangle which will become the next challenge to his dubious gift.

For now, he's not thinking of success or failure. Around the room he's propped his previous efforts on the floor, their faces to the wall. He's sick of seeing them. He can't sell them and has nowhere else to store them. David loves everything else in the room—the paint-stained easel, the old mugs full of brushes, the lids of empty ice-cream cartons he uses as palettes, the bottles of turps and primer, the tubes of paint—all these are the familiar paraphernalia of his rediscovered passion.

But he doesn't want to get carried away with himself. He wishes to avoid self-delusion. And so it's good, he thinks, to be surrounded by stern reminders that passion is only the beginning of art. Technique demands labour. He consoles himself with the idea that each new attempt can be nothing but a step forward. Another assertion of the self in the face of fear and darkness. He thinks of treading through the jungle in Vietnam. Different orders of fear and darkness.

David registers pain in his knees and the muscles in his forearms as he applies pressure to the brush. In a minute he'll have to take a break—stretch, prowl the room—but he's anxious not to make the application uneven. It would be best if he could finish the first coat in one go.

He's glad he refused to march. Glad that today is about this making.

His mates, Glen and Marty, came round yesterday. He only sees them once or twice a year these days. Glen has moved down the coast with his third missus; Marty lives alone in an old weatherboard on the outskirts of Bungendore. All they have in common is Vietnam. Which is more than enough to ensure you can get thoroughly pissed together and pledge your undying loyalty, mateship, brotherhood. But it isn't enough, David knows, to get him through each day. He's learned that's something he has to do for himself.

Anyway, they came round. Had beers, then bourbon. The usual laughs, remembering wild times on leave in Vung Tau. David played along: rolling smokes, downing the booze, oiling the camaraderie. However embarrassing, however juvenile it seemed, they called each other by their nicknames. There was no escaping this regression to young manhood. No escaping how in Vietnam they'd grown old together before their time.

In the army, Glen had been known as Hooter, because of his large and badly broken nose, the result of pub fights and football. Marty was a conventional 'Bluey' in deference to his sandy red hair. David was 'Youngey' for obvious reasons. Their talk took on a nostalgic intimacy. It was only when Glen and Marty, fuddled by drink, started to try to persuade him to go on the march that David dug his heels in. Refused.

'You've got to be in it, mate. Why not? It's about pride in what we done.' Hooter stabbed home his point with the cigarette between his fingers.

'If you can't do it for us, do it for the blokes who didn't come back. I mean, it's about remembering them.' Bluey with the reinforcements, splashing more booze into their glasses.

David clenched his jaw. He raised his glass in salute and drained it in one. 'Time to go home, boys,' he said. 'I'm not arguing, and I'm not marching. End of story.'

They heard his tone. Muttered and grumbled but backed off. As David ushered them out the door and along the concrete walkway, he called after them, 'I'll be thinking of you tomorrow. Have a good one.'

¢

At least that's a promise David's kept.

He grits his teeth as he works towards the edge of the canvas. He thinks about the idea he has for the painting, but then tells himself off; he doesn't want to kill the work before it's begun. He heard a painter, someone famous, he can't remember who, once say, 'Let the painting paint itself.' That's what he thinks he should let happen. That's maybe the problem with everything he's done so far. Too abstract, too cerebral. Too self-conscious. He's talked to his counsellor about this. After all, it was Donna who suggested he go back to painting. She said it didn't matter about that stuff. To do the work was the important thing. 'Please yourself,' she'd said. But David knows he also wants to please others. Pleasing yourself doesn't seem enough.

A sharp, anxious knocking on his front door jolts David from his thoughts. He pauses in his work, aware now that perhaps there's been a previous gentler knock which in his reverie he's ignored. He swears to himself as he lays his brush on the drop sheet and clambers to his feet, his knees clicking as he straightens. He only has a tiny bit of the canvas to go, and isn't expecting anyone. David hates that his solitude is to be interrupted. He hopes it's not Glen and Marty coming over half-pissed for round two.

'Wait on,' he shouts as he moves through the flat, wiping his hands on an old rag. He always keeps the door locked. That way he can't be surprised.

The door opens into the tiny living area of the flat. A narrow kitchenette is separated from the lounge and dining area by a waist-high counter. The place is untidy. The idea of a stranger seeing it makes him tense.

He opens up to find his sixteen-year-old daughter, Josie, standing there. She's wearing a black quilted jacket with the hood up and black jeans with frayed rips at the knee and thigh. Her stance is hunched, as if she's cold, despite the sunshine. She's stuffing the earphones from her Walkman into her pocket.

David tries to hoist a welcoming smile onto his face, but he feels himself failing.

'Why are you wearing that hood? And what's with the hole in your strides?' he says, trying to keep the irritation out of his voice.

'It's good to see you too, Pa.' She leans up to him and kisses his cheek. 'It's called a fashion statement. You wouldn't understand.'

He moves aside and lets her into the flat. She pulls the hood down as she walks past him. David's heart lurches at the sight of her auburn brown hair with its natural curls, just like her mother's.

'Jesus, Dad, this place is a mess. Why does it always feel as if you're camping? Couldn't you, at least, like, unpack?' She kicks at a couple of cardboard boxes, one stuffed with yellowing papers, old photos, notebooks; the other holds pots and pans that he's never got round to using.

David fills the kettle. 'Tea? Coffee?'

'It stinks in here. Can't you open a window?'

'For Christ's sake, Jo-Jo, give it a rest.' He watches as she wrinkles her nose and sniffs melodramatically.

'There's the usual stale beer and tobacco, sweaty armpits, sour milk and ...' she pauses for effect, performing a little pirouette, '... something else, something that might be quite good if it weren't for the other smells. I know. You've been painting again. Can I have a look this time? Please, Dad?'

'No, no, no, there's nothing to see. I've just been priming a canvas. It's a blank rectangle.' He moves round the counter to make sure Josie doesn't disobey him. 'Sit down there and don't move.' He indicates the battered brown velvet sofa he bought courtesy of a Vinnies op shop.

'God, must I? These jeans are clean.'

'Clean but torn. Excellent. Sit.' He takes her by the shoulders and pushes her onto the couch. 'Tea or coffee?'

'Have you got real coffee?'

'Only pretend.'

'I'll have tea.'

'Since when did you join the yuppy set?'

'Since I grew up. Since I went to college. Since I go to Manuka for coffee with my sophisticated friends.'

'Jesus.'

'What are you going to paint?'

David doesn't answer immediately. He pours boiling water onto tea bags in two tannin stained thick white mugs. He slops milk in from a carton and adds the teaspoon of sugar he knows Josie has in her tea. Stirs.

'Look,' he says, as he carries a mug to Josie, 'I can't talk about my painting. It stuffs everything up if I talk about it. I don't know why.'

Josie grimaces as she gingerly accepts the tea. 'You could at least take the bag out.'

'I don't know how strong you like it. Here, put the bag in that.' He gestures towards an ashtray full of butts on the side table next to the sofa.

'Charming.'

There's a silence. David pulls up a chair opposite Josie. It's made of grey painted metal and plastic and goes with the battered formica topped dining table, which stands against the far wall, also courtesy of Vinnies. He begins to roll a smoke, the paper suspended from his upper lip as he takes the tobacco from the pouch.

'I wish you wouldn't do that,' Josie says, sulky now. 'And look at all these grog bottles. I thought you were supposed to be going easy on the booze.'

'Give me a break, Jose. I am going easy on the booze. My mates were round here yesterday. We had a few drinks. Okay?'

He lights up, inhales, blows smoke rings. When she was a little girl, Josie used to love it when he did that. Now she sits and stares at him, exasperated.

'Can I have a ciggy, then?' she says, a mischievous glint in her eyes.

'No, you can't. You'll keep right away from them and any other drugs.'

'It's do as I say, not do as I do.'

'Too bloody right, it is.'

Another silence. David smokes. Scratches his cheek. Josie sips her tea, eyes down.

'So,' David begins. 'It's been a while. Everything all right?'

'All right.'

'School?'

'College. Yeah. Good.'

'BB?'

Josie rolls her eyes. 'Same as usual. Trying to be my best mate and failing dismally.'

David chuckles. BB is their code for 'Boring Barry King'—Josie's mother's not quite live-in boyfriend.

'What about your mum?'

'She's okay. Busy, busy. You know. No time. Must get on.'

'Your love life, then?'

'Haven't got one.'

'Is that a problem?'

'No way.'

'Money. You need some cash?'

'Oh yeah. Like you've got a few thousand to spare. No, Dad. I'm still doing the supermarket at weekends and I hit BB every time I can. I'm doing well in that department.'

David is aware of the conversation hitting a wall. He's out of options. He leans forward and stubs out his smoke. He sits and listens to the quietness settle, wondering why it's so difficult to talk to the person he cares most about in the world.

Josie drinks her tea. David sees she feels as awkward as he does. After a while, she stands and takes her cup into the kitchenette. He watches her clanking yesterday's dirty dishes into the sink. She wrestles with the taps. He's turned them off tight to stop them from dripping. The washers are shot.

'Leave that. I'll sort it,' he says.

'I can do it.'

'I know you *can* do it. I just don't *want* you to do it.'

'I want to help.'

'I don't need any help.'

Josie triumphs over the taps. She squirts in dishwashing liquid. Takes her jacket off and pushes her sleeves up. David sighs. He rolls another smoke. Finishes his tea. Thinks about the corner of his canvas left unprimed.

Josie has her back to him, washing up. On the windowsill in front of her are a few tomatoes, knobbly and green. 'Are these the last from the community garden?' she asks, not turning round.

'Yeah. Always pick the last before Anzac Day. Usually coincides with the first frost.'

'What will you do with them? Make chutney?'

'Don't think there's enough. Anyway, I don't know how to make it.'

'I could come round and help.'

'There we go with the *help* again. I'm not an invalid.'

'I know. I was just saying.'

The jangle of the crockery as Josie works grates against David's nerves. He tries to calm down. Concentrates on his smoke.

When Josie speaks again, her voice is taut and deliberate with the effort, her eyes set on the kitchen window above the sink, her arms straight in the water.

'I came round because it's ... well, you know ... it's *today*. I wanted to tell you how proud I am of you. Of what you did.' Her voice wavers and wobbles.

Josie's words trigger involuntary memories. Jagged images of blood and flayed flesh roar into David's mind. He covers his eyes with his hands and shakes his head as if to banish the flashback. 'Oh, no, Jose. No, no, no. I'm not having any of that. You don't know what I did.'

He takes his hands from his face in time to see her head go down. 'Jesus, Josie,' he says. 'Don't buy into it. All that stuff in the papers and on TV. All written and filmed by people who have no idea. What did I do? Nothing to be proud of, for Christ's sake.'

Josie wipes her nose on the back of her hand, then sneezes and swears as she inhales soapsuds. She looks round for tissues, but there are none.

David goes into the tiny bathroom and comes back with some toilet paper. He hands it to her, awkwardly patting her shoulder. She shrugs him off and turns back to the sink.

'I wanted you to know,' Josie stops and breathes. 'I wanted you to know that I've thought about everything and how it makes me feel very ...' She begins to weep again.

'Don't you get it, Josie? I don't want you to think about it. I want you to forget it. There's no point thinking about it.'

Josie pulls the plug out. She turns to him with her wet hands, tears smearing her cheeks. 'How can I *not* think about it?' She begins to wipe her hands on her jeans.

'Oh, shit.' David goes to the bathroom, finds a grubby-looking hand towel and more toilet tissue.

As she dries her face and blows her nose, David begins to pace up and down the lounge room, trying to control his agitation, hoping Josie has finished with the subject he most wants to avoid. But to his dismay, she's determined to go on. She follows him into the lounge.

'You can't keep treating me like a little kid. What happened to you in the war seems like the answer to everything. That's why you and Mum split up, isn't it? Your drinking and depression and everything? That's what Mum always says. But when I ask her what happened to you, she goes all vague and says she doesn't know. You can't blame me for wanting to know. I want to understand why my family isn't a real family.'

David rubs his forehead repeatedly with his fingers. He goes to his daughter and grips her by the shoulders. 'I know this is hard for you,' he says. 'And I'm sorry for that. But we have to deal with what is, not what has been or what might have been. It's no good dwelling on the past. It's gone. Over. Finished. It doesn't matter how many Anzac Days you have or how many pious words are spoken. We have to move on. I'm trying to. I want you to move on as well.'

'I need to know what happened to you so that I *can* move on.'

'No, you don't. You need to accept who I am *now*. That's all. If I did start trying to tell you about Vietnam, it would just be stories. Some old bloke spinning yarns. There are no words for it. Do you understand? No words for it.'

'I don't believe you.' Josie pulls away from him. She grabs her coat and begins to put it on. 'You could tell me if you wanted to, if you trusted me. If I was a boy you'd tell me. I bet Grandad told you. You're always shutting me out. You won't even let me see your paintings. You're always shoving me away.'

'It's not like that, Josie. I can't tell you anything. I've got nothing to say.'

'Well, neither have I then,' she shouts at him as she heads for the door.

'Don't go. Don't leave like this!'

But it's too late. She's through the door and slams it behind her. He follows. Opens the door, shouts after her, but she's already off down the stairs. He thinks about chasing her but runs out of energy.

He goes back inside, slumps on the chair and rolls a smoke. He sits there cursing under his breath, feeling sick.

After a while, he goes back into the room where his canvas is drying. He looks at the unfinished corner. He thinks about finishing it, but he hasn't the heart. Instead, defeated, he goes back to the kitchen and pulls a quarter-full bottle of Jim Beam from the cupboard. He pours a slug into a tumbler and drinks.

'Happy bloody Anzac Day. Here's to remembering and forgetting,' he says to himself.

II

David wakes in the middle of the night. At first, he thinks he's back in Vietnam. It takes him a moment to realise he's at home, lying fully clothed on the camp stretcher that serves as his bed. The feel of his mouth, as if he's chewed sand, reminds him. The bourbon. Listening to cassettes in his old player. The Stones, Frankie J, all the old blues. Remembering the boozer at Nui Dat. Drinking himself to sleep. He looks at his watch. It's 4.00 am—the hour when sick people die. He can't remember where he read that useful piece of information.

Lying awake—staring at the dark—isn't an option. It gives him the terrors. Reminds him of picquet duty on the gun, hyper-alert, staring into the J, watching the fireflies dance and imagining VC out there, intent on killing him.

He struggles out of his cot.

Not dead yet.

Still, the cold is so fierce he thinks he could be returning from the grave. He hugs himself as he rushes into the kitchen, lights the gas, sticks the kettle on. While he's waiting for it to boil, he takes two Panadol with a pint of water, then gets the fan heater going in his painting room. He seldom thinks of it as his 'studio'. Too pretentious, as well as tempting fate. Those too far up themselves achieve nothing. Another Christmas cracker motto he remembers from somewhere.

He has to finish priming the canvas. After a few sips of scalding tea, he gets to work, cursing the stiffness in his knees, the fur on his tongue. As he works the gesso in, he tries not to think about the previous day, the misery of Josie's visit and her abrupt departure. He pushes the guilt away, says to himself he'll deal with it tomorrow. There's nothing to be done now. Now is the time to enjoy the silence and stillness, the magic of the night, the feeling of being enclosed in his own world beyond intrusion.

It doesn't take long for him to cover the last corner of the canvas. He lifts it onto the easel to dry. He'd like to start painting, but he knows he must wait for the whole canvas to be ready. Though he could start in the opposite corner, he's superstitious about the process. Every step has its mystique. He must be patient, wait for the moment.

Instead, he takes up a drawing block and pencil. He sits in the battered armchair which, along with a stool, is the only furniture in the room, and begins to sketch studies for the painting he has in mind. A man staggering forward out of the darkness, carrying in his arms the limp body of another man. He wants them to be anonymous figures, archetypal. Brothers. One dead, one alive. In an attitude of tenderness. The scene as he wished it could have been. How he imagines it should have been.

Not the brutality of how it was.

Images come back to him, a fragmentary narrative unspooling through his wounded mind. It was only their second operation; the second walk in the jungle: welcome to the Long Green. They bivouacked for the night. Exhausted with heat and fear, the endless peering through whispering foliage, the creak and groan of insects and creatures, the smell of rot, trying to stay alert for movement, for human scent. Their greens dark with sweat so they looked like black pyjamas.

That's where it all went wrong. Billy the Kid. A strung-out youngster behind a big gun. The clearance patrol sent out, lost sight of. Billy sees movement, hears sounds from the wrong direction. Glimpses black. Opens fire. A long cry. Not Vietnamese. Another voice shouting, 'Cease fire! Stop! Friendly!' The sickening realisation through the harbour position. The way they dragged the body in. David's mate, Jez. Gone. Beyond help. His face shot away. What language was there for that? His friend. His comrade. Unrecognisable. They'd become like brothers, going through training together. The bloke who made it all bearable.

And Billy the Kid, nineteen years old, rocking with his back against a tree, pale-faced and gibbering. 'No, no, no, oh shit, oh shit, oh shit,' his voice becoming louder as the tears began and hysteria set in.

'Shut up, soldier,'—this from the sergeant—'someone look after him, for Christ's sake. And keep him quiet. Hit him if you have to.'

The looey, McMaster, said they couldn't call in a chopper until dawn. Ordered them to cover the body with a poncho. Said they had to move, reposition, in case the enemy had heard the shots. They obeyed. In shock. There were no words. David was numb. Frozen. Couldn't afford to feel. Couldn't afford the gestures he now wishes he had made. Wished he could have held his friend. Carried his mate with dignity, instead of the rough manhandling and the winching into the helicopter the following morning. Billy the Kid went too. Nerve gone. Never saw him again.

Sunshine and shadow, jungle sounds, the constant whirring of insects, and the steady *whump whump* of the chopper. Coming to take them away. There and then gone. Sudden and irrevocable. Loss. Like hitting a wall. But you had to keep going. The operation went on. Treading through the J. A slow-motion ballet in big boots, trying for silence, stepping delicately for fear of mines. The dead forgotten in the fear and anxiety to stay alive.

Now, as the dawn begins to stain the light, shifting the electric yellow with its paler grey, David realises he's tired. He has drawn three versions of the two figures he wants to paint. He has tried his best to capture the scene his imagination dictates. He has allowed himself to feel what it might have been like to heft the body of his dead friend.

In the process, he's remembered the advice of Donna, his counsellor. The way to go forward is to go back. Allow yourself to remember. Allow yourself the anger and the grief. Face it. Know the emotions for what they are. Then you'll be able to move on.

David can't will tears. Instead, he lets the pencil weep for him. Tomorrow, the brush. For now, he thinks it's enough to have made a start. With the coming of the light, the sound of growing traffic, the occasional thrilling treble of a magpie truant from Mount Ainslie, the hours of fear have passed. He can go to bed and allow himself to sleep for a while. It's like being back at the Dat or in Vung Tau after an op. There's a sense of relief. He can let go for a few hours.

¢

As he struggles to consciousness through entangling nets of dreams, the first thing David is aware of is a terrible screeching, and the sound of feet pounding the concrete verandah outside his flat. Full sunlight streams in through his curtain-less windows. He glances at his watch. It's nearly eleven. As he struggles to his feet, the noise he heard on waking recurs. He realises it's a kid running up and down outside his flat, imitating the sound of an emergency vehicle at the top of his voice: 'Nee-naw, nee-naw, nee-naw!' David presumes it's a 'he' without really knowing why. The floor vibrates to the pounding of the child's heels.

David hauls on his jeans and a t-shirt. Why doesn't the mother keep the kid quiet? David stumbles into the bathroom. He takes a piss but can still hear the footsteps hammering up and down the walkway, the sound of the child's voice going on and on. David washes his hands. Stares at his face in the mirror, clocking the dark smudges beneath bloodshot eyes, the three-days growth of beard and dishevelled hair, prematurely grey. Enough to frighten himself, never mind some punk of a kid.

Before David reaches his front door, a horrible thought occurs to him. The flat next door has been empty since the previous occupants—a drug-fucked, dreadlocked couple in their twenties—had done a midnight runner. The bloke from housing came and knocked on his door, wanting to know if he'd seen them. David told the truth. He'd had nothing to do with them. He'd been glad they'd gone. He didn't like their taste in music or company. The bloke said they were months in arrears with their rent. The place was left like a pigsty.

But recently there'd been people round cleaning it up. New tenants with a kid were just about his luck. David opens his door. The kid, four or five years old maybe, nearly bowls him over.

'Nee-naw, nee-naw, nee-naw!'

'Hey, watch what you're doing,' David complains.

'My sirens were on,' the kid shouts, aggrieved, over his shoulder, as he skids through the open door of the adjacent flat.

'I'll put my bloody sirens on next time,' David mutters.

'I hope we're not going to get off on the wrong foot.' A young woman emerges, her voice assertive, challenging.

David stands there, suddenly aware of the cold seeping into his bare feet, wishing he had more clothes on, resenting the vulnerability he feels. The young woman who stares at him—red in the face, hands on hips—has short black spiky hair with a purple streak in it. She wears a stud in her nose. Dressed in blue jeans and a black tank top, she is tall and slender. An ex-druggie, maybe, David thinks, or bikie's moll, or both, as he takes in the coloured tattoos down her left arm and the swallow in flight inked above her full and shapely right breast. She must have been working, cleaning perhaps, to be dressed so flimsily.

'There's no need to go off at the kid,' she says, her tone dropping a peg or two.

'I was trying to sleep. I'm not keen on rowdy children.'

'He's not rowdy, he's four.'

David folds his arms across his chest and hunches his shoulders avoiding a shiver. 'Shouldn't he be at kindy or something?'

The young woman bristles. 'He's had a cold. Not that it's any of your business. You a shift worker?'

'No. Not that it's any of your business. You moving in?' David fires back.

'Well, I wouldn't be scrubbing the place out if I wasn't, would I?'

David clocks the impatience on the young woman's face. He stamps his cold feet. The concrete isn't getting any warmer. He thinks about how ludicrous he must look, like some mad derro. No wonder she's sharp with him. Still, the vestiges of pride require a response. In an effort to appease, he says, 'Thought the mob from housing had cleaned it.'

'I'm cleaning it properly,' she replies, putting him straight.

A small tousled blond head, followed by an arm, emerges round the door jamb. The arm finds Mum's leg and winds itself around clinging on. The kid's body follows, his feet just inside the threshold, so that he makes a triangle against her leg. The young woman staggers slightly before taking the weight.

'Zak,' she says, stand up properly and meet Mr—'

‘I’m sorry, I cannot do that.’ The kid is stately and solemn.

‘Yes, you can.’ She begins to unwind him from her leg, and in the end is obliged to lift him so that he’s standing straight in front of her. He’s thin, like his mother, but blond and blue-eyed, his face all angles and already full of character.

‘G’day. David Young.’ David advances, bends toward the child with his hand outstretched.

‘This is Zak. Shake hands with Mr Young, Zak. And I’m Lara.’

The child solemnly shakes hands, as does the mother. Her grip is firm, her look uncompromising still.

‘Have you any brothers or sisters?’ David addresses the kid, keen to know the full catastrophe.

The boy shakes his head.

‘And before you ask,’ Lara says, a resigned frown compressing her lips, ‘there’s no husband or partner. I’m a single mum.’ Her head is up. She’s defiant.

‘Good on you,’ David says, retreating. He doesn’t want to hear anymore. ‘I’ll be seeing you then. I need to get something on my feet before they get frostbite.’

‘What’s frostbite?’ Zak looks up at his mother.

‘It’s when you get so cold your toes drop off,’ David says. ‘Be seeing you. And if you could keep those sirens down, that’d be good.’

Zak looks at his feet and then looks at his mother again. ‘Do your toes really fall off, Mum?’ he says.

‘No, of course not. See you later,’ she says to David. ‘We’ll be moving in properly on Saturday.’

‘Whacko.’

¢

Back in the safety of his flat, David puts on some socks and shoes, a flannel shirt, an old green ex-army jumper. He brews a coffee and rolls a smoke. As he prepares some beans on toast, he alternates between cursing his luck and saying to himself it could be worse. Why couldn't he have some nice old bloke for a neighbour? But he knows why not. These days, the elderly are shunted off to purpose-built places. The housing trust flats are for people like him. Dropouts, failures, the mentally challenged, the unemployed, the unemployable, the doped-up, boozed-up, and fucked up. How could you expect anything else?

On the positive side of the ledger, she didn't look as if she was using hard drugs. But it was often difficult to tell. The kid looked cared for in the sense that he had decent clothes on. She was cleaning, which was a good sign. And there's no drunken or violent father on the scene.

Drunk and violent, like I was, David thinks.

'Fuck it.' He drops ash from the cigarette between his lips into the pot of beans. Gets a spoon and tries to fish it out. Ends up stirring it in. 'Fuck it.'

But a young woman like that. Bound to have friends. Boyfriends. Shenanigans. Noise from the kid, mornings, evenings, weekends, nights. He wonders if she has a job. Pension, more likely, like all the rest of the poor bastards around here. That means she'll be around all day. Playing music, most likely, or TV, mates round, drinking and carrying on. A bloody nightmare, with no waking up. And there's nothing he'll be able to do. He'll just have to wear it.

David scoffs the beans and even before he's finished feels the familiar beginnings of indigestion. Heartburn. He first got it in Vietnam. The potent mixture of ration cans, fear and anger. Acid reflux—what a laugh. He's been chewing chalky tablets ever since. No cure for his burning heart.

Two Rennies and a soda water give temporary relief. Those and his painting, to which he now returns. The arctic white canvas with its chill challenge confronts him from the easel where he left it at dawn. He runs the flat of his palm lovingly across the surface, feeling the tooth, inhaling the smell. He takes the sketches from last night and pins the best one to the top right-hand corner of the canvas. With a piece of charcoal in his hand, he inhales and rapidly begins to draw.

Risk-taking.

It's only for the purpose of mapping, he tells himself, nothing is irrevocable. He will articulate the figures in paint later on.

The bold and uncomplicated design he has for the picture means it doesn't take him long to block in the shapes of the two male bodies right of centre. On the left of the canvas, he shades some abstract shapes where different colours will eventually form a contrast and balance for the whole composition.

David rolls a smoke, sits on a stool and contemplates what he's done so far. Occasionally, he gets up and tinkers with the charcoal or rubs to get different shades and textures. None of it matters at this stage, but already there's a feeling of pride, of investment in the work. He wants it to be good. He wants to do his best. There's so much in his life he's got wrong. He wants to do something to somehow make things right. To show he's not entirely worthless.

The next step requires more nerve than sketching. In order for the painting to work, David wants the figures to emerge from blackness. He begins to mix a quantity of bitumen oil paint with some No.4 medium. When the paint is ready, he takes the canvas from the easel and puts it on a drop sheet on the floor. He kneels with brush and palette knife to hand, and, trying to resist conscious thought, he begins to apply the paint, working at the texture of it, enjoying the impasto, the shades of night. All he knows is that he's going to work from light to darkness.

And then from darkness to light.

III

As he works the paint, David enjoys the vast luminosity of the black. It's good to feel in control of the darkness rather than being overwhelmed by it. Later, he'll have to try to talk to Josie, though he's not sure what he can say to make things right. It's a miracle they're as close as they are given all that's gone on. But David always has this fear the filaments of connection between them can be easily broken. God knows he's done his best to repair things, in so far as that's ever possible. Josie, God bless her, has always done her best to stick with him. But it isn't an easy road they're on, as their last bad-tempered parting demonstrated.

How can he explain? Always the problem. Not just what happened in Vietnam but the aftermath. That was the name of the album: *Aftermath*. The Rolling Stones: *Paint it Black*. He'd heard the song before he went to Vietnam. Listening to it at Nui Dat, drinking with the boys after a few days in the J, it took on a grim irony.

Then he came home.

At first, everything went okay. Margaret had waited for him.

They got married. He got a job. He tried to settle in to middle-class suburban life. It took a few years before Margaret fell pregnant with Josie. It was only after she was born things started to go awry.

David often thinks about this. He's talked to his counsellor about it—whether the pressure he felt, allied with the pressure Margaret was under, their mutual tiredness and anxiety, and the responsibility of fatherhood triggered the onset of the flashbacks, the descent into depression. The drinking to try and cope. He listened to *Paint it Black* over and over again. He would get drunk and late at night play it like an anthem. In the end, Margaret had smashed the record in a paroxysm of fury. She had come downstairs, wrenched the disc from the player, and with both hands thrashed it against the dining table until it was in pieces on the floor. She couldn't understand why he couldn't 'pull himself together', as she put it. Stop wallowing in self-pity. Get over himself.

At the time, this only made matters worse. It confirmed the warped thinking of depression, the sense of isolation and alienation. Now, he realises he couldn't expect his wife and daughter to understand. They were in an impossible situation. When he was depressed it was hard not to resent their inability to empathise. Yet, in a way, he didn't want them to understand. He didn't want them to experience what he had experienced. He didn't want them to feel the black despair that descended on him.

How could you explain then or now? In the bad old days, he drank to get rid of the feelings of uselessness, failure, of loneliness and sexual longing. But the drinking made everything worse.

The blackness was like some dark matter swelling inside him, overtaking him, overwhelming. He became bloated with sorrow. Literally, as well as metaphorically. The beer gut burgeoning as he lost control.

David is grateful he's managed to step back from the destructive path he was on. He knows he still drinks more than he should, but it's nothing like the excesses of the past, and he's made efforts to lose most of the belly. In the early days of rehab, he went to the gym. Now, he has come to enjoy the physicality of his painting as well as aiming for a longish walk every day. He's even tried a few minutes of running in with the walk. Sometime he'll give up the fags. Donna has advised him to take small steps. Not to punish himself. Not to set impossible goals. He's doing his best.

Even so, when he looks back to the stages in the disintegration of his marriage, it makes him feel ashamed. How could you explain the numb inability to communicate, the sense of being separated, trapped behind a glass partition which allowed you to see out but not touch or feel? And when eventually you were provoked into emotion, it was to experience a seething fury against yourself, then against everyone else. The battles with Margaret escalated as she tried to cajole, then harry him out of the darkness. It was as if she couldn't help herself, almost taunting him with her imprecations to forget the past, shoulder his responsibilities, act like a real man. David threw a beer bottle at the wall. Crockery was hurled in retaliation. He remembers sweeping up the shards, thinking of bone fragments.

That was the point. The impossible point.

The memories came back without warning in vivid hallucinatory detail: the dead, the wounded, the maimed. David in the guise of killer. Adrenalin pumping fear and discharge of energy, firing the weapon. The release.

Translate that into the domestic sphere ...

Thank God he'd never struck Josie. But David knows he's frightened her in the past. Frightened her by losing his temper, by shouting at her, by shouting at her mother. He's never struck either of them but has come close. He raised his hand to Margaret but saw the look on her face: the scorn as well as the fear and anger that it should come to this.

There's no doubt in David's mind she would have fought back. Who knows what damage might have been done? Thank God he'd got out of there before he landed a blow. Flung out of the house and, as he did so, saw Josie, aged four, standing in the passageway in her Snoopy nightdress, the tears streaming down her face. 'Why are you fighting, Daddy?'

He hadn't even managed a reply. He rushed out of the house into the dark of a Canberra winter night with frost making crackling patterns on the footpaths. He was a lost soul walking, shivering cold, through the deserted suburban streets. He'd crawled back an hour later, hoping Margaret would be in bed, so he could be alone with the whisky.

David remembers the morning humiliation as Jo-Jo woke him up. He was still fully clothed on the couch. His little girl came to watch her morning cartoons and found him laid out beside the over-flowing ashtray, the empty bottle. She shook him, told him he was stinky. Next, she was tidying up, her little feet pattering between the lounge room and the kitchen, asking if she should put the kettle on for him. And David trying to be normal with her. Giving her a hug, saying he was sorry for last night, aware he was still half-drunk, breathing stale whisky fumes into that innocent, sweet face.

The memories make David work the black paint harder. He uses a palette knife to create striations, roughen the texture. He knows this work is his way of seeking forgiveness. Atonement.

He still finds communication with Josie difficult. How can he really make amends? Certainly not by telling her what happened in Vietnam. How could you begin to tell a sixteen-year-old such things? It's not possible. David hasn't been able to tell his counsellor, never mind Josie. Though Donna has encouraged him to talk about the flashbacks, he's only provided an edited version and this only after much persuasion. He couldn't find the words for some of it. It was like being asked to take your clothes off in front of a bunch of aggressive strangers. He just couldn't do it.

In the early days of the counselling, in response to a direct question, David admitted thinking about suicide. It's not something he's proud of. When he thinks about it now, he can step back and analyse his self-destructive thoughts. It was like being taken over by the darkness, black ink spilling through him, spelling out the futility of his existence, how he's no good to anybody, how Josie, Margaret, his mother, would be better off without him. He knows the script now. Recognises the siren call. Fights back. Knows the life-denying whispers are not true. Knows it would hurt Josie, hurt his mother. Knows it's the wrong end to his story. He's also learnt that when he emerges from these episodes, the blackness disappears and seems to belong to someone else.

That's why he's painting from the dark to the light. Donna says the more he remembers and brings to consciousness, the more he will be able to fight back. He needs to own the images and overpower them. Transform them.

That's what he's doing with his art.

But he doesn't want this to be just about therapy. He wants to make something that will speak to others. Something that isn't only about his ego and his will. Something that shines with its own light. Something that transcends the circumstances of its composition. Something that will live. This is his crazy ambition. He doesn't know if he has the talent or technique to create such magic. But this is what he wants to achieve. This is his purpose, energising his days and nights.

¢

David washes his brushes, then his hands, with turps. He needs to get a move on if he's to catch Josie as she leaves college. The thought of trying to talk to her makes him feel sick with apprehension. He doesn't know what to say, beyond apologising. There's only so much 'sorry' you can deliver. It doesn't seem to do much good anyway. Josie wants explanations. Says she needs to understand.

What more is there to understand? His behaviour in the past, in the marriage, was terrible. He and Margaret had run out of energy, out of goodwill towards each other, and definitely out of love. In David's view it wasn't only the war that came between them, though that is a convenient fiction for them both. He knows he would have a hard time persuading Josie about this. But it's true, nevertheless. Margaret wanted a safe and secure conventional middle-class life, fuelled by the usual middle-class ambitions for material wealth and advancement up the pay scales and career ladders. David wasn't interested. Couldn't see the point.

He doesn't want to broach these matters with Josie at this stage. Soon she will have to make decisions about her future. David doesn't want to influence her, and he definitely doesn't relish the thought of becoming embroiled in some tedious wrangle with Margaret for giving Josie bad or wrong advice. And anyway, he'll be delighted if Josie decides to go to uni and finds a responsible job. He knows trying to live in the margins of society isn't easy.

He also knows for him it's the only way to go.

He's fought hard to find his own small space where he's free to be himself and practice his art. It's not that he's without ambition. He'd love to sell some pictures. He'd love to be able to contribute more to Josie's upkeep. What he's not prepared to do is sacrifice the integrity of his pursuit, his own integrity to the mighty dollar. He hopes by the way he lives he might show Josie there are some values that transcend money, money, money. But the last thing he wants is a discussion of all this so Josie can go back to Margaret and BB with a lot of 'Dad says' and 'Dad thinks'.

It takes several turns of the ignition before David's battered brick-red Toyota ute fires into life. Probably needs the spark plugs cleaning ... again. Once it gets going the engine sounds fine, despite the 250,000 km on the re-wound clock. The sweetness of the motor, though, won't make it any less inconspicuous parked up outside Hawker College. Its well-worn duco, its rust spots, its grimy wheel hubs will make a fair contrast with the polished Range Rovers, the Beemers, the Mercs, the Hondas, and all the rest. Hooley dooley.

David arrives early. He avoids the car park and eases into the kerb about a hundred metres beyond the college entrance, adjacent to the playing fields. He'll be able to spot Josie in his side mirror as she walks up for the bus. He hopes he won't embarrass her in front of her mates. Maybe if he just sits here, or gives a little lean on his horn, she'll see him and come to the car. That way he won't have to get out and confront her.

He winds the window down and rolls a smoke. It's one of those windy autumnal days with the afternoon sunshine paling at the thought of winter, the light a lemon wash rather than the golden glare of summer. A few straggly eucalypts adorn the nature strip across the road. David watches a magpie under one of them foraging for worms, its beak surgical and unforgiving. He thinks of the bird's lovely carolling. Brutality and beauty. The painting he's begun.

When the kids begin to spill out, David experiences a tightening in his gut. He's frightened of missing Josie in the crowd, but he's also horribly strung up about the encounter. He doesn't want to get this wrong. Make another mistake. Make things worse instead of better. He tries to sit still, just watch through his rear-view and side mirrors. But every so often he can't help twisting round uncomfortably, trying to spot her. It doesn't do his back and shoulders any good.

Though the college only caters for years 11 and 12, there are plenty of students flooding into the car park and onto the pavement leading to the bus stop. He marvels at the size of the backpacks they all carry. What can be in there? They look as if they're set for a route march. Must be some bloody huge lunch boxes. Or maybe books have grown since his day.

At last, he sees her. She's with a bunch of her mates, walking next to a tall, gangly young bloke with a mop of curly fair hair. If they were at the coast, David would have said he looked like a surfer. Josie has her head down while the guy is talking to her. She's wearing black jeans, her black jacket, hair loose to her shoulders, Doc Martens. The conversation seems intense. She nods, says something back. She doesn't look at the guy. She doesn't look towards the ute.

David doesn't know what to do. He stubs out his cigarette. The idea of walking down, bailing Josie up, suddenly doesn't seem like a good idea. He doesn't want to catch her off guard, make her defensive. Maybe if he stays put, she'll clock him. She can't keep her head down indefinitely.

There's a whole crowd of kids at the bus stop now. Twenty or thirty milling about. David sees Josie look up at last. She seems to look towards him. In his rear-view he can see the bus approaching. He thinks about getting out of the cab. Surely Josie has seen him. She makes no move towards him. She doesn't want to talk to him. She won't give him the satisfaction. Does he really want to force the issue?

Before he can make up his mind, the bus is pulling up. He watches as Josie and the young bloke mount the step into the bus. Other kids crowd on behind them. As the bus leaves, he looks up to its windows as it passes. He sees Josie staring out, a look of bewilderment on her face. Or is it irony? The eyebrows slightly raised, the mouth a serious line, her eyes posing an unfathomable question.

Impossible to tell—she's there and gone in a blur.

David is left with an inhalation of diesel fumes, the empty road. He bangs his palm against the steering wheel.

Fuck it. Another stuff-up.

He rolls another smoke before driving back to the flat. He registers the familiar vacancy of defeat. His only consolation is the canvas, its black paint beckoning.

IV

Early on Saturday morning, David drives to his patch at the community gardens. The day is grey and raw. There's no frost, but low cloud and intermittent drizzle make the paddocks on either side of William Hovell Drive look dull and bedraggled. A mob of roos look like bent old men in sodden grey overcoats. It's the kind of start to the weekend when the lucky in love stay close together under the doona, making their own warmth and later planning luxurious meals to eat by the fire. David allows the image of his ex-wife and Barry King to flit through his mind before banishing this useless reflection and thinking about the tasks ahead.

Gardening doesn't come naturally to him, but some days it's easier than others to persuade himself that a few hours of physical activity might be a good idea. Today, it's the thought of the movers next door that has convinced him. He wants to be away and out of it before the noise begins and any favours are called for.

Another bonus of his early start is that he arrives at the gardens before anyone else. This suits him. He likes the solitude. He doesn't go there to be sociable. He never has. Though he's obliged to turn up and do his bit for the communal part of the garden, it's his own patch that really interests him. It's here that he can grow what he likes for food and as a homage and memorial to his father, whom he thinks of, not without humour, as the 'master gardener'.

David parks the truck on the grass verge and walks up the slope to the gardens. They are situated on a slight rise overlooking a valley where another scatter of kangaroos can be seen hunched and feeding against the backdrop of Black Mountain with its unmistakable telecommunications tower—the big hypodermic needle some people feel is a neat symbol of the capital's drug problem.

On his left shoulder, David hefts a bag of manure. In his right hand he carries a sack holding the last few days' veggie scraps and other organic waste decanted from the bucket he keeps in his kitchen. He has two compost bins on site which need constant feeding. He drops the manure and empties the sack of scraps into the bin containing unripe compost. He picks some comfrey leaves from plants nearby to scatter across the top to make sure the compost remains sweet smelling. Then, retrieving his tools from the shed in the middle of the communal plot, he sets to work.

His job for today is to prepare the ground for winter sowing. Methodically, he begins to clear the remains of his zucchini plants and his tomato and pumpkin vines. As he digs out the dead stems and leaves and carries them to the compost bin, he thinks of the gardener's mantra: *what once was alive will live again.* Though the thought of making a comeback as spinach isn't much consolation, the general principle appeals to David. And with the inevitability of invariable routine, such thoughts lead back more sombrely to the dead who live with him: his friends and comrades, his father.

The old bloke died about twelve months after the final bust up of David's marriage. David worried that the distress caused by his divorce had contributed to his father's sudden and fatal heart attack early one weekday morning while working in the garden of the family home in Ainslie. There were other unresolved tensions between the two men, which made his father's passing all the more bitter. Their different experiences in different wars, instead of bringing them closer together, had somehow led them apart, each stranded in the fog of their own memories.

After his father died, a chaos of booze and grief followed, from which David only emerged after exploring, at dangerous speed, various highways and byways of self-ruin. He woke one morning in a hospital bed, having been plucked unconscious from an all too literal gutter, following some violent altercation outside a pub. He was so drunk he'd aspirated his own vomit and had only been saved by a passer-by. It was not this humiliation that had pressed upon David the need to change, though, but the fact that his ex-wife, possibly in a moment of inspired psychological insight, or maybe hoping to destroy his relationship with Josie, brought their ten-year-old daughter to the hospital to see him. The little girl's tears had been the catalyst which sent David in the direction of professional advice. His GP referred him to the Vietnam Veterans Counselling Service.

Funny that this progress should lead to compost. He shovels the rich, dark matter from the ripe bin into the wheelbarrow, remembering how the counsellor chuckled when David first spoke of 'unearthing' happy childhood memories of being with his dad in the garden and greenhouse. It was just such recollections that led David back to gardening. The fact that he missed the constant supply of fresh produce from the old bloke was a secondary incentive. It was more the realisation, too late, that his father's obsession with growing plants, flowers and vegetables was somehow related to his war service—a compensatory desire to grow and nurture life, rather than dwelling on the violent destruction of war—that inspired David to try in some small way to emulate his dad. It's a way of feeling close to the hero of his childhood who became, however unjustly, the antagonist of his young manhood.

David works up a sweat as he labours, spreading the compost and then covering it with straw. The weather isn't helping. The morning damp is threatening to become a steady soaking rain. There's no sign of the sky lightening, so David works on, huddled in his waterproof jacket, intent on completing his chores before he retreats to the truck.

When he finishes the mulching, he hurries back to the shed with his wheelbarrow and tools. He takes shelter there for a while, listening to the rain on the tin roof, inhaling the musty smells of damp earth and leaf mould mixed with old oil and tar from the creosote someone has used to weatherproof the place. He thinks about the rest of his day. He doesn't want to go back to the flat, and there's another job he'd like to do before he leaves the garden. His chilli and eggplants are still going; he needs to cover them with a bit of plastic sheeting to protect them from the frost. It won't take a moment, but he doesn't want to get soaked through, so he waits. He watches the swathes of rain drifting like smoke, which never fails to remind him of the tropical downpours in Vietnam.

After ten minutes, there's no sign of any change. Impatience overcomes him. Grabbing the plastic, he bundles out into the rain, padlocks the shed and hurries back to his patch where he sets to work. It doesn't take long, but by the time he's finished his woollen beanie is soaked, as are his jacket and trousers. Anxious now to get out of the downpour, he fills the sack he uses for the scraps with a handful of chillies, a small eggplant, a decent sized pumpkin and a zucchini that's become a truncheon-sized marrow, and hightails it back to the ute. He flings himself and the sack into the cabin, laughing at himself, glad to be out of the cold and wet.

On the passenger seat, there's a thermos of coffee and a ham and cheese sandwich. He pours himself a cup, eats the sandwich, then rolls a smoke. He winds the window half down and tries to enjoy the hot drink.

His wet clothes, and his uncertainty as to what to do next, irritate him. The thought of his new neighbour with an army of helpers, lugging furniture up those stairs, and the kid running wild along the balcony isn't attractive. No thanks. Instead, he decides to drive round and see his mum, telling himself it's a good opportunity. He hasn't seen her for over a week, so the guilt has been mounting. Might as well get it out of the way. He can give her the veggies.

¢

David's mother, Violet, lives in the family home—an old 1920s weatherboard cottage in Ainslie. Though the real estate prices in the suburb have been steadily rising, she hasn't felt tempted to leave. David sympathises. It's been her home since just after the war; she's lived there for over forty years. Why would she want to go? So, until such time as she can't manage the place, he's happy for her to stay where she is. He helps her keep the garden neat and tidy, but it's much changed since his father's day. After his dad's death, his mum had done away with the veggie patches and had easy-care natives planted.

When he pulls up outside, the front of the house has a familiar autumnal appearance—the meagre lawn is pale and weed-filled; the side hedge has a straggling unkempt look to it. The few gnarled fruit trees are leafless, their brown-black branches stark against the iron sky.

David walks round the back, knocks on the door and without waiting for an answer opens it and shouts, 'Hello, Ma! It's only me.' As he steps inside the laundry, he can hear voices. His mum has company.

She shouts back to him, 'Hello, love. Come and see who's here.'

His heart sinks. He hadn't thought she'd have company. But

there's nothing he can do. He dumps his sack of vegetables on the kitchen table as he walks through and into the small dining room beyond. Before he gets there, he knows who the mystery visitor is; he realises it's his daughter's voice he heard as he opened the back door.

'Oh, Christ,' he murmurs under his breath. A flutter of anxiety goes through him. He feels a dill for having sat there in the ute while Josie's bus took off. David's mum bustles to her feet and gives him a peck on the cheek as he enters the room.

'You're wet through,' she says. 'Best get that jacket off. You'll catch your death.'

'Don't fuss, Ma. I'll soon dry out.'

Josie doesn't move or say anything. Just sits there, glancing at him, then back at the table.

'Hello, Jo-Jo,' he says, trying to keep it light.

'Hi, Pa.'

'Sit down, I'll put the kettle on,' David's mum says. 'We can all have some lunch in a minute.' She goes into the kitchen as David and Josie simultaneously begin to decline the offer of food. They both start to speak and stop together. They share a sickly pseudo-grin.

Josie and her grandmother have been sitting opposite each other. As David sits down next to Josie, he takes in for the first time what's on the table. The sight of his father's wooden box in which he kept his medals, uniform buttons and battalion patches from the Second World War gives David a choked-up feeling, as if his windpipe is constricting and he can't breathe. He tries to conceal his distress. He can feel Josie's eyes on him. He takes a large breath, forcing air into his lungs, telling himself not to panic. Still, Josie says nothing.

Violet bustles in with a plate of scones. 'Josie and I have been having a lovely time,' she says. 'We've been chatting about Granddad and the old days. If you won't stay for a proper feed, hoe into the scones. Fresh baked this morning. The tea's on its way.'

David can hear the nervousness behind his mother's hearty bluster. He nods at her as she retreats back to the kitchen.

'Thought you had your job at the supermarket, Saturdays,' David says with a semblance of calm.

'Doing a double shift tomorrow.'

A slight pause. David watches Josie's eyes flicker from the box on the table up to his face. 'I was asking Nana about Grandpa.'

'What about Grandpa?'

'About the war and that.'

David shakes his head. He breathes deeply and vents his frustration in a loud sigh exhaled through puffed cheeks. 'You really do have a bee in your bonnet, don't you? What *is* this all about?'

Josie is inclined to sulk. 'You know what it's all about.' She looks him in the face, challenging.

'I don't know why I can't get through to you. What's your Nan been saying?'

'How Grandpa was on the Kokoda Track and how the Aussies pushed the Japs back into the sea.'

'Well, that's one way of putting it. I reckon we could leave it at that.'

'What I don't understand,' Josie begins, taking up the cudgels, 'is why you *don't* want me to know this stuff. It's my heritage. It's part of who I *am* for God's sake.'

'Nonsense.'

'Why are you being horrible?'

David is saved by the arrival of the teapot. His mother puts the tray with cups and saucers, milk and sugar on the table. She removes the wooden box and places it on the sideboard. David feels as if she's playing with his memories.

'Don't be mean to Josie,' his mother says. 'I encouraged her to ask questions. It's good for her to know about your father.'

'He never said a word about Kokoda.'

'Well, there are some good reasons for that. But there's no harm in Josie knowing he was there. He did his bit.'

'Which bit would that be then?'

'You know what I mean.'

Violet pours the tea. David reaches for the milk and sugar.

'What good reasons?' says Josie.

David and his mother look at her.

'You just said he had good reasons not to talk about it. What were they?'

Violet looks at David, who raises his eyebrows but says nothing.

'Have a scone,' she says, passing the plate to Josie. 'There's some nice butter there.'

Josie takes a cake but fixes her grandma with questioning eyes. David scratches his cheek. He wishes he could smoke, but he knows his mother hates it. He should have gone home. Should have known better.

'So, you were saying,' Josie begins again in between mouthfuls, 'there were these reasons Grandpa wouldn't talk about the war.'

'Oh, he didn't mind talking about the war,' David says. 'Did he, Mum? You remember don't you? When I was a kid. That box, you've had out to show Josie. Every year when I was at school, out it would come before Anzac Day. He'd sit and polish the medals. Tell me the funny stories. How the lieutenant jumped into the latrine pit when the shelling started. How he nearly shot his own toe on sentry duty. All the talk about beating the Japs. Pride and mateship. The Fuzzy Wuzzy Angels. There was no end to the stories. It was just the bit about the fighting he left out.'

Violet looks at David as she begins to speak, a terrible appeal in her fading eyes. 'He didn't like to remember it, you see, Josie, love. Said he *couldn't* remember much.'

'Shell shock, Combat fatigue, whatever you want to call it,' David says. 'The mind protecting itself.'

Josie considers this for a few moments. She looks at her nan and then at David. 'Are you having me on?'

'No.' David's reply is unhesitating.

'So, is that the same as what you've got? That PSDT thingy? Is that why you never talk about it? Cos you can't remember?'

Josie's relentless interrogation threatens to unhinge David. 'Bloody hell,' he mutters, before his mother intervenes.

'Maybe you should leave it now, Josie. Maybe your dad isn't ready to talk about it.' There was barely a pause before Violet went on. 'They look lovely, the veggies you've brought me, Davey. Thank you.'

David sees the sugar spoon shake in his mother's hands as she turns her attention to her teacup. Some of his anger dissipates.

There's a silence. Josie chews eyes down on her scone. David swigs his tea, aware of his mother glancing between the two of them. He wants to leave. Get out of his damp strides. Be by himself. In the quietness with his painting. But he sits there, sticking it out, wishing he could make things right with Josie but not knowing how.

His mother, ever the peace broker, begins again. As she speaks, David remembers how her interventions always made things worse between him and his dad. Now she's taking Josie's part.

'You have to remember Josie's growing up. She's beginning to question things. Trying to understand. I don't know why you can't help her. You were always going on at your dad about his silences. Now you're just the same.'

David feels the spur of anger prick his guts. He takes a breath. He's not going to lose control. He thinks about pride. He thinks about all the conversations with Donna the counsellor about what makes a man. Certainly not losing it and abusing women.

'I'm not just the same, Mum,' he says, measured and slow. 'We were different men who went to different wars. I've told Josie the truth. I have no words. I'm not going to sit spinning yarns about

Vietnam. To understand it, you had to be there. End of story. The best thing for Josie is if she forgets all this, concentrates on her study and goes to uni and takes advantage of her opportunities. Has a happy life.'

'Hel-lo,' says Josie, with a little wave. 'Like, I am actually in the room.'

'Hel-lo,' David waves back. 'As if we could forget.'

'Sorry, dear,' Violet apologises, patting Josie's arm.

'It's time I shot through,' David ventures. He can't wait to get out.

'Why can't you both stay for lunch?' his mother complains. 'It's not often I have the chance to see you together.'

'Sorry, Mum. I need to get out of these clothes. I only popped round to give you the veggies. I'll nip round for a cup of tea sometime in the week.'

'Make sure you do. I'll need some wood splitting by then.'

David rises and kisses Josie lightly on the top of her head. Her hair smells of apples. As he dons his jacket, he attempts an awkward levity. 'Josie will stay for some lunch, won't you, hon?'

'I've just had two scones,' she protests, frowning.

'You're a growing girl. Get your nan to do you a fry-up. You'll be right for a week.'

He bends and kisses his mother's cheek. Throws a parting shot at Josie. 'When you've recovered from the wars, come round and have a cuppa. It'll save me sitting outside college in the truck, looking like a dag.'

David's gesture towards connection doesn't work. The last he sees of Josie as he leaves the room, she's giving him a baleful stare. His mother follows him to the back door. She's not pleased either.

'You need to wake up to yourself. Go easy on Josie. She only wants to feel proud of you. That should mean something to you, surely.'

'Righto, Ma.' He sketches a wave as he strides down the path, eager to be away.

¢

David puts his foot down in the ute. He wants to expend the energy coiled tight inside him. If he had a punching bag, he'd go home and hit it. But he doesn't. He drives round to Ainslie shops instead. He buys a pie and sauce from the bakery and a six pack of beer from the supermarket. He wolfs the pie, sitting in the cab, and then drives back to the flats. His plan is to get out of his damp clothes, have a hot shower, relax with the footy on TV with a couple of quiet ales. Pray that he can get past the neighbours without being waylaid. He reckons he deserves a break having survived the women's tea party without doing his block. He wants to forget his family for a while.

At the flats, he parks his truck in the usual spot and sees the hire van a few spaces up with its back doors open. A couple of youngish blokes in jeans and t-shirts are unloading a sofa, while an older grey-haired man with a beer gut in shorts, workboots and an old brown jumper stands watching, smoking a cigarette.

David doesn't hang about. He's up the stairs well before they begin the ascent and along the concrete walkway to his flat. Young Zak, mounted on a plastic tricycle is guarding his mother's open door.

'G'day, tiger,' David says, as he walks past, glancing inside.

'I am not a tiger,' says Zak.

'G'day,' Lara shouts from her kitchen.

'How's it goin'?' David replies, holding the bag with his supplies under one arm, while he fumbles to unlock his door.

'Good,' she shouts back. 'The boys have nearly finished.'

'First class. See you then.'

'I am *not* a tiger.' Zak stands astride his bike, turning to regard David sombrely. 'Are you very old?'

'GRRROWWWL. I'm an old stuffed-up tiger, so you'd better watch your step.' David raises a paw with a raking motion before disappearing into the safety of his flat, closing the door behind him.

Later on, showered and changed with the heater blowing and the TV on, he cracks the first beer and it tastes like heaven fizzing. Then he hears the rattle of the kid's wheels up and down, up and down outside, and the sound of music and voices through the wall. No rest for the wicked. Goodbye to privacy. Goodbye to peace and quiet.

V

David stands in front of the easel. In his left hand he balances the ice-cream container lid, which is his palette; in the fingers of his right, he wields a fine brush. He regards his work intently, unmoving.

In the last few days, the painting has developed well. He has the figures emerging tentatively from the blackness. They are suggested by the use of sepia tones and burnt umber, their bodies a sequence of smudged brush strokes with no attempt at naturalism. They are more expressionist emblems than fully clothed individuals.

To the left of the canvas, deep crimson weals are overlaid on the black like bloodstains or violent scars, and a jag of pale paint beneath suggests an eerie dislocated bone. David is pleased with the drama of the painting and its sense of mystery. But what he hasn't got quite right are the hands of the walking figure which curl round the front of the body carried in his arms. They aren't shapely enough. They look like bunches of small anaemic bananas.

David decides to take a break. It's about 4.30 am, the electric light garish against the darkness outside. Apart from the swoosh from the fan heater, it's completely silent.

David's been working for a couple of hours. He's pleased with the progress but frustrated by this detail which is ruining the effect of the whole. The composition works by drawing the eye to the limp body held in the arms of the walking man. The focal point, both visually and emotionally, is the hands which lovingly bear the body's weight. But at the moment these look comic and are spoiling everything. It's going to be a difficult and delicate business rectifying the problem. If he can't, he'll have to trash the canvas and start again.

Laying down his brushes, David takes his sketchbook and pencil and slumps in the armchair. He rolls a cigarette, resting his pad on his knee. The tobacco tastes sweet and he inhales luxuriously. He closes his eyes and attempts to visualise his dead friend's hands. The recollection is vague and partial. Quite unlike the certain sense he has of Jez's character and personality: his assurance, his love of the ironic and absurd, his laughter, his quiet confidence with the girls.

David tries to conjure his mate clutching a football or bashing away on an old guitar or grasping a cold tinnie at Nui Dat, but the image that comes to him is of a hand hanging dead and lifeless from the poncho as they winched Jez's body into the medevac. The fingers were larger and squarer than his own, but somehow, David can't fix them in his mind. He finds himself struggling to resurrect the corporeal reality of the dead soldier, forever twenty years old.

As he stubs out his smoke and takes up his pencil, David realises the logical contradiction of giving the living man in the painting his dead friend's hands. He should be trying to paint his own. But something in him is resisting this. He decides to draw some studies, trying not to think too much. He wants to capture the expressive emotion of hands, without borrowing too much from the famous etchings by Dürer that he's looked up in recent days. Instead of helping, these master works are somehow blocking him. He has to work his way towards the appropriate hands for the figure in his own painting.

He holds his left hand up, palm facing away from him. He curls the spread fingers and flexes his wrist back towards his body. He begins to draw, deliberately enlarging, broadening and thickening the bone structure. As he works, he recognises he's been avoiding his own limbs because they're too small and slender for his purposes. Though he's quite a big man, he's what his mother calls 'light boned'; he has smallish hands and feet. He could do with a photo of a big man carrying something so that he could copy the image, but he hasn't got anything suitable. Above all, he wants the hands in the painting to speak of strength and tenderness.

David becomes lost in his work. He's unaware of time passing. His concentration is absolute as he tries to bring his sketch to life. There's nothing else in his world but the paper and the pencil. It's as if he's trying to channel all of himself into the movement of the lead on the thick grain of the sketching block.

The spell is only broken when he hears the irritating sound

of a telephone ringing and ringing through the wall. He glances at his watch. It's 5.30 am and still pitch-black outside. He hears bangs and thuds. Imagines his neighbour stumbling out of her bed, wondering who the hell is ringing her at that time of the morning.

David tries to stop listening. It's not his problem. He can just hear the faint susurration of her voice, like an underwater whisper. It's none of his business. But then there are more bangs. He hears her voice louder now, urgent, peremptory.

'Zak, Zak, wake up.'

There's no way David can go on with his work. He sighs. Goes out to the kitchen, puts the kettle on. All the time he can hear further sounds of hasty activity from next door, and though he can't detect any words, he can sense the mother's tones—urging, cajoling, encouraging. Then the kid begins to wail.

The noise intensifies. David's stomach tightens. He brews his tea. His neighbour's front door opens. Lara is pleading with the kid to hush. Instead of moving away towards the stairs, David hears them and then sees them come past his kitchen window.

'Shit. Shit. Shit,' he mouths to the air.

She's knocking on his door.

David answers, already dreading what's coming. He opens up. Lara is wild-eyed and breathless. She holds the struggling child in her arms and is further encumbered by a green canvas bag suspended from her elbow.

'Oh, thank God,' she says. 'Thank God you're up. I saw the

light. I need you to look after Zak. I'm sorry. It's my dad. Heart attack. They've taken him to Woden Valley Intensive Care. I have to get down there. My brother lives in Queanbeyan. There's nobody else I can ask at this time of the morning. I can't take Zak. Please. Help me.'

As this tumbles from Lara, Zak is bawling. 'No, no, no,' he yells between sobs.

She tries to put him down, but he clings on. 'You have to be a brave little man for me,' she says, 'and stay with Mr Young for a bit. I'll be back soon.'

'No. No. No. I cannot do that,' Zak whines.

His mother attempts reassurance. 'It's only like going to playschool.'

David sees he has no choice. 'You'd better come in.'

'I'm sorry. I don't know what else to do.'

Lara struggles across the threshold still bent over, trying to make Zak let go of her. David watches in dismay before making a desperate attempt to stave off the responsibility coming his way.

'Maybe I should drive you and stay with Zak while you see your dad?'

'Zak won't have anything to do and if he bawls like this, it'll be awful.' Lara is adamant.

She manages to wrestle the kid to the floor, where he clings to her leg. 'Please, mate,' she says to the child. 'Look, we've got Thomas the Tank Engine and Mr Robinson and here's a picture book Mr Young will read to you if you ask nicely.'

'Don't like Misser Young.'

David goes down on his knees, holding his arms out in a clumsy attempt to console the child. 'David, call me David,' he says.

Zak turns his back. 'Don't like Dawid.'

'Look, here's Mr Robinson.' Lara hands the child a soft toy. It's a battered brown and cream monkey with a long tail.

Zak hurls the monkey to the floor and stamps his foot.

Lara looks frantically from Zak to David. 'I have to go. They said Dad is critical.'

'Jesus.' David isn't ready for this.

'Jesus, Jesus, Jesus!' Zak shouts at the top of his lungs.

Lara ignores her son and addresses David, desperation lending an edge to her voice. 'It'd be good if you could manage not to swear. Maybe read him a story or something. He'll get tired of bawling eventually.'

As Lara moves to the door, Zak runs after her, grasping for her leg. David prises him away. Lara kisses the top of her son's head. 'Be a good boy. I'll be back as soon as I can.'

And then she's gone.

Zak sits on the floor by the door and cries. David can see real tears. Snot bubbles from the boy's nose. While David is getting some toilet tissue, the child raises the volume even further. A weighty feeling of helplessness descends on David. Beyond cleaning the boy's nose, he has no idea what to do.

Even wiping the kid's face becomes an ordeal. As David approaches with the tissue, Zak screws up his face and turns away, refusing to cooperate.

'Zak, mate, hold still. I'm only trying to clean you up.'

'I cannot do that. Mummy is very naughty. I want my mummy.' The decibel level is high and intense.

'Come on, tiger. I'm trying to help.'

'Not a tiger. I want my mummy.'

This is followed by more gulping, shuddering wails. Panic begins to churn David's guts. He wants to control the situation and he can't.

'Calm down, for Christ's sake,' he says. 'Big boys don't cry and carry on like this.'

The child continues to yell, winding himself up into a state of hysteria.

David tries to pick the child up, but Zak resists, pummelling David with his little fists and screaming. David feels fury rise in him, the impulse to hit back and impose his will. The violence lurches in him, frightens him. He stops himself. He dumps Zak roughly back on the floor, and retreats to the bathroom.

Staring at himself, dishevelled in the mirror, David splashes cold water onto his face. How could he feel such anger towards a little kid? He remembers his father hitting him. They'd be playing with something and suddenly his dad would lose his temper and smack him on the legs over and over again. The memory is still painful. He doesn't know why.

Like father, like son.

Thank Christ I never hit Josie, he thinks, remembering all those times he'd come close.

As he towels his face dry, David realises that Zak has

quietened down. When he re-enters the room, the child still hasn't moved but is only whimpering softly now. It's as if being sat on his backside has shocked Zak into silence. David retrieves Mr Robinson and dances the monkey in front of Zak's face, making ape noises and smiling as he does so.

The child, still snivelling, reaches out for his toy. David gives him the monkey and then goes into his own simian impersonation. He bends his knees and bows his arms and pretends to scratch under his armpits, all the while making high-pitched whoops. He cavorts and capers in front of the kid, who stands up clutching Mr Robinson. David beats his chest with his fists and then, bent double, drags his knuckles along the ground and takes a banana from the wooden bowl on the table.

Zak watches with wide eyes as David theatrically peels the fruit and takes a bite. He offers the banana to the kid. 'Whoop-whoop. Wanna bite?'

Zak reaches out, but David snatches the banana away.

The child tries again. 'Gimme,' he says.

'Whoop-whoop. Gimme, *please.*'

'Monkeys don't say please.'

'You're not a monkey, I am.'

Zak reaches for the banana again. David relents, afraid of further storms. Bugger the hygiene too.

The kid takes the banana and begins to eat, still clutching Mr Robinson to him with the other hand.

David sits down on the edge of the sofa, infinitely relieved.

He could do with a smoke but supposes he'd better not. 'Do you want a story?' he asks.

'Not really.'

Zak comes and sits next to him. 'Why are you a monkey?'

'Because it's fun.'

'Why?'

'I dunno. You get to eat bananas. I bet Mr Robinson likes to eat bananas.'

'Mr Robinson cannot do that. He isn't real.'

'He looks real enough to me.'

'He's a toy. You said before you were a stuffed tiger. Now you're a monkey. I think you're funny.'

'I think you're pretty cute.'

'What's cute?'

'Never mind.' David looks at the little boy, searching for something to say which might entertain him. 'Have you ever seen a real monkey or tiger?' he asks.

'Nope. I have not.'

'I've seen tigers in the zoo and monkeys in the jungle.'

'What's a jungle?'

'It's where there's lots of trees and grass and plants all growing wild with no real paths or fields. It's where creatures like to live.'

'Mummy says there is no monkeys in Australia.'

'Only in zoos.'

'Where did you see monkeys?'

'In a funny place a long way away.' David realises he's heading into difficult territory. But happily, Zak seems satisfied with this answer. He doesn't ask another question immediately. David takes advantage of the respite. 'I know what we can do,' he says. Let's boil some eggs for breakfast. Do you like boiled eggs?'

'Can we have soldiers as well?'

'Yes, we can have soldiers. Come on. You can help. After breakfast we can play with Thomas the Tank Engine.'

¢

By the time Lara returns towards midday, Zak is asleep on the couch and David is sitting on one of the dining chairs, trying to keep awake by reading a biography of Joan Miró. The connections Miró makes between painting and gardening intrigue him. Still, David's pleased and relieved to see Lara. The burden of responsibility for Zak's welfare lifts from him. This, and the dark bruises under Lara's electric blue eyes, encourages an overeager hospitality. He sits her down, asks after her father and makes a brew.

The emergency is over. Her father is stable. She will go back and see him this afternoon, but she'll be able to leave Zak with one of her mates for an hour. All is well.

'Could you use a little something medicinal in your tea?' David asks, waving the bourbon bottle at her.

'In my tea?' she asks, her eyes wide.

'It'll be good for you,' he says. 'My mum swears by whisky in a cup of tea to settle the nerves.'

'Just a drop then. I have to drive later on.'

David brings the two mugs to the table. Zak sleeps on, completely out to it after his early morning and all the excitement.

'It looks as if you two got on fine,' Lara says, sipping her tea.

'It was a bit hairy at first. He screamed quite a lot. I'm not very good with kids.'

'I don't think he'd be asleep like that if you were no good with kids.'

'I reckon he's just exhausted.'

They sip their tea in silence for a while. Though she looks strained and has no make-up on, and though he finds the stud in her nose distracting, David can't help registering how attractive she is. He tells himself off. She is years younger than him and covered in tattoos, for God's sake. For now, though, they are hidden by her thick maroon jumper, which she's wearing over a pair of tight blue jeans.

'This is good with the bourbon in it,' Lara says. 'Gives the tea a kick.'

'You must be relieved about your dad,' David ventures. 'Sounds as if he might be okay.'

'Yeah. He wasn't much of a father to me, but he's the only one I've got.'

'I know what you mean. Is your mum with him?'

'Mum died when I was a kid.'

'I'm sorry. That's hard.'

Lara pulls her mouth into a tight little grin. 'It was at the time. Are your parents alive?'

'Just my mum. Dad's been gone a few years now. Heart attack

as it happens. Just like that. In the garden. A good way to go for him, I suppose. Not so good for us.'

'No goodbyes.'

'No goodbyes.'

Silence falls between them again. David wishes he could think of something to say. He's hungry for a smoke but decides Lara might not approve. Zak begins to stir, diverting the attention of both adults. Lara goes to the sofa and perches on the edge as Zak wakes. She smooths the child's brow. He struggles to his feet.

'Mummy, Mummy,' he says. 'Did you now that Dawid is a monkey? And we had boiled eggs with soldiers and then we did Thomas the Tank Engine? And Dawid says he's seen monkeys in the jungle?'

Lara gives David a quick interrogative look, then says, 'That's great. But you mustn't call Mr Young a monkey.'

'No, no,' David intervenes, 'I was playing with him, monkeying around.' He lapses into his ape act again, for a moment, whooping and scratching under his armpits. Lara laughs. 'And,' David adds, 'we can drop the Mr Young bit. The name's David or Davey, if you prefer.'

Lara nods. 'We should be going, anyway. We've taken up enough of your day. You've been very kind. Hasn't he Zak? I honestly don't know what I would have done. You're a lifesaver.'

David experiences a warm thrill of pleasure. It's a long time since anyone's been grateful to him. But then he remembers Lara's desperation. She hadn't much choice. It's not really about *him*.

They pack Thomas the Tank Engine and the picture book into the green bag. Zak has Mr Robinson under his arm.

'Say goodbye to David now, Zak, and thank him for having you round.'

'Thank you, Dawid.'

'That's all right, tiger.' David ruffles the kid's hair.

'I am not a tiger. I'm a monkey, like Mr Robinson.' Zak goes into a monkey routine, imitating David's earlier antics.

'Now look what you've done,' Lara says with a smile at David.

David opens the door for them. As she's passing, Lara leans up, and kisses him on the cheek. It's like the remembrance of a half-forgotten melody—the softness of her lips, the warmth and scent of her body—and then she's gone, thanking him again as she leaves, saying she'll see him around.

The flat seems to echo with emptiness when they've gone.

David finds himself straining to hear Lara and Zak next door. He rolls a smoke and pours himself a small tot of bourbon. He's shattered. He's been up since the insomnia kicked in and he started work at 2.30 am or so. But he needs to settle down before he can think of sleep. The experiences of the last few hours have provoked a jumble of emotions that he now finds difficult to contain. His play with Zak has reminded him of the few good times he had with Josie when she was small, and fills him full of regret for all he missed of her childhood when he was too miserable or drunk to take any notice of her. He thinks too of the mess he made of his marriage, and all the comfort lost by that.

David grinds his cigarette out in the ashtray and drains his glass. He deserves to be alone. That's the point. He's not fit for company. He pours himself another tot of bourbon and goes into his workroom. He hasn't the energy to paint now. But if he can get some kip in, he'll get up again tonight and have another try at the painting.

The drawing block is on the chair where he flung it down when the drama began next door. He picks it up. He looks at the hands he's sketched. With a shock of recognition, he realises what he's drawn. He has to fight back the tears.

He finds himself staring at his father's hands.

VI

David is working. It's late in the afternoon with the light beginning to fall. In the last two days and nights he has laboured to improve his painting. Mustering all of his willpower and patience, using his finest brushes, he has obsessively returned to the task of re-shaping the carrying fingers curled round the limp torso of the dead man. He's intent upon the fine lines at each joint, the network of tendons and veins across the back of the strong square hands.

Impatiently, he switches on the electric light. The sickly pale yellow that stains the room won't deter him. Colour's not an issue. He's using the same mixture of white and burnt umber to mark his ghostly figures emerging from the deep and shining darkness.

As David works, his father comes back to him in different guises. With photographic clarity he remembers the way his dad used to cup a chrysanthemum bloom, the delicacy of the flower petals making a strange contrast with the wide workmanlike fingers underneath. Or he sees his father's hands tending the tomato plants with slow deliberate movements, checking for greenfly and black spot, the clean antiseptic tang of the vines entering the small boy's mind as he adoringly follows his dad's progress through the gardening chores.

David recalls everything that went wrong between them, too. Sometime in the midst of his adolescence they became strangers to each other. His father couldn't understand David's interest in rock music and art, wanted his son to follow a sensible career in accounting or banking. David began to see his father as a strict and mostly silent disciplinarian, out of touch with the modern world, lost in the mental torpor of the 1950s. Looking back, David understands his father's attitudes were a reaction to the awful experiences he'd endured at Kokoda. Having survived the ordeal, all his father wanted was a quiet life. His home, job and garden. If he had to trade boredom for safety he would. He wanted safety for his son as well.

When David was called up, to his amazement, his father had tried to persuade him that he could refuse overseas service. Said that all war was dirty, but this one was dirtier than most. There would be no disgrace in staying in Australia.

But how could David *not* go? After doing all the training, what would it look like?

Simple cowardice.

There was no way David could refuse to go to Vietnam. Anyway, at the time he'd wanted to go. His dad and his grandad had both fought in their wars. David felt he couldn't refuse the family tradition. He was curious. He wanted to test himself. He was lured by the excitement of it, an excitement that seemed legitimate, honourable. There was a romance to soldiering; no matter how laconic, sardonic, self-deprecating you might be—that was all part of the image. He wanted to enter what he thought of as a sacred brotherhood. You were donning the uniform your father and grandfather had worn, putting on the guise of ultra-masculinity, putting yourself on the line, prepared to kill and be killed for your country.

Now he realises how naïve he was, but back then David was puzzled and angered by his father's evident disapproval of his decision to fight. He expected his father to be proud of him. Instead, he continually harped on about the risks, the worry to his mother and the dubiousness of the cause.

After all, it was his dad who had infused David's boyhood with a sense of awe when it came to the idea of soldiering. When his father's medals and stories came out, the young David had been enthralled. But when it was his turn to earn his place in the tradition, there seemed to be a turnaround. Prior to his embarkation for Vietnam, David found himself being warned that war wasn't all 'spit and polish, drums and bugles.' Most infuriating was his father's refusal to say anything about the experience of fighting.

David had challenged him. 'Come on then, Dad. Tell me what it's really like to be in combat.'

But his father ducked the question. 'I've told you before, it's a filthy business, and you're a bloody young fool if you think any different. It's about killing and being killed. What more is there to know or say?'

Tenderly now, David paints his atonement. When he came

back from Vietnam, his relationship with his father remained difficult. The older man was grieved to see his son struggling but had no advice to offer beyond the dictates of stoicism.

'You've just got to get on with it. You can't live in the past. Put it behind you, concentrate on your family.'

David's failure to 'get on with it' successfully led to further friction. And his father's untiring adherence to the rituals of military remembrance added fuel to the flames. They did their best to get on and be civil to each other, but there was always tension between them. When they were alone together, the silences seemed to stretch forever. There was no easy conversation to be had.

It was only when his dad died and his mother handed David a letter from the old bloke that the journey towards understanding began. And then, of course, it was too late for the words he wished he could have exchanged.

David has had to learn to live with the old story of 'if only'. He recognises this painting as a stage in that story, a homage not only to his fallen comrade in Vietnam, but also to honour his first comrade, his father, as a man and a soldier.

¢

With such passion and purpose guiding his hand, David is lost in the process of his making. Only a series of bumps and bangs and voices from next door breaks the spell of his concentration.

'Damn, blast and bugger,' he shouts in frustration.

He tries to continue, but finds himself distracted, listening to what is happening on the other side of the wall. He can hear Lara's voice and Zak and someone else, a man's voice. It can't be her father; he's still in hospital. Her brother, maybe? Or maybe a boyfriend.

David berates himself for letting his attention wander. He lays down his brush and palette and goes into some back and shoulder stretches. He has a tendency to hunch at the easel, so he takes some time, attempting to unwind himself. He hears adult laughter from next door. They're enjoying themselves. It will soon be dinnertime. He wonders if Lara's guest will be staying and what they'll have to eat. David has a pot of chilli beans on the go. He'll have that with some rice and a couple of glasses of red. Watch some TV. Go to bed. He's done a good few hours at the painting. There's no point going on tired. He doesn't want to make mistakes.

Sitting in his battered armchair, David rolls a smoke. He looks at the painting and likes what he sees. It's nearly there. A few more hours on those hands and then it will be time to start the next one. He has a series of three or four paintings in mind. When he's done them, he'll have to decide what to do with them. Maybe they can form the basis of an exhibition.

Maybe they won't be good enough.

Maybe he should just give them away.

He's already thought of giving one, if not all, to Josie. Since he can't talk to her about his war, maybe he can share this gift with her. But would she like such dark offerings? Bitter gifts. He doesn't know.

Thinking about Josie makes him feel low. He wants to reach out to her but can't see the way. He doesn't want any more futile conversations with her about Vietnam or his father's war. Sometime, he'll show her the letter his father wrote for him. Sometime. But not yet. She needs to be older before she has to deal with that testimony. In the meantime, he's stumped. She hasn't taken him up on his invitation to tea. Presumably, that means she's still got the shits with him.

These needling reflections are brought to a halt by a peculiar noise from his front door. It sounds as if someone is playing with the handle. The door is locked, but still a surge of panic rushes through him as he moves to find out what's going on. Suddenly, David is in a Vietnamese village with his mates herding women and children into a group, cordoning off the area and searching the huts, wondering all the time about booby traps, not to mention hidden VC.

When he sees the slow and tentative rotation of the doorknob, he has an intimation of the likely culprit. He flings open the door to find Zak standing there in a Spiderman suit with his large blue Thomas the Tank Engine tucked under one arm. The boy looks up at David with wide eyes and a serious demeanour. David stands there while the banging of his heart subsides and the adrenalin rush dissipates. It doesn't take much to put him into this hyper-alert state, even after all these years.

'My mummy says I can come to play.'

Zak's words dispel the flashback, but David is still dazed and disoriented.

'Does she now? And did Mummy say anything about knocking on the door before trying to break and enter?'

The child shakes his head, eyes serious. 'I'm sorry,' he says, 'Spiderman cannot do that.'

'Spiderman needs to learn.'

Zak regards David uncertainly now. David is aware of looking and sounding less than friendly. The kid's expression makes him relent. 'You'd better come in, then.'

'Have you got any ice-cream?'

'Jesus Christ.'

'Jesus, Jesus, Jesus Christ,' Zak chants and rolls Thomas the Tank engine across the floor.

'Better not tell Mummy I said that.'

'Mummy's busy. Zak wants an ice-cream. Zak wants an ice-cream. Jesus, Jesus, Jesus Christ.'

David restrains himself from swearing again. 'I haven't got any ice-cream, mate. Have you had your tea?'

'No tea yet. Mummy's busy. Busy with Bobert.' David wonders who the hell Bobert is and what his busy-ness with Lara involves. Maybe it's nothing important. He finds himself unreasonably interested, then chastises himself. He needs to look after Zak. At least that might keep him in Lara's good books.

'Would you like a jam sandwich?' David offers.

'No, thank you. I cannot eat that. Spiderman only eats ice-cream and chocolate frogs.'

The kid retrieves Thomas from under the table and whizzes it back across the floor. David stops the engine with his foot. Bends down and bowls it back.

He goes to his kitchen cupboard. There are a couple of chocolate biscuits in an old Tupperware canister. They look past their best. The chocolate has melted and solidified again.

'This is all I've got, mate,' he says to Zak, holding up one of the biscuits.

Zak comes over. 'Thank you,' he says, solemnly, and takes the proffered cookie. He sits on the edge of the sofa, licking the chocolate off the biscuit, while contemplating David, who puts the kettle on.

'Mummy kisses Bobert. It's 'isgusting.'

'I bet it is,' David says with feeling. 'So, Robert, Bobert— whatever— is your mum's boyfriend?'

'Don't know. Don't like Bobert. He's silly. He is always kissing Mummy.'

David sighs. 'Yeah, well, there you go, mate. There's not much we can do about that.'

Zak has a ring of chocolate round his mouth and his fingers are sticky with it. He discards the biscuit on the coffee table. David advances on the child with a wet dish cloth, and cleans him up. Zak submits without complaint.

'You not going to eat that?' David gestures at the biscuit.

Zak shakes his head. 'It is not chocolate or ice-cream. Spiderman cannot eat it.'

'Have you heard about all the starving kids in Africa who would be grateful for a biscuit?'

'Nope.'

'I dunno. My mum would have shot me for doing that.'

'Has your mum got a gun?'

David has a sudden vision of a woman toting an AK-47. It's not funny.

'No. No. No. It's just a manner of speaking.'

'What's a manner of speaking?'

'Never mind.'

'Where is Africa? Can we send the biscuit there?'

David raises his palms high. 'Okay. Okay, I surrender. Let's play with Thomas the Tank Engine. I'm sure it'll soon be time for your tea.'

'What's surrender?' asks Zak.

¢

Later that night, long after Zak has been retrieved by his flushed and flustered mother who is profuse, if not a little shamefaced, in her thanks, David lies awake on his camp stretcher, listening to the unmistakable sounds of Lara and her boyfriend making love. It's both horrible and compelling. It fills David with loneliness and desire. He feels his cock growing hard and despises himself.

As the intensity of his neighbours' pleasure increases he gets out of bed and goes to the bathroom. He splashes cold water on his face. He tries to forget what is happening on the other side of the wall. But he can't.

After a few minutes, he returns to his bedroom, hoping that it will have quietened down. But he's underestimated their stamina. He's just in time to hear the strange, unearthly moans and cries of their climax, followed by the murmur of their voices in intimate communion.

Soon there is silence, and then perhaps the faint rumble of a snore. Uncharitably, David hopes 'Bobert' is making a pig of himself. He also hopes that Zak is fast asleep and hasn't been disturbed by the adults. What that kid needs, he thinks to himself, is a father. He wonders if Bobert is destined to play that role. David thinks of the time he spent playing with Zak that afternoon. It makes him regret how little time he gave to Josie when she was small.

More 'if only's.'

Unable to sleep, David rises and shoves his jeans and a top on. He goes into the kitchen and takes the whisky from the cupboard. He pours himself a slug and goes into his painting room. Switches on the light.

With the darkness outside interrupted only by the orange glow from the streetlamps, the painting looks more impressive than it did in the late afternoon. The glossy black and reds shine, the white and umber look more ghostly.

David sees the man carrying his dead friend. He thinks of his father and the way the memories of his father are carrying him forward. What he wants most in the world is to somehow be a proper dad to Josie. He wants to protect her from the kind of life Lara is living next door. He wants to make sure that Josie is safe and makes the most of her opportunities. But he doesn't know how he is to do this.

His art is helping him come to terms with the loss of his father. He can't see how to paint a way back to his daughter.

VII

A week later, Friday afternoon, David has finished work for the day, had a shower, a shave, worked hard to remove the paint from his hands, under his fingernails, his hair. He's put on clean jeans, a check shirt, a blue jumper. He's polished his ten-year-old R.M. Williams boots. He's as smart as he's ever going to be. Now he's pacing, having a smoke, resisting the temptation to risk a calming beer or better yet, a bourbon before Josie arrives. She's due about five-ish. He's elated she's coming round. They're going to have dinner together. David has no idea what he'll say to her, how it will go. He's just thrilled she's coming round.

Josie rang yesterday, said she wanted to ask a favour. She explained she had an evening out in Manuka planned with her mates. She needed a lift to get there. She didn't want to ask her mother and BB because they made such a fuss.

'They do know what you're up to?' David had asked. He couldn't risk colluding with Josie in some kind of deception. 'I mean, they know you're going to Manuka and who with?'

Josie reassured him. It was just that she wanted to be there around 7.00 pm and BB would make an issue out of it as it would interrupt their usual dinner routine. She was fed up with him and Ma.

David didn't ask any more questions. He offered to pick her up from college, but she said she'd make her own way to Civic and meet him at the flats. They could grab some tea before he dropped her off. It seemed a good opportunity. Maybe they could avoid the recent difficulties and move on. Re-establish the *entente cordiale.*

David checks his watch. Josie said she'd be at the flat about five. Not long now. He continues to pace. He hears his neighbour's door bang, followed by a timid knocking and the turning of his own front doorknob.

'Oh, no, bloody hell,' David exclaims. He's left the door unlocked in anticipation of Josie's arrival. Zak has pushed it open and is over the threshold before David can get there. There's nothing he can do about it.

'Hello, Dawid,' Zak says. 'Can we watch cartoons? Is there chocolate frogs?'

'Zak, mate. Sorry, not today. I have to go out in a minute.' David places his hand on the boy's shoulder, ready to steer him back out.

'I brought Mr Robinson specially,' Zak says. He swings the soft toy by its leg head down by way of demonstration.

'Yes, I can see that,' David says. 'I'm sorry, Mr Robinson. Sorry, Zak. It will have to wait for another day.'

David tries to turn the boy round but he won't budge.

'Why are you going out?' Zak asks.

'I'm taking my daughter for tea.'

Zak considers this for a long moment. Mr Robinson is swung more violently. David is frightened the kid is going to start crying. But he wants Zak safely back next door before Josie arrives. He doesn't want to have to enter into explanations about the little boy's presence in his flat.

Before David can usher the kid out, Zak says, 'Can I come? Mummy and I could come.'

'Another time, maybe,' David says. 'Not today. Come on. Let's get you back home.'

'Don't want to go home.'

'Well, I'm afraid you have to go home. Nothing else for it.'

Zak collapses theatrically to the floor. 'I'm sorry I cannot do that,' he declares emphatically.

The coil in David's stomach winds tighter. He recognises the spark from which anger might ignite. He doesn't know what to do. He's wary of manhandling the child—doesn't want to hurt him, doesn't want to be accused of hurting him.

David decides to enlist Lara. He steps round Zak and says, 'Come on, mate, help me out here, or else I'm going to have to get your mum.'

'I want cartoons and chocolate frogs.'

David props the front door open with a cardboard box of old kitchen utensils he hasn't bothered to unpack and bangs on Lara's door. She opens up. She's wearing a black tank top over blue jeans. Her heating must be on. David shivers. The autumn evening has a chill edge. He outlines the difficulty with Zak. Lara apologises.

'No need,' David says. 'It wouldn't be a problem, usually. It's just that I'm due out in a few minutes.'

Lara follows David into his flat. 'Come on, mister,' she says to Zak. 'Time to go home. You can't expect David to always be here for your entertainment.'

'Don't want to go home.'

'This isn't about what you want. Come on, little man, before Mummy gets cross.'

David isn't enjoying this. Lara gets hold of Zak and hauls him to his feet. She takes his hand, but he fights back, pulling away from her with all his might. They tug each other.

'Zak,' she says, 'this is very naughty. What is Mr Young going to think?'

'Don't care. Don't like Dawid. He's not nice to me.'

'He is so.' Lara looks at David, rolls her eyes. 'I'm so sorry,' she says again.

'No need. I just have to get going.'

'Righto.' Lara picks Zak up in her arms. He's heavy for her and giving her a hard time, still struggling against her. As they leave, Zak starts screaming at the top of his lungs.

David is standing at his door watching Lara's retreat when he hears footsteps along the walkway. It's Josie. Just his luck. Before she goes inside, Lara turns and mouths, 'See you later.'

Josie gives him an interrogative greeting in the form of a frown.

'Don't ask,' David says. 'I'll just get my coat then we're out of here. I thought we'd have a bowl of pasta in Braddon before I drive you over to Manuka. Is that okay?'

'Sounds good to me'.

¢

At the restaurant, David orders spaghetti matriciana and a glass of red. Josie chooses carbonara. David offers her a glass of wine. She refuses. Has a glass of sparkling mineral water. All very sensible. It doesn't take her long to get stuck into him though. While they wait for the food to arrive, Josie begins her interrogation.

'So, what was going on? It looked as if that kid had been in your flat. And that chick with purple hair. Who's she? She looks like a bikie moll with all those tatts.'

'Her hair isn't purple; she only has a purple streak,' David protests. He goes on as best he can. Tells Josie that Lara seems okay. How he baby sat Zak during the emergency over Lara's father. How the kid has taken to wandering into his flat.

'Isn't that driving you crazy?' Josie asks.

'Not really.' David can guess what's going through Josie's mind: the fact that he rarely played with her when she was little. Never seemed to like small children. The way he's avoided most social contact since he left Margaret. Josie is surprised. It's only natural. David tries to make the situation sound normal, ordinary, of no particular significance. He's just being a good neighbour. Doing the right thing.

Josie isn't going to let go that easily.

'How old do you reckon this Lara is? She looks very young. Twenty-five, tops.'

'Oh, I dunno. I think she might be a bit older than that.'

'Does she do drugs?'

'I don't think so.' When Josie looks sceptical, David goes on. 'Listen, how should I know? I don't think so, though. She seems a decent sort to me. Nice. Friendly. Quiet.'

'But what about the tatts and the piercing?'

'You don't miss much do you?'

'Well, it's not every day I see a young woman walking out of my dad's place carrying a kid.'

'We're neighbours,' David protests. 'Enough. It should be the other way round. Me asking you about that tall young bloke I saw you with the other day coming out of college.'

Josie doesn't answer immediately. The tucker arrives. David hoes into his. He's suddenly very hungry.

Josie approaches her plate less enthusiastically. 'God, these bowls are humongous.'

'It's good for you,' David asserts. 'Ballast. If you're going drinking with that young bloke.'

'I won't be drinking,' Josie says too quickly. 'Or if I do, not much. I'll be breath- tested by Ma and BB when I get in. There's always an inquest if they smell booze on my breath.'

'Extra strong mints are the way to go.'

'Bit of a giveaway.'

'Well, yes, but then there's the burden of proof. Anyway, I'm not going to be accused of encouraging you to get pissed. Particularly if there's a bloke involved. I know a thing or two about young men. How careful you need to be. Protection. You need to look after yourself.'

Josie blows out her cheeks theatrically. 'I don't need the sex ed chat, Dad. Been there, done that, got the certificate. Condom on the banana, no probs.'

'So, you're thinking of having sex with this guy?'

'Whoa. Stop. Enough. The guy you saw me with is Dylan. He's a mate. A good mate. That's all.'

David slurps up a string of spaghetti. Looks at Josie over his fork and spoon.

'You going to eat some of that?' he says, as he watches her picking at it. 'You need to eat.'

'Get off my case, Dad. No anorexia here. Just not very hungry.'

David puts on a wheedling voice as if he's talking to an infant. 'Eat a few spoonfuls for Daddy. There's a good girl.'

She pulls her tongue out at him. Eats a few spoonfuls.

'So it's this Dylan character you're meeting in Manuka. You seemed to be having a very intense conversation with him the other day.'

'I'm meeting a bunch of mates. Not Dylan. And by the way, while you're like giving me the third degree, you haven't explained why you were sat outside school spying on me.'

'Spying's a bit strong.'

'Well, what *were* you doing?'

'If you must know, I'd come to apologise for being cranky with you.'

Josie gives a little half-smile. 'But then you decided not to?'

'I decided maybe it would embarrass you if I bailed you up in front of your boyfriend.'

'He's not my boyfriend.'

'He looked pretty interested to me.'

'Oh, God. Don't start.'

'He looked intense, as if he was quizzing you.'

Josie pauses. 'Yeah, well. He is intense. Maybe too intense. He was asking me about this other guy I've seen a couple of times.'

'Aha. Now we're getting to it.'

'To what?'

'To the boyfriend scenario,' he says, keeping his tone light, hoping for a confidence.

Josie pouts her lips as she gives an exasperated sigh. 'You're obsessed, do you know that? I *haven't got* a boyfriend. I mean, is this like reverse psychology or something? Is this because you've got a girlfriend?'

'What? No? Course not.'

'What about the babe next door? The punk rocker, the bikie chick?'

'Her name's Lara. She's my *neighbour.*'

'I'd say you were pretty interested. I saw the way you looked at her. And she's not much older than I am.'

'She's much older than you are. I reckon she might be older than you think she is. Anyway, it's not an issue. She's got a boyfriend. Let's move on.'

'Happy to do that,' Josie says.

David finishes his spaghetti, drinks his wine. He watches Josie fiddling with her food. She eats a few strands, head down. He's disappointed. She doesn't seem to be enjoying it. At least they haven't had an argument. There's been no mention of the wars, for which he is truly grateful.

'Tucker no good?' he says.

'It's fine, Dad. Just too much of it. Puts me off.' She pushes her bowl away. Looks at her watch. It's obvious she wants to be on her way.

'Righto. Let's go.' He calls for the bill.

'Thanks, Pa. Thanks for doing this.'

'No worries. Don't suppose it'll make me *numero uno* in the popularity stakes with Barry and your mother. Never mind. Maybe I never have been. Maybe I don't want to be.'

Josie gives a wicked grin. 'I don't know why you would. They're boring as bat shit.'

David can't help smiling but feels obliged to say, 'Steady.'

Josie gives him a quizzical stare—the raised eyebrow treatment again.

¢

By the time they reach Manuka it's dark, the sky indigo against the lights of the restaurants, bars and cafés around the square. The pavements are busy with young people beginning a long night out. Josie asks to be dropped in Furneaux Street. She wants to walk round to the café where she's meeting her mates. She says she doesn't want them to see her being delivered by her dad. It would be too uncool. 'I'm not a child anymore.'

David asks Josie how she's getting home.

'I'll share a cab.'

'You could always ring me.'

'Yeah, I could. But there's no need.'

David frowns. 'You need to be careful. Drugs, booze, blokes—it's a jungle out there.'

When he sees the wry smile on her face as she goes for the door handle, he puts a hand on her arm just above the friendship bands she wears. 'I'm serious,' he says. 'It's easy to make mistakes.'

'I'm not an idiot, Dad. I'm nearly seventeen. I can take care of myself.'

'Good for you. I was an idiot at sixteen, eighteen and twenty as well.'

'What do you mean?'

'Never mind.'

There was a pause, Josie looking him in the face, challenging.

'I made mistakes with girls. Hurt them. Hurt myself. I don't want anything bad to happen to you. The world is full of young blokes stoked up with hormones. They can be very persuasive. You don't need to rush into anything. Get caught. End up a single mum like Lara.'

Josie gives him a play punch on his upper arm. 'I'll be careful. I'm not going to end up like Lara. Promise. I've got the shining example of my old mate Sharon to keep me grounded.'

David can't remember Sharon. Says so.

'Pregnant at fourteen. Not a good look. Don't worry, Dad. I'll be sensible. I'm gone now.' She leans over, pecks him on the cheek. Climbs out of the truck. Before she slams the door, she looks at him, mischief in her eyes. 'You be careful with Lara,' she says. Then she's off.

David sits for a minute or two. He watches Josie in his rear-view as she walks down and turns into Franklin Street. David fires up the motor and flings a u-turn. He moves slowly back down Furneaux over the speed humps, then right into Franklin, following Josie's route. The busy street suits him. There's no way he can gun it.

Instead, his eyes are everywhere, trying to spot Josie. He sees her standing outside a pub. Not a café. No mates in sight. She's just standing there on her own, looking up and down the pavement.

As he passes, David accelerates, hopes she hasn't seen him. He drives round the block—a complete circuit. He's back on Franklin Street in time to see a tall dark-haired bloke greeting Josie. She leans up and kisses him. He looks older than Josie, more mature, confident. It certainly isn't the blond-haired surfie boy he's seen her with outside college. Josie and the bloke disappear into the bar together.

David doesn't know what to do. He drives round the block again. On an impulse he turns into the car park on Furneaux Street. It's Friday night, busy. He has to wind his way up to the second tier. Money-grubbing bastards make you pay Friday nights as well. He fumbles for change, feeding the machine, cursing. Then he's back on the street. As he walks briskly down to the pub, past the bustling night spots, he works to persuade himself this isn't like the sleaze joints in Vung Tau. This is upmarket, prosperous, full of middle class kids. He hopes that makes it more innocent.

In his heart he doubts it.

The pub is crowded with people. This is where he has to be careful. Doesn't want Josie to spot him. He follows a couple of big blokes in and stands in the crowd at the corner of the bar. He takes a look around. There's a mirror on the far wall. He spots Josie and the bloke, head-to-head, deep in conversation. Josie is drinking some clear liquid: vodka, gin, water? The bloke is on a beer.

David pushes out of the pub and away. He realises the pointlessness of what he's done. He's been spying. Invading Josie's privacy. And for what? Nothing is going to take the anxiety away. He just has to wear it. He wonders if the bloke is driving. Josie said she was taking a taxi home. But then, she said she was meeting her mates ...

It doesn't seem right, but what can he do? Reluctantly, he drives back to the flat. At least he has some idea of what's going on. Some intel. He tries to persuade himself no action is the best action. Rest and regroup. Wait for an opportunity to talk to Josie again.

¢

After all the excitement, David has a couple of beers then goes for an early night. Mercifully, sleep comes quickly. It doesn't last long. The phone ringing breaks into his dream and brings him to sudden consciousness. He glances at the illuminated figures on the digital clock at his bedside. It's quarter past midnight. His heart starts hammering. The adrenalin begins to flow as he clambers from the cot and hurries into the kitchen where the phone is still belling insistently from its wall mounting. By the time he's picked it up he's absolutely certain something unspeakable has happened to Josie.

'Yes,' he bellows into the receiver.

'We are absolutely furious,' the voice on the other end of the line announces. He realises it's Margaret. The tone is icy but has a weird calm. 'Your daughter's just arrived home drunk. We told her she had to be here by eleven-thirty at the latest. We told her no drink, no drugs.'

David says nothing. He's busy trying to process the information, work out what Margaret wants. What she expects him to do. He's also aware of an incoming tide of relief. There's a lot worse things Josie could be. Drunk now means sober, even if sick, tomorrow.

'Well haven't you got anything to say,' Margaret continues, obviously even more irritated by his lack of reaction.

After another pause, David says, 'I'm not sure what you want me to say. It's not really my fault is it? She had no booze while she was with me. I told her to be careful as well.'

'We're hearing you told her to suck extra strong mints. Of all the stupid irresponsible things to say to her after your wonderful example with the booze all through her childhood. And now you're saying, "Oh, well, nothing to do with me." Really, you're hopeless. Absolutely hopeless. Barry and I are doing our best with her. It would be good if we could count on you to help, not you giving her advice to undermine us.'

'All right. All right. Calm down, will you? The main thing is she's okay.'

'She's not okay! She's staggering, slurring, vomiting in the toilet, drunk, for Christ's sake.'

'Well, thanks for letting me know. I'll have a word with her next time I see her. Okay? I don't really know why you felt the need to ring me now.'

'I wanted you to share our pain. To take some responsibility. To know there are problems.'

'Thanks, Margaret. Terrific.'

David hangs up. He stumbles back to bed. He lies awake, staring into the dark, sweating, thinking of all the things he did wrong as Josie was growing up, thinking what a lousy dad he's been. He knows he's just been unfair, unreasonable with Margaret. It's her tone. They push each other's buttons. But when his irritation and anger dissipate, he recognises Margaret has always been there for Josie.

It *is* all his fault.

If it weren't for Margaret, God knows what shape their daughter would be in. It's only since Barry's been on the scene and Josie's entered her mid-teens that mother and daughter have been at loggerheads. What can he do to help? If Josie really has a problem with booze, with this young bloke, with bloody Barry, what can he *do*?

VIII

David wastes Saturday in a welter of uncertainty, thinking about Josie, wondering if she's okay, trying to decide if it's a good idea to attempt a phone call or go round to see her. Either strategy risks having to deal with Margaret and/or Barry. It's not an enticing prospect. If they try to stop him speaking with Josie, there'll be a row. David knows he can't risk losing it with Barry. He's lost count of the number of times he's imagined hitting the smug bastard. He knows he shouldn't. Knows he shouldn't even feel like that. But he can't help himself. There is also the question of what state Josie might be in after her bender. If she's hungover it might not be the best time for a serious chat with Dad, particularly as Josie would have had to endure an earbashing from her mother and BB. David doesn't feel like adding to an unwanted chorus.

In the end, he decides no action is the best action. But somehow the whole of Saturday disappears before he comes to this conclusion. By the time he arrives at his decision he is exhausted with anger, anxiety, frustration. After a troubled sleep, he spends Sunday morning at his allotment, trying to dig out his fury with the weeds. He returns to the flat calmer, more grounded. *Earthed,* he grins to himself.

Now, he's ready to spend the afternoon with his work. He's laid aside the picture, provisionally titled *Bearing the Weight*, the first of what he thinks of as his 'Vietnam' series. Someone famous, he can't remember who, once said a work of art is never finished, only abandoned.

That's what he's done. Abandoned it—for now.

He's pleased with it, but he knows such pleasure might fade with time and he'll be compelled to try to improve it or start again. For the moment, he has begun another canvas. Again, in black. He's in the early stages, working the bitumen paint as he did before with the thick brush and palette knife, sometimes smearing with his fingers. He enjoys the work, the direct connection between his body and the effects he wants to create.

As he adds texture to the dark, David considers the way relationships, situations, like art are never finished, only abandoned. They don't end until you do. Both the living and the dead who have touched your life never cease to do so. You might try to abandon the past, but it won't abandon you. You can change perspectives, change your angle of vision, but there are no conclusions. You might think you've forgotten, moved on, but memories are never finally deleted until you die.

David thinks of the way his dreams and his waking mind are populated by people from his past. Margaret is a case in point. She's often busy in his dreams. He's entangled with her and will never be free. Even if he never saw her again, didn't have to negotiate with her again, he knows she would walk into his mind just as surely as other previous girlfriends do.

He wonders if one day he'll be able to express the wreckage of his marriage through art—the journey of his own degradation and reclamation. Now seems too soon, too close. He hasn't sufficient distance to gain perspective. For now, images of the deeper past are calling him, scenes that have haunted him for twenty-five years and won't let him be. It's as if he has to conjure and transform the horrors of Vietnam first. Paint them out of his system before he can move forward.

He remembers a day that began badly and ended worse. In a morning of stifling heat and humidity they did a cordon and search of a village. David hated this because it invariably involved upsetting all the inhabitants. The women, children and old folk, not to mention the few young men about, had to be corralled, while their huts and storage spaces were searched. Though David knew how to play the tough guy role, and the fear of booby traps or springing hidden VC made him aggressive, the sight of the women and children wailing, the sense of violating what little dignity the people had in their poverty made him feel ashamed.

On this particular morning, it was made worse by the fact that they found nothing. It hadn't taken David and his mates long to work out the central problem of soldiering in Vietnam: it was impossible to tell who the enemy were. Men and women in these villages, young and old, might be small farmers by day and VC or VC sympathisers by night. There was no way of knowing unless you caught them in the act.

And the VC were clever. Their bunker and tunnel systems were extensive, so supplies and ammunition were often moved and stored underground, well away from the prying eyes of the 'round eye' soldiers.

The patrol moved on. David remembers the sheer physical labour of it. The weight of their equipment in the sullen heat oppressed them, the insects and the fronds of unknown, unnamed foliage pricked and tickled and irritated. Their clothes chafed where straps and webbing rubbed. Over all was the constant state of tension, the attempt to maintain concentration on your arc of vision, the necessity to do your part to keep the section safe.

Fear was ever present and never spoken. It was the motivator and the scourge. In a contact, it was the stimulus to fury. On that afternoon, the monsoonal rains hadn't begun. Hooter, who was scout for the platoon, had reported 'sign'. Tracks that looked recent. Their platoon commander signalled they needed to be totally switched on. And it *was* like a switch being thrown. David experiences again the raised heartbeat, the adrenalin sparked electrical thrum of every nerve stretched taut to breaking point – the human animal, hunter and hunted.

They moved forward through the breathless air, the pitch and intensity of hide-and-seek raised to the level of anguish. Each slow step in this weird ballet might be his last. David's shoulders ached. His mouth was parched. A sudden impression of movement to his right swung David round, stopping Bluey behind him. But it wasn't anything. Or nothing definite. There was no smell. No untoward noise. Only the dense tracery of branch and leaf, the shrill demented concerto of insects, the mottled light that half-revealed, half-concealed.

A brief hand signal of apology to Bluey and they were moving again, half-bent in a tense crouch, high-stepping over dead fall, they placed their feet with manic deliberation. David was a slow-motion character in a never-ending movie. It was more and less than real, a walk on the edge of language where the old words, *courage, endurance, willpower* were as full or empty of meaning as you cared to make them.

David didn't care. Once you said yes to being a soldier, once you were committed to infantry, there was no choice. You had to go on. The only places to run to were lonely places in the mind, empty rooms labelled *failure, weakness, cowardice.* So, with wide staring eyes and silent prayers, they went on.

CONTACT FRONT.

The jungle erupted.

Slow-motion to fast forward. Gunfire, screams, movement.

Contact drill. Machine gun group one way. David another.

Adrenalin burst. On his belly now. Firing.

Feeling the brutal kick of his rifle. Concussed by noise.

Heart hammering. Shouting and orders. Wounded crying out.

Splintering. Showered by wood and leaves.

Bullets whining. Grenades percussion.

Fierce hatred. Fierce joy.

The abandoned power.

He squeezed the trigger again, again, again.

A sudden silence. A pause. The enemy running.

Everything slowing down.

It ended as quickly as it began.

David's mind began to clear.

He lay there, listening to the cries of the wounded, aware of his heart rate beginning to ease, and the ache from his kidneys as the adrenalin rush subsided. The medic was trying to help the wounded soldier. David attempted to stop his limbs from trembling.

The injured man, Danny Johnson, was whimpering, whacked with morphine. He made soft snuffling moans. The sound of torn flesh and dying creatures. David was relieved when he and his mates were ordered to join the search for enemy bodies and blood trails. Anything to get away from the sounds of that suffering.

He hauled himself to his feet and with shaking legs followed his comrades into the scrub and along a small winding path the VC had used. They found a slight figure that lay broken. To their dismay, they found it was a young woman. In briefings they'd been warned that young women fought with the VC. They could and would kill you with the same efficiency as any other soldier. They were to be treated accordingly.

Still, it seemed all wrong.

She looked about eighteen. She was wearing a black pyjama style suit with black rubber thongs on her feet made from old tyres. Her shirt was stained with blood and body matter. She'd been hit in the stomach by a 7.6 mm bullet.

No words for the violation.

No words for the damage.

Her deep brown eyes stared at the jungle canopy, unseeing. Already the giant ants were at their task, feeding from the blood between her palate and her tongue. Hot bile rose into David's throat. He swallowed it down. He wouldn't puke and lose face.

David and his comrades were tasked with burying her. They took no chances. They tied a rope around her wrist and, moving some distance away, pulled the body over to make sure it concealed no grenade or booby trap. Then they dug a shallow grave and flung her in without ceremony. They had to use a shovel to scrape some of the remains into the pit.

'*Xin loi,*' said Bluey. 'Sorry about that.' A linguistic shoulder shrug. Hastily they covered the remains.

'*Xin loi.*'

Been there, done that with death.

This unknown, unnamed woman in her shallow grave has been a constant companion of David's for the last twenty years. It doesn't matter how often Donna says to him, 'it was war, she was a soldier, she would have killed you if she'd had the opportunity,' he can't stop the grotesque haunting.

Now, as he smears the black paint, he thinks it is time for mourning, for tribute and for exorcism. Another atonement.

¢

David is distracted by the sound of his neighbour's front door closing. He freezes, waiting. The frequency with which he's being interrupted by Zak is increasing and he doesn't know what to do about it. Sure enough, there comes a knock on his door.

Cursing, David wipes his hands on a rag as he moves through the flat. He's going to have to talk to Lara about this. But when he opens the door, he's surprised to find Zak *with* his mum.

Lara smiles at David, disarming him. She nudges Zak. 'Go on, mate. Ask Mr Young, like we said.'

The child gazes up and speaks nervously, a rehearsed recital. 'Dawid, would you like to come to my house for a cup of tea to thank you for playing with me?' Zak giggles, having completed the flawless sentence.

Lara continues to smile, the question also in her eyes.

'Great, mate,' he says, addressing Zak. 'I'd better get cleaned up first.' He gestures at his paint-laden fingers and shirt.

'Walls or canvas?' Lara asks.

'Canvas, as a matter of fact.'

'Well, we'll see you in five, then?'

David nods, still twisting the rag in his hands. 'Yeah. No worries.' He tries not to sound overeager. His eyes meet Lara's for a moment as she ushers Zak away. He can't read her expression. Is it a knowing look? Can she tell how interested he is? Is she laughing at him?

David retreats. Washes his hands in turps. Flings on a clean shirt and jeans. Some deodorant. Wonders about having a shave then thinks he hasn't time. Splashes on a bit of Old Spice. Takes a deep breath. Plunges next door.

Lara ushers David to a seat on the couch. Asks whether he'd

like tea or coffee. Zak is playing on the floor with some Lego bricks, seemingly content to let the adults do their adult thing.

While the kettle boils, David has time to appreciate the way Lara has transformed the sparse utilitarian contours of the flat into a home. The place is redolent with what he thinks of as feminine mystique. And he loves it.

The couch and chairs are covered in throw rugs made from Indian textiles in warm reds and browns and greens. There are matching cushions. The walls have been covered in draperies and reproductions. A large, framed print of Klimt's *The Kiss* is hung by the entrance that leads to the bedrooms. On the end wall is the reproduction of a tapestry. It looks like a Pre-Raphaelite design, showing Flora scattering fruits and blossoms. William Morris, perhaps. There is a faint musky smell of incense which competes with the more homely aroma of lightly burnt toast. Everything in the room seems designed to suggest warmth and comfort.

Lara makes tea properly with leaves in a pale-yellow ceramic pot. She brings it over to the couch on a tray, which she props on the occasional table. She kneels on the rug opposite David and pours. They talk about art for a while. It turns out it was Lara's favourite subject at school, but since she left at sixteen, she's had to rely on a few night classes in art history and her own interest to further her knowledge. She laughingly explains how her attraction to body art and tattooing led to other fascinations. How tribal myths and symbols made her think about later kinds of painting and representation. She asks about David's work.

He tries to answer without giving too much away. He is vague and self-deprecating. Mumbles about expressionism and hoping to do some good stuff one of these days. He's saved by Zak, who comes over to them with his Lego model.

'Look,' he says. 'My robot.' He waves the toy in front of David.

'Robert the Robot,' his mother says.

'Not Bobert. Bobert's gone home. I don't like Bobert. Bobert's 'isgusting.'

'Hey, hey, hey! That's enough of that.' Lara's finger is raised, her voice sharp.

The little boy is shocked into silence. He regards his mother with round, uncertain eyes.

David notices Lara has blushed bright red. He tries to defuse the awkward moment. Asks Zak if the robot would like a cup of tea.

Zak is hesitant. 'Robots don't drink tea.'

David responds with more playfulness. 'Some oil then for his joints. We could call him Castrol GTX.'

The boy considers for a moment then relaxes. 'You're silly, Dawid.'

'Castrol's a good name for a robot.'

'Castrol, Castrol, Castrol. I'm going to make another robot.' The kid scampers back to his bricks. Lara rolls her eyes.

'I'm sorry. He's cheeky sometimes.'

'He's a good kid.'

'Most of the time. He has his moments.'

'Don't we all.'

There's a silence. Lara has her head down. She's no longer

kneeling, but is propped on her right thigh with her legs bent and her elbow on the low table. It gives David the opportunity to look at her. She's wearing black canvas jeans and a powder blue t-shirt with a thick chunky knit navy blue cardigan over the top. The colours look good on her. Her complexion is dark and David finds himself wondering if she hasn't got some Italian or Greek in her. But her eyes, when she glances up at him, are electric blue, which take him back to Ireland.

Her ancestry hardly matters.

What he knows beyond doubt is that she makes him feel breathless, off guard, vulnerable. Frightened of the power of his attraction to her.

He wants to ask about the boyfriend. Struggles to frame a question that won't sound impertinent. She beats him to it.

'Have you got any kids?' she asks.

David tells her about Josie.

'That must have been the young chick I saw you with the other day.'

David agrees. Soon he's sharing all his worries about his daughter drinking and the older guy who might be her boyfriend. It's a relief to talk to someone about it. He finds Lara a willing and sympathetic listener.

It's only when he begins to explain his anxiety about Josie's safety and how he has to fight the compulsion to watch and follow her that Lara baulks.

'The easiest way to alienate her is to show you don't trust her.'

'Old habits die hard,' he says. 'Reconnaissance is never wasted.'

Lara looks at him through narrowed eyes. But he keeps talking, as if he can't help himself, as if he needs to confess.

David describes driving round and round Manuka on Friday night, then parking the truck and footing it round the place till he caught sight of Josie with the bloke in the back of the pub. How he retreated then endured the call telling him Josie had gone home drunk. How he spent the rest of the night sleepless with worry.

Lara responds without hesitation. 'You can't carry on like that. If she thinks you're following her, you'll spook her and she won't tell you anything about anything. You have to keep the lines of communication open.'

'Like in battle.' The words escape David, a reflex response. As soon as they're spoken, he wishes them back. Lara is looking at him again, puzzled and uncertain now.

'That's a funny way to describe talking to your daughter.'

'I meant I should communicate with Josie to keep her safe.'

'Safe from what, exactly?'

'The world. Booze, drugs, dope, men, sex.'

Lara colours again. 'Canberra's not that dangerous, is it? The best way to keep her safe is to tell her and show her you love and trust her.'

'Maybe you're right.'

'I know I'm right. I have a dad. He drove me away from him. He was never the same after Mum died. When he was drunk he got violent and abusive. I never really felt he loved me, you know. Felt he blamed me for Mum's death somehow. I was left and she was gone. I don't know. But that's what sent me off the rails for a while. I was just looking for love. Looked in the wrong places as it turned out. But things are okay. Out of that muddle came Zak, and he's the most beautiful thing that's ever happened to me, so there you go. I've made mistakes, but I'm all right. I'm not a victim.'

David nods. They seem to be in deep water already, and part of him wishes for the shallows. He's unnerved by the turn the conversation has taken, back from Josie to Lara. Yet, just as he feels compelled to understand Josie's situation, he is now even more desperate to know how things stand between Lara and her boyfriend. But he can't find the words. Instead, he asks after her father's health. She tells him that they've let him go home, but she's worried he won't take care of himself.

David makes sympathetic noises, after which a silence develops. The idea of asking questions about the boyfriend seems even more remote.

'Are you a Vietnam vet?'

The question lands like a percussion round.

David swallows. He doesn't answer immediately. Looks at her. It makes her nervous. She goes on. 'I mean, you mentioned monkeys in the jungle to Zak and there was the stuff about reconnaissance and battle ...' Her voice begins to tail off as she loses confidence. 'I mean, it seemed to add up.'

'It does add up.' David tries to keep his voice neutral. 'I was in Vietnam. But there's no need to be frightened of me.'

'I'm not frightened. Just curious.'

'Curiosity killed the cat.'

'Not this one. I'm a survivor.'

'Good for you.'

'It is. I'm my own person, these days.'

'So where does the boyfriend fit in?'

Lara's eyes widen, and she kneels up again, as if bracing herself. David realises he may have stuffed up. 'I'm sorry. It was just since we were getting to know each other, getting personal …'

'Yeah. Well, it *is* personal.'

'Sorry. I just thought … it must be hard with Zak and everything. To find a boyfriend. It's easy to get hurt.'

'Thanks for the concern. I can look after myself.'

'Oh, well. That's good.'

There's another silence. Lara looks at the floor, and then back to David, her lips compressed.

'Maybe I should be going,' David says.

Lara relents. The tension in her face slackens. 'You don't have to rush off,' she says. 'I didn't mean to sound sharp.' She pauses. 'To tell you the truth, I don't really know what I'm doing with Rob. A casual affair … maybe.' She gives a little laugh, aimed at herself. 'He seems like a nice guy. I've been on my own quite a while. Apart from Zak, I mean. It gets lonesome sometimes, you know?'

'I know.'

'Rob kept coming into the café where I work. After a while, he made it clear it wasn't just the coffee he was interested in.' She gives another little laugh. 'Like I say, he seems like a nice guy.'

The mood is broken by Zak, who comes over with his rebuilt

robot now touting a space age gun. David plays with the kid, while Lara makes another pot of tea. The talk is desultory over the second cup since Zak won't leave them alone. Before David goes home, Lara thanks him again for playing with Zak. Says it means a lot to her.

'Friends, then,' he says.

'Of course, we're friends,' Lara replies.

¢

Later that night, David contemplates his work. His encounter with Lara earlier in the afternoon has shifted his angle of vision. When he began his new painting, he thought he knew what he was doing. Now, he's not so sure.

The thought of Lara swirls round his mind like the whisky in his glass: sharp, sweet and warm with promise and danger. He aches with emptiness and desire. But when he thinks of the Vietnamese girl-soldier dead in the jungle, and when he thinks of the bar girls in Vung Tau, he thinks he doesn't deserve love. He has no chance.

David sits in the armchair and takes up his sketchpad. Rapidly, he begins to draw. He can't render Lara's face with any accuracy from memory, but he does his best. It's easier to remember her body shape and the way she knelt in front of the coffee table or reclined with her legs tucked and bent beneath her. He tries to capture the casual elegance of her limbs, the sensuality of her pose.

At first, he draws the figure, who is simultaneously Lara and not Lara, clothed. Then, having rolled and lit another cigarette, he draws her nude, imagining the lovely swell of her breasts and buttocks, trying to capture the poignancy of her nakedness as well as the beauty. The work is both exhilarating and troubling. He feels like a voyeur, a perv. He feels as if he should ask permission. Maybe he should suggest that she sit for him. But he can't imagine having the nerve. And anyway, he reassures himself, it's not really Lara. The point is to work towards representative figures. He's not a portrait painter.

After three or four studies, another series of images comes into his mind. He turns over the page. There's an urgency to his sketching now. He begins again with an added vehemence and intensity. Dimly, he intuits that he's working his way back to the painting he's begun, but he stops himself going back there yet.

Instead, there's another Vietnam scene.

As he roughs out the shape of a bar, he's back there in his mind. Vung Tau. Rest and recreation. After the fear and tension, the witnessing of violence, wounds and death, a trip to the dingy seaside town of Vung Tau was supposed to provide a panacea. Its principal attractions were booze and sex. There was pool and table tennis at the Badcoe Club or a dip in the grey and dubious ocean from the grey and dubious beach, but mainly there were the filthy streets of dimly lit taverns with their scantily clad girls, the urge to get pissed and forget everything.

But David can't forget. He remembers with vivid clarity. Wandering the narrow, neon-lit sleaze strip, through the crowds of servicemen, street sellers and hustlers, half-drunk already, before taking the plunge into a long thin room that smelt of sweat, stale smoke, and fish sauce. The bar was made of plywood covered with lime green lino. There were brown vinyl booths for the drinkers. Behind the bar was a mirror in which David could see the painted flowers of the bar girls' faces as he ordered a round of beers.

Back at the booth, one of the boys was regaling the company with an enthusiastic account of his dealings with a prostitute the night before. David stopped listening, drank his beer and stared at the mirror behind the bar. Soon he was drunk enough to become obsessed. He became mesmerised by the lips and eyes of the girls. He adjusted the angle of his gaze to look at the legs and breasts of a young woman dressed in a red miniskirt and floral top. Fuelled by grog, he imagined how it would feel to hold her close. He imagined passion.

She caught him staring at her, raised her eyebrows and smiled. It was more than enough. All the cautionary tales about VD were put aside. He went to her and ordered Saigon tea for her. Several times. He drank more beer.

'You very handsome,' she said. 'You lonely boy. You want come with me, short time, long time?'

'Long time,' he said. What a joke.

She led him by the hand, out the back and across a small patch of dusty ground into another shabby room with clapboard walls and a single unshaded lightbulb dangling from the ceiling. There was a narrow bed with a yellowing sheet on it and a dirty blue-striped pillow without a pillowcase.

David recalls the rest of the transaction with grim irony, as he works with his pencil to capture the seedy lust-driven squalor of the bar.

Once she'd hooked him, the girl was intent on transacting her business as quickly as possible. He wanted to talk to her, but she was insistent. He paid her and she hurried him to get his clothes off and to lie with her. He lay beside her as she struggled to get a condom on him. Not even the sight of her small, pointed breasts could arouse him.

Drunk and bewildered, he said, 'You're beautiful. Why do you do this?'

'You very nice, you very handsome,' she said and continued to suck him into action. He held her head and stroked her hair and tried to think of the exchange as erotic. She straddled him.

Contact, he thought.

But still he felt nothing. He inhaled cheap scent mingled with the oyster smell of her sex. The girl manoeuvred so that he was on top of her. He looked into the almond eyes with their fine brown pupils and remembered the dead girl they'd buried on the track. He wilted. He couldn't do it. He dressed quickly, flung some more money at her, and rushed back to his mates who greeted him with cheers.

Then he lied to them about how great it had been and drank more beer until nothing mattered any more.

And they said that soldiering made you into a man.

In his sketch, David has tried to preserve a point of view where only parts of the bar girls can be seen. As he looks at what he's drawn, a sense of excitement and discovery begins to agitate his mind.

The possibility of three paintings to make a triptych begins to take shape.

None of the pictures would be naturalistic. Rather, there would be a movement from fractured forms to wholeness. The broken body of the girl on the track would form the centrepiece of the first painting. The second would be a version of the bar room he's just drawn. And the third would be based on one of the figures of Lara, the kneeling or reclining woman in umber and white, emerging from the darkness.

Somehow, he realises, he has to mend the wounded women in his heart and mind.

IX

Friday evening. David is cooking up a casserole with eggplant and chilli from his garden together with some mince and tomatoes and kidney beans. As he works, he has a smoke and a beer on the go. He's spent the day at his garden and then splitting some wood for his mum, so he's feeling pleasantly tired. There's footy on the TV later, so the only irritation is the noise coming from next door. Even though he's got his portable cassette player on, he can hear Lara's stereo and the sound of multiple voices through the wall. There seems to be a small party in full swing. She's had people round since earlier in the afternoon. No sign of Zak. David wonders if she's farmed him out for the night.

Once the casserole is assembled, David leaves it to develop for a while, and wanders into his painting room. He's trying not to feel resentful about Lara. She could have invited him if she was having a few friends round. But then she probably reckons he's too old to enjoy young company. And maybe she's right. That's the trouble with women, he thinks as he contemplates his painting: they can hurt you whether they're carrying a gun or not.

The first of his paintings in the planned triptych is on the easel.

In this picture, the figure emerging from the darkness is that of a woman splayed face down with the suggestion of long hair down her back. By her outstretched right hand there is a weapon. David has restored the rifle the VC removed from the body of the dead girl in the jungle. But there is nothing naturalistic about the depiction. Violent splashes and streaks of crimson suggest bloodshed. The bitumen paint erupts through the body at the joints suggesting a broken doll. The effect is macabre and disturbing. David has already named the painting, 'The Woman Warrior.' It isn't finished yet, but it's well on the way. The composition is still missing something, but he's not sure what.

David switches out the light and goes back to his cooking. The noise from next door bubbles on, as David prepares some spuds to go with his casserole. Thinking of the painting and thinking of Lara brings scenes from his failed marriage to mind.

Things began to unravel when David made it clear he wasn't interested in having a nice cosy Canberra career and a nice cosy Canberra life in one of the more salubrious suburbs. He chucked in his job shuffling bits of paper for an insurance firm and took up painting and decorating the houses of friends and acquaintances instead. In between, he drank and gambled.

As the mutual antagonism in the marriage escalated, their sex life went awry. David remembers the anguish after a drunken row; trying to make up, trying to make love, he looked into Margaret's eyes and saw not his wife, but the Vietnamese girl, dead on the track, then the Vietnamese bar girl in the shanty in Vung Tau. Not for the first time, his ardour failed. After that, he began to avoid sex with his wife. He was afraid of such intrusive memories. Afraid of sexual failure. And the more he avoided Margaret, the more angry and dismissive she became of him. He drank with increasing fervour to forget Vietnam. To forget the misery of his marriage. A downward spiral.

As he serves up his meal on a tray and screws the top off another stubby of VB, there's a sense of thankfulness and relief. Despite the party next door, there's something to be said for being alone. He can please himself. He switches on the footy, grateful for the intensity of the sport. Part of the trouble after Vietnam was that ordinary life seemed both over-complicated and trivial. The stark simplicities of kill or be killed, of living hand-to-mouth in the bush for survival were completely at odds with middle-class mortgage and matrimony, with all the trappings of taxation, superannuation, the scrabble for promotion, the fevers of material acquisition. Watching the Swans take on Geelong has a brutal simplicity, which David is happy to enjoy.

¢

The tucker is good. The footy is good. Small pleasures but real ones. The phone rings. For a wild moment, David thinks it might be Lara inviting him round to join in the fun. But as he clambers to his feet, puts his tray down and goes through to the kitchen he dismisses the idea as fantasy. She'd just knock on the door, wouldn't she? It's probably a cold-caller flogging something.

‘All right, all right,’ he says, as he plucks the receiver off the wall mount.

‘Hello.’ He’s abrupt, business-like, a tone designed to abbreviate any incoming bullshit.

‘Well, hello to you too, Pa. Lovely to hear you sounding so … welcoming.’ Josie giggles.

David’s eyes narrow as he clenches the receiver. ‘Sorry, Jo-Jo, I was having my tea. Wasn’t expecting a call. Are you okay? You sound a bit …’

‘A bit what?’

‘I dunno. Never mind. What’s up? Are your mother and BB there?’

‘Nope, they’re out. I’m grounded. They say they’re going to call every hour to make sure I`’m here. Gaolers. I hate them. I hate Boring Bastard Barry most of all. The way he talks down to me as if I’m some little girl who he has proprietorial rights over. The way he orders me about. Honest to God, I’ve nearly had enough.’

‘Staying out late and coming home pissed the other night hasn’t really helped, has it? It gives them ammunition. Landed me in the shit as well—not that that matters—I’m always in the shit with your mother. It’s par for the course. But you know what I’m saying, Josie?’

There’s a pause. David imagines her winding a strand of hair around her finger, winding herself up. He braces himself for a further tirade. It’s not long in coming.

‘I know what you’re saying, but it pisses me off. Mum and BB are out drinking. I’d bet any money you’ve got at least a beer on the go in front of the footy. So, it's only little old me who has to be a good girl? Well, fuck that."

'Josie.'

'Don't, Pa. Don't "Josie" me. I've had it with all the hypocrisy, the sanctimonious crap. So *please* don't start preaching about the evils of drink. And by the way what *were* you doing coming into the bar and, like, spying on me? Stalking me? I mean, really? What the fuck? It's no wonder I had a few vodkas after that.'

David hates that he's been sprung. It makes him defensive. He struggles to keep his voice even. 'Oh, I get it. Your drinking is my fault and you've called to let me know. And what's with the language? You think that makes you sound like a grown up?'

'Fuckety, fuckety, fuck, fuck, fuck!'

'Are you drinking now?'

'Might be having a sip.'

'Christ, Josie, you're not into Barry's booze are you? They'll ground you for life.'

'Don't worry. I've got my own supply.'

'How am I supposed to not worry?'

'You haven't told me what you were doing stalking me.'

David takes a deep breath. He'd like to roll a smoke but hasn't got the makings to hand, and anyway, it might send the wrong message. 'Look, Josie, I'm sorry about that. I get anxious, okay? I just wanted to make sure you got to where you were going—that you'd met your mates. I shouldn't have done it. But I tell you what, the boozing and the secrecy don't make it easy for me or your mum. Who's the guy you were with? Boyfriend? He looks older than you.'

Josie sighs theatrically. 'How old do I have to be before I can have a *private* life?'

'It's only eighteen months before you leave college. I reckon you might claim to be an adult then. Maybe. Who's the guy?'

There's silence on the other end of the line. Thick and heavy. David wonders how much Josie's had to drink, what she's been drinking, and how to proceed. When she still doesn't speak, David decides he has to plunge on.

'Okay. I get it. Let's pretend this is about me, not you. How about you reassure me? I need to hear he's not mad, bad and dangerous to know. How old is he? Does he do drugs? Is he a boozer? What does he do for a living? Are you sleeping with him?'

Josie gives another snigger. 'Are you sure that's all you want to know?'

'It'll do for starters.'

'I'm not even sure he's my boyfriend.'

'You sound as if you want him to be.'

'What chance have I got being held prisoner here? Like, he wanted to see me tonight. I told him I was grounded. I could have just gone out, but he said not to—it would be better if I played along with Mum and BB, not make things worse. That's how sensible he is. But I'm frightened he'll get fed up. Find someone else. He's at uni. Plenty of chicks around. Don't really know why he's interested in me, but he says he is. And no, no drugs as far as I know. He didn't drink as much as me the other night. I don't think you need to worry about him, Dad. The thing is I need you to help me. That's why I rang. I want you to talk to Mum. I want you to persuade her and her horrible partner to treat me more like a grown up. If they don't, I swear to God, I'm going to jack-up. I can't stand much more of this.'

David doesn't want to encourage Josie's seething. He decides to backpedal on his approach to the maybe boyfriend. Start from the beginning. Keep his tone reasonable. 'Does this bloke have a name?'

'His name's Michael. He's really cool. I think you'd like him. He's doing politics and history. Likes footy. He's kind of quiet, but confident. He's like, so much more grown up than the boys in college.'

'You sound keen.'

'Will you talk to Ma?'

'I'll see what I can do. But you have to play the game, Josie. Meet us halfway. I can't go persuading your mum to be more relaxed with you, if you're going to start rolling home drunk every time you go out. How's it going to go tonight when they come in? Are you going to be stinking of booze again?'

'I've got some extra strong mints.'

'Yeah. Good on you. Glad you told your ma and Barry about that.'

Another giggle. 'Sorry 'bout that. I must have been drunk!'

'How was the hangover?'

'I was fine. I puked up. No problem. Mum and BB fuss. I'm fine. I just want a bit of freedom. Respect. I want a life, for God's sake.'

'Okay, okay, message received. I'll do what I can with your mum. You make sure you don't drink anymore tonight.'

'Same to you, Dad. And steer clear of you-know-who next

door. She's too young for you. You're middle-aged. Way, way too old for the likes of her.'

They say their goodbyes. David goes back to the TV. His dinner is cold and his beer warm. He eats and drinks anyway. He watches the footy, but he can't concentrate. He keeps going over the conversation with Josie. He thinks he did all right. But it's hard to tell. And what the hell is he going to say to Margaret? He thinks about Josie giggling. Was she making that exaggerated effort to enunciate like a drunk trying to be sober? Did she nearly slur a couple of times? How much *had* she had to drink? No way of knowing. Nothing to be done. At least she's obeyed the curfew. Maybe this Michael lad is sensible. He gave Josie good advice. Who knows? It's in the too hard basket for tonight. He tries barracking for the Swans, but his middle-aged heart isn't in it. They scrape home by nine, but he hardly cares.

¢

After the game, David has a few more drinks and falls asleep on the couch with the TV on. He's woken by the sound of doors banging and raised voices. Some of Lara's guests are going home. It's 1.20 am and David feels cold despite the fan heater steadily whirring away.

He struggles to his feet, drinks a schooner of water in the kitchen and swallows some Panadol. The music's stopped next door, but he can still hear voices. He stands for a moment, trying to make out the snatches of conversation. It sounds like only

Lara and Robert now. David hopes he's not going to be treated to hearing them having sex. For now, though, they seem to be in earnest discussion.

David has a piss, switches off the lights and heater, stumbles into his bedroom. He can't be bothered taking his clothes off. He stretches out and pulls the doona up round his ears. He wills himself to ignore the voices through the wall. But it's not as easy as that. He finds himself tossing and turning, wondering what they're talking about, wondering why they have so much to say to each other. They might be in bed already or perhaps they're still in the lounge room. The smallness of the flats makes it difficult to tell. The only certainty is that silence is a long time coming.

As he attempts to doze, the voices begin to spike. David sits up, strains to hear. He still can't make out any words, but the intonation of the voices has shifted. They're having an argument. Or at least an animated discussion. This goes on for a while and then there's a silence. He hears the toilet flush. Maybe now they're going to settle.

David lies down again and tries to compose himself. But the noise begins again. This time it's louder still, as if the stakes have been raised. The row is escalating. David feels sick as he remembers his own battles with Margaret. The way they'd begin having a semi-civilised discussion and how slowly, slowly the fire would burn brighter and more intensely and then *whump*. Someone would say something and it was like a napalm strike. There would be an eruption of pure flaming anger, and then the crockery throwing and glass smashing would be on.

Next door, they haven't quite reached that stage yet. But David is edgy. It seems to him it's going in that direction. He wonders what he should do. He hears Lara shout, 'Get out! Get out, now!' Robert's reply ends with 'you fucking bitch,' snarled with horrible ferocity.

David is up now. He goes into his lounge room and puts his ear to the wall. He thinks they are in Lara's lounge room. They're still exchanging words, but the volume has fallen again. He hopes for a moment the row has burnt itself out. But then they start again. There's more shouting and screaming. It seems clear to David that Lara is trying to get the bloke to leave, but he's not having any of it. Instead, he's hurling insults and abuse. David hears, 'prick-teasing slag', 'uptight, frigid cow' and 'lying, cheating little whore.'

He hears Lara crying now, and begging the bloke to go home and sober up.

There's another pause.

David listens in an agony of suspense and indecision. He tells himself he should leave them to it. It's none of his business. Maybe the guy is getting his coat and pissing off. The sound of ceramic exploding into the wall ends that hopeful speculation. Lara screams. There's more smashing and more screaming.

'Christ,' he says aloud, feeling panicky, still wondering what he should do.

Then he hears, 'Get off, get off! You're hurting me!' The sound of further bangs and struggles and high-pitched cries sends David rushing out. He thumps on Lara's door with his fist.

'Stop!' David shouts. 'Stop now or I'll call the cops. Let me in!' He hammers on the door some more.

The bloke shouts, 'Fuck off!' and Lara is yelling, 'Help me! Help me!'

There's the sound of a slap landing and another yelp of pain from Lara.

The door's locked. David bangs against it with his shoulder, but it won't give. The sound of scuffling and panting and swearing is still clear. 'Right,' David shouts, 'the cops it is then, you silly young bastard! What kind of a coward are you?'

That does the trick.

The door flings open. Robert stands there wild-eyed, his shirt half unbuttoned. He's opened the door with one hand and has Lara by the other. He has the hair on the top of her head bunched in his fist so she's bent double. A livid weal down his cheek betrays the spot where Lara has caught him with her nails.

'Let go of her,' David says, 'and fuck off home.'

Robert looks at him, dazed, as if he doesn't quite understand. He's taller than David, but less solidly built. David knows he also has the advantage of relative sobriety.

'Let go of her,' David repeats, still quiet but more emphatic. 'Before I deck you.'

'Who are you, cunt?' Robert still has Lara by the hair.

'Don't be a silly little prick. Let her go.'

Robert releases Lara and lurches towards David.

'Get the cops, Lara,' David says.

Lara disappears into the flat. Robert takes a swing at David.

It triggers all the old training. Unarmed combat. David parries the blow, grabs the arm, swings Robert round and trips him to the ground over his leading foot. Within seconds, the younger man is facedown with David's knee in the middle of his back, an elbow across his neck and one arm halfway up his back.

'If you keep struggling, I'm going to break your arm,' David says in the bloke's ear.

Lara emerges and flings Robert's coat out of the door.

'Have you called the cops?' David asks.

'No,' she says. There's no need. I don't want the cops. Just make him go home.'

'Where's Zak?'

'At my brother's. Queanbeyan.'

'I still think you should get the cops. Sort this prick out.'

'No. I've had enough.'

By this time more of the neighbours have congregated by the door to see what all the fuss is about. Robert has stopped struggling. David leans into his ear.

'If I let you go, sunshine,' he says. 'You're going to pick up your coat and piss off and never come back again. Got it? And if I ever see you near her again, I'm going to sort you properly. Understand?' As he finishes his little speech, he lifts Robert's arm a fraction further up his back, eliciting a sharp yelp of pain.

'Do you, understand?' David says again.

The bloke nods his head. Murmurs a grudging, 'Yeah.'

Still holding him by the arm up the back, David gets off Robert and hauls him to his feet, using the back of his shirt. He throws him through the door, where his jacket has landed on the concrete.

'You can all go back to bed now,' David says to the neighbours. 'Excitement over.' He raises a warning finger to Robert, who stoops to pick up his jacket. 'Remember what I said. You come near her again, and I'll lose my temper.'

'You're welcome to the bitch,' Robert flings over his shoulder, as he stumbles off along the walkway.

David goes back inside Lara's flat and shuts the door. She's sitting on the couch, weeping, her head in her hands. He finds a box of tissues and puts them beside her, then goes into her bathroom and wets a flannel with cold water. He sits beside her.

'Let's have a look at you,' he says. There's a bruise developing high up on her cheek, where Robert hit her, and her lip is cut and swollen. David cleans her face up for her. She says nothing, just looks at David with eyes of pure misery. She's in shock.

'I'll make some tea,' he says. She's stopped crying now and sits bent forward, her hands clasped tightly together, a tissue balled in between them.

David puts some sugar in the tea. Figures she doesn't need any more alcohol, though he could kill for a belt of whisky. Promises himself one later. Delivers the tea. Sits next to Lara again. 'Some party,' he says.

'I'm so sorry.' She begins to cry again. 'Why am I such a fuck up? He seemed like a nice guy.' She sniffles and sips her tea.

'Didn't look too good to me just now. What was the blue about?'

Lara grins, rueful. 'I told him I thought he was getting too serious. I wanted him to go home, so I could get up early and collect Zak. I told him I was only interested in a casual affair. He wanted to stay. Said he was in love with me, that I'd led him on. Started accusing me of using him and prick-teasing and all the rest. Then he started losing it.'

'The trouble is you never know what people are like until it's too late. Life's little ironies. It's not your fault.' This is the best David can do by way of consolation.

'But I always choose the losers,' she says, her head down, staring at the tissue she's worrying between her fingers 'There's some instinct in me. Every time I meet a bloke, I say to myself, "well, is this another one like Dad? Am I trying to get a man like Dad to love me?" But I never pick it. I thought Rob was nothing like Dad. But I've never seen him so pissed before.'

David doesn't know what to say. He's sorry she's hurt. After a moment, he responds gruffly, 'Anyway, it's good that you've found out what a prick he is before you got sucked in any further.'

Lara glances up at him. 'I guess. I just feel like a fool. Look at all the trouble I've caused you.'

'That's no worries. What are friends for?'

'You should go home. Get some sleep. I'll be right now.'

Lara puts some strength in her voice. She's got some spirit. Still, David doesn't feel it's right to leave her alone. 'I reckon it might be better if I have a kip on your couch,' he suggests. 'Then you can relax. If he comes back, I can deal with him.'

Lara hesitates. Then she says, 'Are you sure?'

'Sure, I'm sure. No worries.'

Lara brings pillows and a doona. Before she retreats to her room, she leans up on tiptoes and kisses him on the cheek and thanks him.

When she's settled down, David takes his shoes off, turns out the light and arranges himself as best he can on the sofa. He doesn't care about the discomfort. He thinks about Lara, Josie, his painting. He remembers the weight of the gear he hefted through the scrub in Vietnam. The heaviness literal and metaphoric.

Sometimes it feels as if he's still carrying it all.

To persuade himself to sleep, he remembers the luxury of returning to Nui Dat, taking the pack off, sleeping on a camp stretcher instead of the ground. Bloody luxury. Like this couch. And here, unlike the Dat, he can think of Lara, sleeping in the room next door, which is a beautiful thought.

X

David walks through Civic on Tuesday morning, shoulders hunched and hands in pockets. It's a bright clear day. The morning winter sunlight is citrus lemon. There's a knifing breeze blowing off the Brindabellas. The glittering air smells of snow. But it's not only the weather that makes David hunch within his battered leather jacket. The prospect of a rendezvous with his ex-wife is just as chilly.

When he first rang on Sunday afternoon to suggest a meeting, Margaret talked about Josie's drinking and her boyfriend: 'I'm afraid she's coming off the rails. I'm just not sure how helpful a conversation with you will be. Let me think about it. I'll get back to you.'

Then, this morning, having been up and working on his painting since five, David had been having a smoko, full of ideas and energy when the phone rang. It was Margaret interrupting his morning shift, saying they should meet at 10.30. Though he hated the peremptory tone and the way Margaret had somehow managed to wrest the initiative from him, David couldn't complain. He decided not to fight her on the phone. If Margaret wanted to make it seem as if the agenda was hers, so be it. He knows the interview will be difficult enough without starting on the wrong foot. The point is to follow through for Josie. He isn't confident speaking to her mother is going to help. He promised to try. What else can he do?

David is always behind the eight ball in these conversations. The fact that he contributes so little to Josie's wellbeing financially is always an unspoken issue with Margaret and part of the ritual humiliation she inflicts upon him. Her income, not to mention Barry's, give them power. There's not much he can do about it but dream of one day selling some paintings so that he can redress the balance and salvage some pride.

David thinks of the work he's done this morning. The first canvas in his planned triptych is developing nicely. He's worked carefully on contrasting textures and colours to create the emotional tones he's after—thick smears of black and red dominating the painting with the pale whites and umber of the woman's broken body emerging delicate and fragile into the menacing light.

Though there's still some fine work to do, David is impatient to start the second and third painting. He has to wait for his pension cheque on Thursday to buy more supplies. He has an idea that working on all three paintings at once might help the development of each, so the images work with and against each other.

David walks into Garema Place and turns left at the carousel, its colourful creatures all stationary at this time of day. He wonders if it's possible to paint it without producing sentimentality or the cliché of the sinister carnival. It reminds him of going to the show in Queanbeyan when he was a kid, about Zak's age. How the wooden horses of the merry-go-round, tan, white and black with their bright and bizarre decorations, spots and stripes in reds and blues and yellows—together with the hurdy-gurdy music, had both attracted and frightened him. And then, the ride itself. The plunging, circling motion, the giddy music had made him feel sick.

Nearly as sick as he feels now, approaching another turn on the ups and downs of his relationship with Margaret.

David hurries on. A scruffy youth with a beard sits by a wall on a blanket with a dog, begging. Further down, a painfully thin young woman is busking with a battered guitar. The drug dealers and their clients will be doing business by the public phones at the other end of the plaza. There aren't many other people about. Most are already ensconced in their offices and shops and other places of employment. It's only the lost and the lonely who are on the streets. And one or two smart people hurrying to have meetings in the kind of flash joint Margaret has nominated for their rendezvous.

On the rails. There's a phrase to conjure with. All the set paths and directions. Start the train rolling, stop at only the major suburban stations—university, career, marriage, children, career, retirement—don't waver until the express pulls into the terminus. Yet, David doesn't want Josie to end up begging or busking or on either end of drug deals. How do you teach someone to find the little places of freedom in a society which punishes everyone who won't conform?

As he strides towards the place of fashionable glass and steel, David struggles with his own conflicted emotions. He needs to calm down. It won't do to begin the conversation feeling unsettled, wound up. He arrives at the café *Force Majeure* adjacent to the Tax Office where Margaret heads up a fraud investigation team. He's been here before and hates the place. From its pseudo-sophisticated joke name to its suited, tied and bound clientele. It's not his scene. It's a place for those who want to be considered part of the smart set, the Canberra wannabes who sit round discussing the performances and peccadilloes of politicians and public service mandarins with an air of knowing authority. He can just imagine all the chatter about Hawke and Keating, Hewson, Reith and Peacock—all the current gang. It's a place for those who get a rush from the merest shoulder brush with power.

David isn't interested in any of it.

Margaret is already there. She waves him over to a table. David hasn't bothered to shave or change. His hands are paint stained, like his jeans. He wears a black round-necked sweater over a black t-shirt and his leather bomber jacket, which he's had for years.

'Glad you've dressed for the occasion,' are Margaret's opening words.

David doesn't bite back. Sits down. Clocks his ex-wife's outfit. Though she's over forty, she still has a figure which can get away with a short, tight grey skirt, cream blouse and matching grey jacket. Her tights are charcoal with woven patterns. She wears high-heeled patent leather black shoes. Her red-brown hair is worn long and blue eye liner emphasises her brown bitter-chocolate eyes.

A young bloke comes over. They order coffee. David's is a long black, Margaret's a cappuccino. She looks at her watch. Says she hasn't much time. 'You want to talk about Josie,' she says. 'I'm interested to hear what you've got to say. Like I said on the phone, Barry and I are nearly at the end of our tether. She's out of control.'

David rips a paper finger of sugar and pours the granules into his cup. Follows it with another. Stirs. He's playing for time, hoping to get the tone right, not to be incendiary. He looks at Margaret as he speaks. 'Don't you think you might be exaggerating a tad? Overreacting? I mean, most kids experiment with booze, dope. Test the boundaries, that kind of thing.'

'Jesus.' Margaret mouths, under her breath. 'That's easy for you to say. You don't have to live with it. And then there's the boyfriend. Phone calls at all hours that go on forever. I sometimes think the bloody thing is welded to her ear. No consideration for other people or idea about the bill. Barry's very generous, he helps out, but there's a limit—'

'Have you met him? The boyfriend?'

'No. Have you?

'No. You realise he's a uni student. Older than Josie?'

Margaret looks genuinely surprised. 'No, I didn't know.

I thought it was a boy from school. How come you know about this?'

'Josie told me about him.'

'Oh, did she? And what else has she been talking to you about?'

'Being grounded. I promised her I'd talk to you about it.' David pauses for a moment, gathering energy. 'Are you sure it's the best way forward? Don't you think you might be making her even angrier than she is to begin with? I'm not sure treating her like a naughty kid is going to work. It's forcing her into a corner, making her feel she has to fight back.'

Margaret's eyes ignite. She leans forward, her hands pressed hard to the tabletop as if she might spring at him. 'Jesus Christ, you've got a nerve. You weren't even *there* half the time when she was little and now you're some kind of expert on parenting? Unbelievable.' She flings herself back in her chair and folds her arms tight.

David says nothing. Margaret's barb stings. It was one of her beefs when they split up that he'd left her too often literally holding the baby. He knows it's true. He has no defence. There's no point biting back.

He allows the silence to continue, hoping Margaret will simmer down. He stares round the place with its polished floors, its glass and mirrors, its hard and brutal reflections. A good venue for the hugger-mugger of politics, the endless discussions in which masquerades of transparency conceal the devious power plays, the half-truths and the lies.

Then he sees Lara. 'Fuck me.'

The words escape him in a passionate whisper, a mindless reflex. He's just spotted her behind the counter. She's wearing regulation black trousers and a white long-sleeved shirt to cover her tattoos. This must be where she works. He watches her emerge with a tray of drinks. She's carrying them to the tables outside where the smokers are sitting under gas burners.

'I don't think there's any need for that.' Margaret is still indignant.

'I wasn't talking to you. I've just seen someone I know.'

Margaret relaxes a little, looks round and frowns. 'I wouldn't have thought this was the kind of place your mates frequented.'

David doesn't respond. Margaret sighs.

'Look,' David begins again, trying to sound reasonable. 'I'm as worried as you are about Josie: the booze, the blokes and all the rest of it. I'm just not convinced that prohibition and trying to lock her up are the best ways forward. It just antagonises her. Makes her angrier.'

'So, what do we do? Let her do as she pleases, no matter what? That's not on. You know it's not.'

David closes his eyes. Rubs his face with his hands. 'There must be some other way. Maybe if you tried to talk to her a bit more. Get her to open up with you. Women are supposed to be good at that, aren't they?'

'Bloody hell, David.' Margaret raises her eyes to the heavens. 'Don't you think I've tried? I can't get through to her. It's like talking to a wall. She's still upset about Barry. She pretends not to be, but I can tell she is. She resents him. He does his very best, but she's so defiant. We can't let her do and say anything she feels like.'

Margaret pauses, her mouth a thin, hard line, her gaze skewering David. When she goes on, her tone is truculent. 'We have to be strict with her. You would be. You'd soon lose patience if you were living with her, dealing with her attitude on a daily basis.'

'Would I?'

'You know you would. I mean, anger management's not exactly been your specialty.'

'Thanks for reminding me.'

There's another antagonistic silence. David can't see any advantage in continuing the conversation. He's done his best. He's tried to make a point. He can't think of anything more to say. He doesn't want to inflame the situation further.

In the end, Margaret is the first to speak. 'Anyway,' she says, her tone moderating, placatory, 'I think it would be good if we could agree to sing from the same hymn sheet when it comes to Josie's drinking and spending time in clubs and pubs.'

'I'll do my best,' David says earnestly, fighting back the impulse to ridicule the silly metaphor. 'I still think you might be better off trying to relax a little with her.'

'Yes, well, we'll see.' Margaret sips her cappuccino. Looks at her watch again. She pauses, considering. David can tell she's gearing up to say some more. She has a peculiar look in her eyes. A steely determination. Yet she seems wary.

Out of the corner of his eye, David sees Lara come back in and walk back round the counter. Thankfully, she hasn't seen him. He doesn't want to make any awkward introductions. He also doesn't want her getting any wrong ideas.

Margaret clears her throat, compelling David's attention. 'I think you should know,' she says, 'that Barry and I have decided to get married.'

David looks at her. Takes a minute. It's not entirely unexpected, but still, he's rocked. 'It's your decision. Nothing to do with me is it?' he says. He begins to bounce his spoon on the rim of his saucer.

'Of course it's my decision. But I thought I should tell you. I don't know how Josie's going to take it. She might come running to you.'

David shrugs. 'I can't make her like Barry.'

'No.' Margaret is beginning to sound exasperated again. 'But what you can do is tell her that in the long run what makes me happy is likely to be good for her. You can also tell her what a thoroughly decent man Barry is, with a good income and good prospects.'

'Ah, yes, the income.'

'Don't be an arsehole, David. His money is contributing to Josie's upbringing. He's very fond of her, you know.'

'Oh, yes, I know.' David continues his percussion with the teaspoon.

Margaret takes a breath. 'I'm not going to let you needle me into a row. All I'm asking is for a little bit of cooperation for Josie's sake. And will you please, for Christ's sake, stop it with that spoon.'

David surrenders, raises his hands palms up. 'Understood. I'll do my best to sell Jose the idea you're the perfect couple. When will you be making the announcement?'

'I don't know. We've not decided. So don't say anything to Josie. We're going to talk to her about it soon.'

'Bonzer.'

'I should have known better than to expect any sense from you. I've got to get back to work.' Margaret starts rummaging through her capacious designer handbag.

'It's okay. I'll get it,' David says. 'A treat to celebrate your engagement. Congratulations. I hope you'll be very happy.'

'The last of the big spenders,' Margaret says, as she sweeps out of the place.

¢

Once she's gone, David sits for a few moments, trying to remember the young woman he married all those years ago. As he does so, he watches Lara's movements and wonders whether he's mad to be thinking about her so much. She's obviously got some baggage. So has he. But then, who hasn't? David loses patience with the futility of his speculations. He decides to make a run for the till while she's there and say g'day.

When he does, Lara looks up and blinks, as if she can't believe what she's seeing. David offers the bill and some cash.

'What are you doing here?' she says. 'I wouldn't have thought this was your kind of place.'

'You mean you didn't see me over there with that rather smart woman?'

'Well, I …'

David lets her off the hook. 'It's okay. She's my ex. We were having a summit. It happens now and again.'

Lara nods. Gives him his change. She seems discomforted by his presence.

'Pretty flash joint to work,' David ventures, pocketing the coins.

'It's not really my kind of scene,' she says. 'But it pays better than most.'

David nods. For a moment, they look at each other, weighing each other up in these peculiar circumstances.

'Heard from Robert, have you?'

'He rang a couple of times, but I've been strict so far. Told him it was over.'

'Good on you.'

David rubs his forehead with his fingers. He's standing there just looking at her. An inspiration comes to him, compelling but risky. The silence is becoming awkward. He stuffs his hands into the pockets of his leather jacket. He has to speak now or shoot through.

Trying to maintain his cool, he says, 'I tell you what. Just so's you don't fall into temptation, why don't you let me cook you and Zak a feed on Saturday night.'

'I don't know if that's wise.'

The free fall of disappointment makes David push back. 'Can't see what harm it can do. Friends, remember?'

She smiles. The tension goes out of her face and shoulders. 'I'm a vegetarian,' she says. 'Can you cope?'

He suppresses a grin. 'You'll have to wait and see. About six-thirty then, so it's not too late for Zak.'

'I'll bring some wine.'

'Now you're talking.'

David walks back to the flats, trying not to feel too pleased with himself. It was only when he used the 'F' word that Lara had relaxed. Maybe they were destined to be 'just good friends'.

So what?

At least he has something to look forward to, besides his ex-wife's wedding.

XI

David sits back and tries to relax, cradling a glass of red. He's feeling good but nervous about what comes next. Dylan's *Shelter from the Storm* with its haunting images and mixed messages plays low on the stereo. Lara is settling Zak down. The evening, so far, has been a success. Instead of Lara and Zak coming round to his place to eat, on Saturday morning Lara suggested he should bring the food to them. That way they wouldn't have to disturb Zak so much. It was a proposal that suited David. It meant he didn't have to spend hours tidying and cleaning his flat. And it meant, after dinner, the immediate proximity of Lara's bedroom. Neither his sofa nor his camp stretcher provided a remote possibility for romance. Lara's rooms with their shawls and scents are a more enticing prospect.

But David is unsure of himself and the situation. There's no question that the vegetarian lasagne he cooked and the apple crumble have been enthusiastically received. Zak's antics have provided a focus for the adults' attention, minimising any potential awkwardness between David and Lara. They haven't been able to talk seriously or personally. Instead, there's been banter and laughter. Even the one moment of potential embarrassment passed without too much difficulty. As David was organising the apple crumble and Lara was stirring some custard, Zak had come into the kitchen, looked at David and said, 'Are you going to kiss Mummy like Bobert did?'

'What, like this?' David said, and then kissed Zak on the top of his head.

The child chuckled and rubbed the spot with his hand and said, ''isgusting.'

'Or like this?' David leaned over and kissed Lara on the cheek. She went bright red.

Zak laughed again. ''isgusting, 'isgusting, 'isgusting,' he chortled.

After dinner, David read Zak a Thomas the Tank Engine story while Lara washed the dishes. Now, the question is where things will go when Lara emerges and they are alone together.

The worst thing for David is he doesn't know what he wants to happen. He's torn between his fantasies of sex with Lara and his fears. He thinks of the preliminary sketches he's been working on for the second painting in his triptych. The interior of the bar in Vung Tau suggested in black shapes, punctuated by mirrors of light in which partial portraits of the bar girls can be seen. In one, the lap and legs; in another, the head and shoulders; in a third, the torso and breasts. He worries about the entanglements of sex. He worries about his ability to perform. Yet he aches with desire.

He tells himself to chill out. Remembers advice from his

counsellor. Let what will be, be. Sexual failure with his ex-wife doesn't mean sexual failure forever. Relaxation is key. Making love is about pleasure not performance. Concentrate on pleasure.

Easier said than done.

Anyway, it's more than likely Lara is only interested in friendship. Maybe that's for the best after all.

These reflections are brought to an end when Lara comes back into the room. Her physical presence creates a charged atmosphere, like a dramatic change in the weather. She's wearing blue jeans and a black tank top, which shows off the vermilion, yellow and blue inks of the tattoos on her left arm. She walks with her bare feet turned outwards slightly, like a gymnast or a dancer, her toenails painted bright red. The music's stopped, so she goes to the player, stoops to change the CD. David's eyes are drawn to the curve and swell of her buttocks against the tight denim. He tells himself to settle down.

Clapton's *Unplugged* begins with some intricate finger-style playing. David has a fleeting vision of his mate, Jez, crooning the blues to a battered old acoustic in the boozer at Canungra. He thinks about the mysteries of friendship, the mysteries of love. It was music and art that first brought David and Jez together. David loved to hear Jez play and sing. Jez admired the drawings he caught David making. An all too familiar sequence follows these memories with its bitter title: *Friendly Fire*. Jez eviscerated; his body winched into the helicopter, his hand flopping, the last wave of the dead.

'You look miles away,' Lara says, as she subsides onto the sofa next to him, tucking her legs up beneath her, and placing a pack of playing cards on the table in front of them.

'Miles and years,' he says. 'I'm sorry.' Shakes his head as if to lose the memories.

'I thought we might play cards. Poker's my favourite.'

'Poker? You're full of surprises. I hadn't pegged you for a Dylan or Clapton fan. And now poker? Bring it on.'

'I didn't think you'd appreciate my punk collection.' She laughs, self-deprecating. 'I've mellowed with age. Shall we play for matchsticks or money?'

'Money, if you can afford to lose it?'

'Can you?' Lara jumps up and goes into the kitchen. She returns with a plastic bag full of five cent pieces. 'Here we go. I'll sell you some of these.'

David digs in his pocket and comes up with a two dollar coin. She counts out the silver.

'Here's to the high rollers,' David says, taking a swig of wine.

They play, Lara sitting next to him, square on, cross legged while he ostentatiously guards his cards. Most of the time, they're not worth guarding. But he's in it for the fun. If he's going to lose, he might as well lose bluffing on bad hands. Folding too often is boring and his antics make Lara laugh. Worth more than a couple of dollars, that is.

The game also means they are constantly looking into each other's faces, their eyes catching with the light of mutual scrutiny. And all the time David is wondering where the cards will lead and whether he's prepared to raise the stakes and gamble on a kiss.

The CD finishes. Lara yawns. They play another hand. His attempt to persuade her that he's holding more than a pair of eights fails dismally. Lara wins with a straight flush. She yawns again. Apologises.

'Drinking wine always makes me sleepy,' she says.

'Perhaps I'd better be going?'

She looks at him, appraising. He meets her eyes for a moment, but her candid inspection makes him self-conscious and he can't hold the gaze. He looks down and shuffles the pack.

'There's no need to, not right now.'

He glances at her, trying to read her intention, feeling like a schoolboy paralysed by the fear of stuffing things up. She smiles at him and leans forward, unfolding herself, so that she's on her knees. She kisses him on the lips, David aware of their ripe softness before she kneels up and away. Something in her eyes invites him. He turns and holds her shoulders, eases her towards him. They kiss again, more passionately this time, the moist invitation of touching tongues.

Lara breaks off the engagement. She kneels back on her heels. David slumps back into the sofa. There's a long pause, a breathing silence.

'Look,' she says, 'I've had a great time tonight and I think you're a really nice guy, a really nice *sexy* guy, but after the disaster with Rob, and with us being neighbours and all ... I don't want to make another mistake.'

David pulls a comic face. 'I know what you mean. I'm scared to death.' He's telling the truth, while trying to hide it, repeating to himself Donna's mantras about relaxation and pleasure.

'All I'm saying is, I think we should go slowly.'

'Slowly sounds good to me.' He turns to her again. Something in her face, her demeanour, gives him confidence. She seems at ease with her sensuality. He reaches and lets his fingers trail across her cheek. They kiss again, this time with more intensity, more commitment. His hand is on her breast when she peels away and struggles to her feet. David thinks he's offended her, until he sees her face and her outstretched hand.

'Come on,' she says with a grin as wide as a river. 'Remember, it's just a casual affair, okay? You can manage that can't you?'

'I dunno. I'll give it my best shot,' David says, as he takes her hand and she leads him to the bedroom.

She takes gentle command, unbuttoning him, stroking, releasing, until the power of her desire gives him assurance and he loses himself in the miracle of her, wanting only to give back the passion she's aroused.

¢

When David stumbles to consciousness, disoriented in the middle of the night, three things impinge upon his consciousness in quick succession. First, the surprise of being entirely naked; second, the warmth of Lara's hand on his stomach; third, a small face with blond hair staring at him.

'That's my mummy,' Zak says. 'Not yours.'

'Oh, shit. It sure is, mate.'

'What's the matter,' Lara murmurs.

'It's Zak.'

'Mummy, have you been 'isgusting with Dawid?'

'No, darling, we've just been having a cuddle, come on back to bed.'

'I think I should go,' David says.

'I want to get into bed with you, Mummy,' Zak sounds on the verge of tears.

'You stay where you are,' Lara says to David. She's up and round the bed and takes Zak by the hand. 'Come on, little guy,' she says to him. 'Back to your own bed. Let's go and see Mr Robinson.'

By the time Lara returns, David is sitting on the edge of the bed hauling on his jeans.

'There's no need to go. He's asleep again. It's half-past three. Nice and warm in here.'

David doesn't take much persuading. Lara is naked too, and in the half-light with her hair tumbled about, she looks to David like all the beauty in the tired world.

'If you're sure,' he says, and pulls off his jeans.

As they settle together to sleep again, he curls into her back. 'I've never liked the word "cuddle",' he whispers, 'but suddenly it's taken on new meaning.'

He feels her giggle in his arms, before the night, suddenly delicious, envelops them both once more.

XII

'David, wake up! Come *on*. There's someone hammering on your door. I think it's your daughter.'

David struggles to surface, snared by dream. For a moment, he's completely disoriented—naked, alone in a strange bed. Lara comes into focus. She's up and dressed and standing at the bedroom door, yelling at him. The bedside clock says 8.34 am.

He swings up and out, pulls his strides on, trying to reassemble himself. Memories of last night with Lara collide with rising anxiety about Josie. What the hell's she up to at this time in the morning?

'Don't let her go,' David says to Lara, who stands watching him.

'Not much chance of that. Can't you hear her yelling?'

As he leaves, they exchange a brief kiss. 'Thanks,' David says. 'Thanks for everything.'

He's still pulling on his sweater as he emerges onto the concrete walkway between the flats. Josie looks distressed, beating on his door with her closed fists, shouting, 'Dad, Dad, are you all right?'

'Whoa,' he says. 'Take it easy. No need to break the door down.'

Instead of looking pleased to see him, Josie looks stunned. She stares at him, brings her hands up to her temples, her face frozen.

David moves to hug her. She stands unresponsive, resisting, tears leaking down her face.

'Hey, hey, hey,' he says. 'Everything's okay.'

'I thought you might be ... I thought you might have ...'

'Don't be daft. Come on, let's get you inside.' He unlocks the door. Ushers her in. 'Sit. Breathe. Calm down. I'll get the kettle on.' He stoops to switch on the fan heater. Places his hand on Josie's shoulder, gives her a squeeze. 'Let me sort out a brew.'

David bustles about in the kitchen, washing mugs, distributing teabags. As he waits for the kettle to boil, he's aware of Josie sitting hunched on the edge of the sofa, knees together, head down, blowing her nose quietly, getting herself together. It's just his luck, he thinks, she should turn up this early and catch him next door. It's embarrassing. Complicates things. But when he thinks of all that happened last night, he can't be sorry. He has no regrets. None at all.

David dishes up the tea. He pulls up a straight-backed chair, so he's sitting opposite Josie. 'All right,' he says. 'Let's have it. What's the trouble? It's pretty early on a Sunday morning to be banging on my door.'

Josie gives him a look. 'Well, yeah. I can tell you weren't expecting me. I thought it would be okay. You're usually up early, aren't you?'

'Usually, yeah. Last night was ... unusual.' He grins trying to make light of it, win her over. It doesn't work.

Josie shakes her head. 'I can't believe it.'

'Believe what?'

'That you're shacking up with the bikie chick next door. She's only a few years older than me.'

'Lara isn't a bikie. I'm not shacking up with her. And she's older than you think she is.'

Josie looks at him with scornful eyes, cradling her mug with both hands. 'How old is she, then?'

'I don't know. It's not necessarily polite to ask.'

'So, you don't *know* if she's older than I think she is?'

'Never mind. Can we move on? I'm guessing you didn't come round to discuss me and Lara.'

'No, but it makes everything so much worse.'

Josie's voice tails off. She looks miserable, head down, her hair hanging either side of her face. She's staring into her tea mug as if it might hold the answers to the world of pain she seems to be in.

'I can't see how,' David says. 'I reckon you'd like her if you gave her a chance.'

Josie looks up, stares him in the face. 'I'm going to be getting to know her, then?'

'I dunno. Up to you. Not if you don't want to.'

'I don't want to.'

'Fair enough.' David pauses. Decides he can't wait any longer. He rolls a smoke, aware of Josie watching him, her lips compressed, her eyes hostile. He lights up, exhales.

'Why don't you tell me why you're so wound up?'

'Mum and Barry are getting married. Made this big

announcement last night. Champagne, roast lamb dinner, red wine. They let me drink. Tiny amounts, but. And then they say we're going to make a new start as a family, sell up in Flynn and move to some new fancy-smanshy place in Red Hill. So, I say what about college, what about my mates? I've got my HSC next year. And Barry's like, oh, we'll sort something out. So, I say nothing. Drink the champagne. Play along. It was sickening the way they were looking at each other.' Josie shudders. Takes a breath. Before David can say anything, she goes on. 'So, I decided to get round here early to talk it through with you and what do I find? My dad has lost his mind as well and is fresh from a night of passion with Ms Tattooed-Single-Mum next door. Then you ask me why I'm upset. Why *shouldn't* I be upset?'

'Will you calm down and give me a chance? They haven't wasted much time putting you in the picture.'

'You *knew*?'

'Only since Tuesday. Your Ma asked me not to tell you. What was I supposed to do? She said she wanted to wait for the right moment.'

'There is no right moment.' Josie raises her voice, almost yelling.

David struggles to smother a flare of anger. 'There's no point shouting at me. You need to take your foot off the pedal. I understand you needing to vent, but there's not a lot I can do about your mother's arrangements.'

'I don't want to live with bloody boring bastard Barry full-time, and I don't want to live in Red Hill!' Josie glares at David.

After taking another long drag, David tips his head back, blows smoke at the ceiling. He tries to hose her down. 'It's a nice area. Close to Manuka and the night life. Maybe if they buy a McMansion up there, you might score a bigger room. More privacy.'

'I *hate* Barry. And what about college? I can't travel to Hawker from there everyday. I've got my exams. And like I say, there's my mates. I'm just not doing it. I'm not going.'

David is at a loss. He stubs his cigarette out. 'Fancy another cup of tea?' he offers.

'No.'

'Righto.' He allows a silence to fall. It's his turn to stare at the bottom of his mug, hoping for inspiration.

'The thing is,' Josie's voice is small now, but intense. It makes David sit up. He looks at her, still with her head down staring at the floor. She looks vulnerable. The sight of her makes his heart sore. He wants to hold her and comfort her and make everything all right for her. He knows he can't. It's bitter knowledge.

'I was thinking,' she goes on. 'Like, before I've seen you coming from next door, I thought maybe, if Ma and BB insist on moving to Red Hill, I could come and live with you. I could get the bus from Civic to Hawker. Or you could give me a lift. I thought maybe you'd like some company. We could, like, help each other, you know. But now that idea's down the pan. I don't know what I'm going to do.'

'Oh, Josie, Josie, Josie. Oh, *shit*.' David is blindsided. Didn't see this one coming. He has a hollow, breathless feeling, as if someone's punched him in the gut. His mind races through the implications. The impossibility of it. What can he say? He has to say *something*. He tries not to bluster, attempts to sound reasonable.

'Look, first off, I want you to know this isn't about Lara, though I've no doubt your mother might make it an issue, if she gets wind of it. But that's the thing. It's your mum and Barry who would make it difficult. Your mother won't let you go without a fight. And I can see her point. A girl your age—you need your mum.'

'Like a hole in the head,' Josie chimes in. 'I need my dad too.'

'Yeah, that's great. But look around.' He flings his arm out in a wide gesture. 'Look at this place. You've said yourself what a mess it is. It's not fit for you. There's nowhere for you to sleep, apart from anything else.'

'We could clean it up. I'd help you. I could sleep in your studio, or you could move in there and I could have your room. There's room for two, if you want to do it.'

David swallows. He feels nauseous. 'It's not a question of what I or you want. It's about practicalities. The place isn't big enough. It isn't right. I don't want to start a war with your mother and Barry.'

Josie stands up, red in the face. She loses it. She's seething. 'What you really mean is since you've found a ready-made family next door and you've got your painting, there's no room for me. That's what you really mean. Ma and Barry don't want me either.' She moves towards the door.

David's on his feet, too, his voice raised, pleading. 'That's bullshit, Josie. Don't go. Don't leave like this. Sit down. Stop being a drama queen. I'll make us some breakfast.'

'There's nothing more to say. I've had it with all of you. I've had it with feeling like a parcel with a bomb in it being chucked between Ma and you. I'm gone.'

She moves away. David tries to grab her arm, but she shrugs him off. She's at the door. David goes towards her, arms held out. 'Please, Josie, wait on a bit. We can work something out.'

But she's gone—slams the door. David opens it. She's running down the walkway, her lovely auburn curls bouncing as she goes. He thinks about chasing her but then hesitates, considers what he would do when he caught up. He doesn't want a physical altercation. He can't easily surrender and say, 'Sure, come and live here.' He can't see the right way forward. He stands there feeling lost and horribly alone—the beauty and promise of the previous evening erased. He looks at the sky, concrete grey with clouds scudding. He shivers, registers winter fingering his skin, reaching for his bones.

XIII

Days go by. David hears nothing from Josie or Margaret. Their silence weighs on him. Every day, anxiety coils and clenches and won't go away. The worst thing is feeling helpless, not knowing what to do. At least in Vietnam on ops or picquet duty, he had a role, a job to do, however fearful. He knew what was expected. It was often tense and hours upon hours were spent impossibly strung out, but thanks to your training you had this self-reliance, a confidence that if things kicked-off you'd know how to react.

Now, he is bewildered by the situation. He has no idea. He spends hours in fruitless self-examination and self-persuasion. Surely he *is* right. It *is* wildly impractical for Josie to come and live with him. All his arguments against it are good. There would be ructions with Margaret and Barry. The place isn't fit. *He* isn't fit. He's getting along okay on his own. But living with someone else is another matter. He can't imagine how it would work. He keeps such erratic hours. There's his painting. The way he likes to smoke and drink. All the strategies he's developed for getting through the day and night. Having Josie around the place full-time—he can't imagine it working out well for either of them.

And then there's Lara. David knows it isn't fair, but he resents the way Josie's troubles have impinged on what seems a miraculous development in his personal life. But then David remembers the look of misery on Josie's face.

The knot tightens in his gut.

He can't, he won't apologise for sleeping with Lara. He repeatedly tells himself she isn't the primary reason he doesn't want Josie to move in. But is he being honest with himself? He doesn't know. He doesn't know anything.

Painting is David's way of trying to cope with the whirligig of emotion which churns his stomach. But with so much on his mind, he's finding it hard to settle to work. He stands in front of the canvas, brush in hand, feeling flat and defeated. He's been trying to work on the picture of the dead Vietnamese girl, adding to the composition by enhancing the suggestion of a track leading across the painting, through darkness to the broken body, and from the body towards a horizon of light. David remembers the way the jungle sometimes seemed like a tunnel in its claustrophobic embrace. It's this effect he's after, the blackness encroaching on the shattered body. Yet he also wants to lead the eye away towards a lighter future. It's a question of creating the right colour values for this emergence, and avoiding any 'yellow brick road' sentimentality in the rendition of the path.

So far, he thinks, it isn't working. The voices of Lara and Zak through the wall provide a constant siren song, tempting David to give up the solitary struggle with his work. He finds himself not concentrating, straining to hear what's happening next door, wishing he was with them and cursing the decision he's made with Lara to be 'sensible', and to take a 'softly, softly' approach to their relationship. Recognising the dangers and temptations of their propinquity, they've agreed on the fiction of 'a casual affair' to be conducted at the weekends, with maybe the odd cup of coffee in between.

In fact, they see each other every day but so far have resisted all temptations to spend a weeknight together. It's like a form of slow torture to David.

Fuck it. It's no wonder he can't work. David flings brush and palette to the floor sending vermilion paint frittering across the bare boards like blood spray. He slumps into his chair and stares at the painting, his belief and confidence draining away like leaves carried by dirty rainwater down a gutter, his work overwhelmed by the raw immediacy of his feelings for Lara and Josie.

He goes into the kitchen, pours himself a whisky. He drinks standing up, propped against the draining board, staring out the window at the walkway and beyond to the crouched buildings of the Gorman House community arts complex where the middle-class wannabees play. The light is late afternoon, winter grey. It will soon be cold and dark. Maybe he's just a wannabee too.

As he raises the glass to his lips, he notices his hand is shaking. He needs to get a grip. He tries to tell himself the right stories.

How the painting will come good if he keeps going; failure is assured if he gives up. This is just a negative mood, part of the process. If you want to create anything worthwhile, you have to be prepared to battle. He needs to be patient, wait on his imagination, wait to be in the zone again.

He drains the whisky, goes to the fridge and finds a beer. A wave of fizzing cold ale refreshes the dry whisky burn on his tongue. It's early for this kind of drinking, but he doesn't care. He needs to take the edge off his frustration, put a stop to his stomach churning with doubt and anxiety.

The stubby is nearly empty when David hears Lara's door bang. It'll be Zak. David opens the door before the kid has a chance to knock. He's a welcome guest, since in recent days he's become the emissary between David and Lara. It's as if neither of the adults want to take the lead in initiating meetings, each waiting for the other to make a move. But Zak has no such compunction. Early in the mornings, or when he's back from kindy, he often calls, opening up the opportunity for Lara and David to see each other without too much pressure.

The kid wanders in, swinging Mr Robinson by an arm. Zak is wearing blue wellington boots and a red anorak. 'Hello Dawid,' he says, 'I've got new boots. Are you drinking beer?'

'Yep. Good boots.'

'Can I have beer?'

'Nope.'

'Why not?'

'It's only good for tigers. What you need is Cola.'

'All right then.' Zak doesn't sound convinced and trails Mr Robinson along the ground until he's sitting on the battered old couch opposite the TV. 'Can we watch cartoons?'

David brings over the Cola and another beer for himself. He twists the top off the beer, switches the TV on, and sits down.

Zak says, 'If you keep drinking beer, you'll turn into a beer bottle.'

David grins. 'Half-full or half-empty?'

Zak looks at him, puzzled. 'You're funny.' And then, in his curiously formal way, 'I do not know what you mean.'

'Never mind. You will one day.'

As they settle down to watch cartoons, David thinks of himself as a beer bottle and tries to answer his own question. The hectic scrambles of *Tom and Jerry* provide an accompaniment to his maunderings, the violence of their combat never quite comic enough to David's mind.

Jerry is winding Tom through a mangle when Lara knocks and enters.

'Hi guys, what's happening?'

'Mummy, Mummy, Dawid's turning into a beer bottle.'

'He doesn't look that green to me.'

'He will be. He will be,' Zak shouts and bounces on the settee.

She turns her smiling attention to David. 'So, how was your day? Good?'

He hears the tone, just a little forced, too bright and breezy, and understands her nervousness. Every encounter since they slept together has been like this. They're dancing round each other, trying for a cool he knows he doesn't feel and strongly suspects Lara doesn't either.

'How was yours?'

'Same old. Same old.'

'Can I get you something?'

Lara stands uncertainly eyeing the beer bottle. 'I'd love to, but I'd better not. Better get Zak home for his tea.'

'You could have something here.' He tries not to sound too hopeful.

'Better not. Best keep to the agreement. Save ourselves for the weekend.' She gives him a knowing look, conspiratorial.

'Whatever you think's a fair thing.'

¢

Lara and Zak bustle out. David ruffles Zak's hair, says he'll see him tomorrow. As they leave, Lara turns and mimes a kiss. It's better than nothing and enough of a promise to be going on with. David decides to celebrate with another beer and a small whisky chaser. He knows he's in a dangerous mood and he doesn't care. He feels like tying one on. He wants to forget his work, lose himself for a while. Put some music on and make some dinner for himself. A baked spud perhaps, with some cheese and beans.

He's into *Cold Chisel* and emptying a can of beans into a pan with a fag hanging out of his mouth when the phone rings. He answers, reaching for the ashtray. He hears a pause, an intake of breath.

'It's me,' Josie says, her voice nervous, tentative.

David's heart bounces. 'G'day. How are you going?'

'Okay, I suppose.'

'What does that mean?'

David hears the sigh before Josie says, 'It means I'm okay. All right?'

'Keep your hair on. I was only asking. You weren't okay when I last saw you.'

'No, well. No wonder, really. I was in shock.'

'And you've got over that now?'

'I wouldn't say I was over it. I'm working on it.'

'Good on you. What can't be cured must be endured.'

'Jesus Christ, Dad. What's that crap?'

'Just something my dad used to say. There were Presbyterians in his family.'

'Presby—*what*?'

'Never mind. The point is to roll up your sleeves and get on with it.'

'Yeah. Well, thanks for the advice.'

There's a silence. David is unsure where this is going. 'Look, I've no idea what's going to happen between Lara and me. We're taking it easy. I'm sorry if the idea of me being with her upsets you. But I'm not going to apologise for my feelings. And about your mother's marriage, like I said, there's not a lot I can do about her arrangements. I *did* try to talk to her about going easy on you, not grounding you and so on, but you have to meet us halfway, Josie. Use some smarts. It's no good deliberately antagonising your Ma and BB. Going easy on the booze would be a start.'

'Thanks, Pa. You've taught me all I know about booze.'

'Okay. Maybe I deserve that one. But you're sixteen, Josie. I don't believe in prohibition, but I want you to look after yourself. And obviously, rolling home pissed isn't going to do your cause any good with your ma and Barry.'

'Yeah, I get it. But like I said, I've nearly had it with Ma and BB. I'm not going to live in Red Hill. No way.'

'I'll have another talk with your mum about that. But after all's said and done, you might have to wear it. The main thing is to concentrate on your schoolwork and do your best not to make things worse by mounting some kind of disobedience campaign. Think about it. It's not in your interests to back your ma and BB into a corner.'

David hears the sigh before the reply.

'Message received and understood.'

Another silence. David searches for a way forward past the attitude. It's still not clear why she's phoned him. Before he can ask, as if she's read his thoughts, Josie says, 'I didn't really call to talk about all that.'

A pause. In the whisper of her breath, David can almost hear Josie gearing herself up to speak.

'The thing is, Dad, I'd like you to meet Michael. I wondered if we could come round?'

David resists his immediate impulse to ask why. He takes a minute to order his response. 'Sure,' he says. 'Any particular reason?'

'Well, obviously, I've talked to him about you. He'd like to meet you. And I'd like you to see what kind of guy he is so you can stop worrying and being suspicious. I think it might make things easier.'

'Has he met Barry and your mother?'

'No.'

'Why me?'

'Because you won't embarrass me. Ma and BB are so like, unrelaxed, uncool. I think you'll like each other. I think it will be good. And it might help when you talk to Mum. I mean, you'll be able to reassure her.'

Though he's aware of nebulous misgivings, David can't see how he can refuse. 'I'm flattered,' he says.

They agree on next Sunday afternoon. David says he'll have the scones and jam and cream ready.

'Don't make a fuss,' Josie says before she rings off. 'And thanks, Pa.'

¢

Off the phone, David finishes his whisky and his beer. He holds the pan and spoons beans into his mouth, an avid wolfing while his mind races. He wonders if Josie has some ulterior motive. The horrible idea occurs to him that she might be thinking of moving in with this guy. She couldn't, could she? Not at sixteen. David pushes the thought away—puts it down to paranoia. Maybe Josie really does want to reassure him.

He paces up and down. Another notion occurs to him. Josie

didn't talk about Lara at all. Made no response to what he'd said about her. Is Josie thinking that if she introduces Michael, maybe it will pave a way for David to introduce Lara to them both? A foursome? Safety in numbers? That wasn't going to happen any time soon. David would need to feel pretty confident about Lara and about this Michael guy first. He'd also need to feel confident that Josie wasn't going to go off at Lara. He needed to know her attitude was receptive.

The thought of Lara makes him pause in his agitation. He listens for sounds from next door. She's listening to some music. It's quiet. He can't quite make out what it is, something gentle. Zak will be in bed by now.

Suddenly, he can't contain himself any longer. He needs to see her. He taps on the wall. She taps back. The next minute, he's knocking lightly at her door. When she lets him in, he says, 'Maybe the weekend can start on Thursdays?'

'I thought you'd never work it out,' she says.

XIV

Sunday afternoon. David is scurrying round the flat trying to tidy up. He shouldn't have agreed to meet here. They could have arranged a rendezvous at some café—neutral territory, a public place. Why he didn't suggest it, he can't think. Maybe it was because he was so surprised by Josie's request in the first place. He'd been anxious to say *yes,* build bridges, not start another row. His efforts now largely consist of piling stray cardboard cartons of unpacked possessions in his studio. Moving them from the kitchen and lounge room. Trying to create the illusion of order. As he stacks the boxes, his unfinished painting stares back at him from the easel like a reprimand.

Part of the process, he says to himself. He'll get back to it next week. He can make the work come good. He's learnt that he has to keep repeating positive affirmations. If he doesn't, if he allows all the negative voices in his head to have their say, then he'll give up. He'll never finish, he'll never paint again.

When he stops for a breather and takes time to really look at the unfinished picture, he sees enough there to make him think he should go on. Keep trying. It has promise. It isn't a complete failure. The central image of the broken body has an eerie power. It's getting the pathway right, the movement towards the light which is tricky. He needs to avoid prettiness. There has to be a sense of loss, pain, struggle, otherwise the suffering depicted will be glossed over too readily. The painting will become too easy to look at. It will become decoration rather than art.

As he says this to himself, he's aware of the irony it is decoration that sells. It's exactly what one of the gallery owners in Canberra said to him last time he summoned the courage to show some of his work with a view to selling.

'I can see the merits,' said Mr Barclay, 'but it's not really the kind of thing people want to hang in their lounge rooms, is it?'

David cares and doesn't care. He'd love to sell some work. But he can only paint what he's been given to paint. It's not possible to be pretty. He can't do it. And anyway, if he can get the triptych right, someone might see something in it that will persuade them to part with their cash. Or maybe he'll just give the paintings away. Give them to Josie, maybe. Wait and see.

Having got the cardboard boxes out of the way, David decides he'd better clean the kitchen floor and put a desperate vacuum over his dusty, faded rugs. It doesn't matter what he does. It's never going to make the place look flash—it's all too dark and dowdy for that. But at least he can try to create an impression of cleanliness. He hopes the young man isn't allergic to house dust.

Escaping the drudgery of his chores, David's mind wanders back to his painting and from there to Lara and the ecstasies he shared with her last night. He thinks about painting her, trying to capture the magic of her loveliness. As he does so, he recognises it would be an image, a simulacrum, a transformation. No painting in the world could capture the living breathing warmth of her. The emotional and physical intimacies of their sexual exchange are something else again. No paint or words could ever suffice.

Still, the idea is tantalising. David imagines Lara's warm skin tones and the palette he'd need to reproduce them. He would begin with Titanium White, Alizarin Crimson, Yellow Ochre, maybe Cadmium Lemon, Burnt Umber and French Ultramarine. He'd need at least a photograph of her to achieve the precise shades, mixing with a palette knife, seeing the subtle transformations, the magic and romance of colour.

It would be even better to have her in front of him. But that would mean having the courage to ask her. Risking refusal. He imagined placing her at an angle in soft lighting, just as he'd seen her perch on the edge of the bed, one knee over the other, brushing her hair. But maybe Lara would be self-conscious and think of it as a surrender to the male gaze. He would have to try to explain his painting as an act of love, of homage. He wasn't interested in the idea of 'possession' or 'capturing' her.

How could you? He thinks of the smooth softness of Lara's skin under his touch, the way he'd have to work to deliver the illusion of texture and translucency through the play of brushwork, the application of the paint. He rehearses the softness of her belly, the slight bulge and roundness where she's carried Zak, the shape of her breasts, the exact colour of her dark nipples. He would accentuate umber or raw sienna in the palette. Apart from the technical problems though, David considers there is a kind of abandonment of the self in the contemplation and creation of the artwork. There is sensuality too.

David remembers the feel of Lara's long elegant fingers on him, the press of their limbs. He can't help himself wanting to recall the unexpected wonder of her, the luxurious silky curls of her bush against the skin, her cries of pleasure as his tongue explored her, finding and teasing her clitoris, while she held his head, the taste of her making him want to drown. And then, when he entered her, the look in her eyes, the mutual recognition of passion, tenderness, growing in wave upon wave.

David has to stop his arousal. He's mopping the floor with an absurd fury. He sits, rolls a smoke, tries to laugh at himself.

Fails.

It was beautiful, that was the point.

Making love, giving themselves to each other, the blissful transcendence of ego in mutual exchange, the aesthetic and erotic in harmony. If sex wasn't like this it was reduced to the brutal or mechanistic or cold gymnastics. David thinks of his failures with Margaret—the way their attempts to recover intimacy ended in reflections of their battle—the collision of will and ego.

He makes himself switch focus. Thinks about the impending interview with Jo-Jo and this Michael character. Wonders if they're having sex. He doesn't want to deny Josie pleasure. Love. How could he? But she *is* only sixteen. Just a kid. He wants her erotic experience to be safe, warm and fine. He wants to protect her from the wrong kind of bloke. Thinking about this is detumescent. Something to be thankful for, at least.

When David goes back to his cleaning, he schools himself to think in more abstract terms about physical experience and representation. Just as there's no use talking about his experience of Vietnam, there's no use talking to a third party about sexual encounters. There is something ineffable that remains elusive and resists. Art might try to capture the unnameable, the unspeakable, but it always falls short.

This is the essential difficulty of David's paintings about Vietnam. He has never wanted to even try to capture the 'reality' of violence. He knows it can't be done. People get off on graphic attempts. That's why there's so much mayhem depicted on the TV, in movies, in books. The audience experience a vicarious thrill. It's only when reality impinges the awfulness takes over. And even then, if you're not the one hurt, if you're the one inflicting the violence, you feel no physical pain, only the psychological trauma—the awfulness of the terrible sights and sounds of the wounded and dying.

This is the problem with all depictions of war. To leave violence out is to cleanse the experience, yet to try to reproduce the violence risks prurience, inaccuracy and a different kind of cleansing. There is no physical pain attached to watching movies, reading books, looking at pictures. People do that for pleasure. There's the paradox.

Pleasure brings David back to his beautiful night with Lara and the equally difficult issue of depicting erotic sensuality.

Is it possible to portray the beauty of sex without becoming pornographic? And yet not to try to image sensual experience seems to somehow suggest shame, belittlement, negation.

David has no answers to these dilemmas. His ambition in his triptych is to explore, come to whatever temporary solutions he can. He wants the broken doll-like image of the woman warrior to be disturbing, to provoke thought rather than the frisson of shocked revulsion. Can he make it work? He doesn't know.

For now, he needs to dig out his crappy old vacuum cleaner and give the rugs a going over.

¶

It's 4.00 pm. David hasn't baked scones. He's bought a packet of Tim Tams instead. Josie's favourite. He's boiled the kettle and has mugs primed with teabags. He just needs Josie and Michael to turn up. Get this over with. He's resisted the temptation to settle himself with a drop of whisky. Stone cold sober he is, and has all the strung-out nerves to prove it. There's nothing to do but wait.

He wonders what Lara is doing. Probably her ironing for the week ahead. Zak will be playing with his robot or watching cartoons. David knows he wouldn't necessarily want to join them right now. He'd want to be painting if it weren't for this meeting. Cosy domesticity is okay in small doses. He isn't sure he wants it full-time. He wonders what Lara wants. Will she be content going forward to be together but separate? Particularly given how much older he is than her?

This fruitless speculation is terminated by a knock on the door. Okay. Operation Boyfriend commencing. As he strides to let the guests in, David's heartbeat becomes an uncomfortable thudding tattoo in his chest.

Josie bustles in followed by her bloke. She's as nervous as David is, making the introductions before they've caught their breath or taken their coats off. David clocks she's dressed for the occasion. The black jeans have gone, replaced by a long hippy-style flounced skirt in dark maroon which falls nearly to her ankles where the Doc Martens take over. Her jumper, though, is black worn over a blouse, which, from the look of the collar, has some kind of floral design. She doesn't quite look like herself.

Michael, whom, Josie keeps referring to as 'Mickey' (Mouse, David wonders) is tall, dark and handsome.

Bastard.

He's over six foot with a mop of brown curly Heathcliff hair and eyes like shining mahogany beads. He has fashionable stubble instead of a beard. He's dressed in blue jeans, a check Ben Sherman style shirt like a tablecloth and R.M. Williams boots. He can't be all bad, David thinks, or can he? Michael's teeth look white enough to be used in an advert for Dulux gloss: are they really natural?

David is assimilating all this as he gestures to them to sit. He apologises for the cramped and insalubrious space. Brews the tea. He proudly proffers the Tim Tams.

As they settle down with their tea and biscuits, Josie and Michael hunched together on the battered sofa, David wonders what the fuck he's going to say to them. He starts with some anodyne questions, playing back to Michael what Josie has already told him about the bloke. In this way it's established that 'Mickey' is indeed a student of history and politics with the added detail, somewhat alarming to David, that he's in his third year and thinking of doing Honours next year. This means he must be at least five years older than Jo-Jo. Obviously, there's nothing he can say to Michael on this subject. He'll save the commentary for Josie later, though the issue of age difference is going to be tricky, given David's situation with Lara.

Having established that the young man lives in Hawker (of course he does, *upper* Hawker by the look and sound of him) that he met Josie in a pub in Manuka (the same one he'd seen them in) and that he wants to be a journalist when he grows up (if he grows up), David finds himself falling into a well of silence.

Josie doesn't help out. She's nibbling sedately on a Tim Tam, which, David notices, she refrains from dunking in her tea—her usual modus operandi—before sucking the chocolate off. Obviously, standards are being maintained.

David's worry about how to construct a rope ladder to climb out of the social chasm he finds himself in doesn't last long. Josie's friend is all smooth smiling confidence. Having dealt with David's minor and gentle questioning, Michael starts in on his own investigation.

'Josie tells me you're an artist. That must be great.'

David gives Josie a look before he replies. 'I dunno about

that. I'm never quite comfortable with that word. I worry about being pretentious. I'm not sure I'm good enough. I'm certainly not one of the smock and beret brigade. I'm a painter, but. Not a decorator.'

'Wow, Dad,' Josie says. 'That's the most I've heard you say about your art *ever*.'

David doesn't respond, regards his daughter with cool eyes.

'I'd love to see some of your work,' Michael says, the white teeth shining sweetness and light.

David tries not to sound ungracious. 'Yeah, well. Maybe one day. I don't like showing unfinished pictures.'

Michael greets this remark with silence. He seems to consider for a few moments, before edging forward slightly in his seat and turning to angle more towards David as if wishing to engage him more closely.

'It seems quite a leap from the army to art,' Michael says. 'Kind of unusual.'

David glances at Josie again. What the hell has she been telling this bloke? 'If you say so,' David replies, trying to keep his tone even. 'My stint in the army was a long time ago.'

'Yes, Josie was saying ...'

David regards his daughter not bothering to keep the displeasure from his expression.

Michael doesn't notice or ignores the exchange. He's relentless, as if on some kind of a mission. 'So, do you think of yourself as a war artist?'

'No, I don't.' David hopes the curt reply might bring the

interrogation to an end, but it's clear Michael is not to be easily deterred.

'Do you think it *helps*? Painting, I mean,' the young man says, a look of concern assembled across his face.

'What do you mean?' David asks. 'Helps with what?'

'With the PTSD. Josie was telling me about it.'

David gives his daughter another narrow look. She reddens. Darts Michael a glance. She looks as uncomfortable as David feels. He experiences the flint-sparks of anger, takes a breath. Trying to maintain his cool, he says, 'I'm not sure that's any of your business,' and then with a wry grin aiming for a little self-irony, 'I don't like to talk about it.'

'Sorry, yeah, I understand that,' Michael says. 'But it seems a pity. I'm genuinely interested. I'm writing this long essay on Vietnam—the history and politics of Australia's involvement in the war. I've been reading a lot. But it's not the same as talking to people who experienced it firsthand. Don't you agree? I mean, it's not often you get a chance to talk to a Vietnam Vet. Do you know what I mean? I've talked to my dad a lot about it because he was involved in the protest movement, the moratorium marches and that, so it's really interesting to meet someone on the other side. But I don't mean to intrude.'

'Not wanting to intrude is good. I don't know if Josie put you up to this or not, but I'll give you the drum right now. I'm not talking about Vietnam and that's final.'

Josie is shaking her head as if to deny responsibility, but she doesn't speak. Instead, she looks at Michael imploringly.

Places a restraining hand on his arm. Michael gives her hand a pat which maybe is meant to be reassuring but just looks condescending to David. Michael shuffles forward another inch and shrugs Josie's hand away. It's evident he's not prepared to give up yet.

'Yeah. I get it,' he says. 'But it seems a waste somehow. I mean how are people to know what it was like, to understand, if those who were there won't talk about it? And even if you don't want to go into what it was like fighting, I'd be really interested to hear your views on the validity of the war, the cause. Do you think it was right for Australia to be involved? Do you think it was a just war? Do you think it was in Australia's interest?'

'Jesus,' David says. 'I reckon you'll make a good journalist. You've got more front than David Jones. But you've picked the wrong bloke. I'm surprised Josie's not let you know. I'm not talking about the war. Not the politics, not the fighting. None of it. There are plenty of books on the subject. If you go to the War Memorial you can read letters, diaries and all the rest of it. You don't need to hear from me.'

'Do you think you were duped? I mean there's a lot of stuff which suggests PTSD is worse because the war, the cause, was controversial. Do you think you were conned into fighting an unjust war?'

'He doesn't give up easy, does he, your mate?' David addresses Josie. 'Did you know he wanted to interview me?'

Josie shakes her head. She looks miserable. 'I knew Michael was interested,' she offers weakly.

'That's great,' says David. 'An interested student is a good student. And I suppose in the final analysis we do need journalists. God knows they need thick hides. So, the only problem here is me. My answer to your question as to whether I was duped or not is *fuck off*. I'm not your subject. I refuse. I don't know you from a bar of soap, yet you think it's okay to come into my home and start insulting me. Fuck off.'

'No insult was intended.' Michael sounds wounded, defensive-aggressive.

'Well, that's good to know. It doesn't change my answer.'

'I think we should leave,' Josie says.

'I think that might be for the best,' David agrees.

'I didn't mean to cause any trouble,' Michael offers.

'Come on,' Josie urges. 'Let's go.'

David has had enough with Michael's mealy-mouthed remarks, which don't actually include an apology. 'You seem pretty intent to me,' he says. 'I can't make up my mind if you're stupid or just very insensitive.'

'Stop it, Dad. There's no need.'

David holds his hands up in surrender. He stands by the door while they struggle into their coats. Josie mouths 'Sorry,' as she walks past him. Neither David nor Michael offer to shake hands.

When they've gone, David feels sick with anger and frustration. He can't tell where Josie stands. He's pretty sure she didn't put Michael up to this stunt, but it's also obvious she's been blabbing to the guy.

Christ, it's not David's fault. Surely he has a right to silence. Even criminals have that.

Was he duped?

What a fucking question.

XV

David lies in bed watching Lara as she undresses. She's still talking to him as she undoes the top button of her jeans and pushes them down. He loves how unself-conscious she is with him already. As if they've been doing this for years. Yet the scarf she's draped over the bedside lamp, making the light subdued and rosy tells a different story. He tries to concentrate on what she's saying, but the emergence of her long and finely muscled legs as she steps out of her trousers proves too distracting. He's already painting her in his mind, even though he knows he can never do her justice. At the same time, he wonders whether 'love' means this entrancing ability to be at ease with each other.

They've spent the last couple of hours engrossed in conversation about David's problems with Josie, the row with Michael. Over a glass of wine, David has relived his anger and indignation, while Lara has tried her best to calm and placate. When she said that Michael and Josie's curiosity was 'understandable', David had threatened to lose his temper with her. But she managed to talk him down, soothe him and smooth him.

'I'm not saying *I* want to know,' she said, 'I'm just saying I can feel where the kids are coming from.'

But David sensed Lara's curiosity, which forced him into further attempts to explain his unwillingness to voice the details of his war. 'I'm afraid,' he said. 'Afraid of her, of you, of anyone misunderstanding because you weren't there. Thank God you weren't there. But being there is the only way to really understand.'

Now, Lara's still talking as she pulls her jumper over her head, but David isn't listening. He's watching, memorising every gesture, every movement as she emerges from her clothes, noting the stretch of her arms, the ripple of muscle, the play of light on her skin against the maroon wool. Then, she's standing in black bra and pants at the foot of the bed with her hands on her hips. 'You haven't heard a word I've been saying, have you?'

David places his hands behind his head. 'Fair go. It's difficult to concentrate when you're ripping your gear off. And you *are* so, so lovely.'

'Don't think you can flatter your way out of this. Nothing else is coming off till you tell me what I've been talking about.'

'Er. Okay. Let's see. There seemed to be a long meandering ramble—'

'Careful, buster.'

'—you were thinking aloud about curiosity, how natural it is if you're close to someone to want to know things about them.' David pauses.

'So far so good.'

'But no reward?'

She shakes her head. 'More needed.'

'I dunno.' David rubs his forehead with his fingers in mock despair. 'It was the lead up to a question.'

'Good, now we're getting somewhere.'

'But that's when you were pulling your jumper off. I couldn't hear. It was like you were talking under water.'

'Nonsense. You weren't paying attention.'

'It was some bloody thing about the army.'

'Very good. Well done. I asked if you'd mind telling me whether you were a conscript or not?'

'Oh, I get it. If I was a conscript, I'm off the hook, is that it?'

'It is a bit different from volunteering.'

'Maybe. As it happens, I was a conscript. But don't be fooled. I wanted to go. I mean, once I was conscripted I wanted to be in the infantry and I wanted to go to Vietnam.'

Lara frowns. She sits on the end of the bed with one leg folded beneath her, facing him. 'But why? I don't get it.'

'Family tradition. My grandfather, my great-uncles, my dad; all the Young men had fought. Why should I be any different? I would have felt bad, not to go. I wanted to test myself. Might even have volunteered if I hadn't been conscripted. I was bloody bored on civvy street.'

'But you must have known it would be awful.'

'You know in your head, but not in your guts. You know it in a kind of abstract way. But that's part of the curiosity. You only really *know* what it's like if you're in it. That's my point.'

Lara looks down, considers for a moment.

'Let me ask *you* a question,' David sits up, eager now, engaged. 'Have you ever been to the War Memorial?'

She looks at him, frowning. 'Well, yes. I've been once or twice.'

'Why?'

'I don't know. Curiosity, I suppose.'

'Curiosity. Exactly. And, if you're honest, excitement. The emotional buzz. I reckon we've all got it, this part of our ancient brain, a strange attraction to warfare and violence. People love it—as long as it's vicarious, as long as they're not experiencing the reality of pain, the reality of the consequences. For that you have to be there. End of story.'

Lara nods, quiet now. 'I've never really thought of it like that. I don't know. I think I understand.' She's silent for a moment, thoughtful. 'Have you ever said any of this to Josie?'

'I've told her over and over again you had to be there to understand it.'

'I mean *why* you went and everything you've just said about curiosity and violence.'

'Well, no. But she is only sixteen.'

'I think she's old enough to understand some of this stuff. You don't have to describe your experiences to her. Tell her some more about how you feel. Explain yourself to her. She might get off your case then.'

'You make it sound easy, but it's not. And now with this Michael bloke on the scene it's particularly uneasy. I dunno. I'll think about it.'

'Attaboy.' Lara smiles as she stands, reaches behind her and unclasps her bra. She stoops to take off her knickers. Her breasts fall forward and sway slightly.

'What I *don't* understand,' David says, 'is how anyone as beautiful as you can think about getting into bed with me.'

She smiles as she slides in next to him. It's easy, she says. 'I like you. And I think you're wise.' And then he feels the blissful embrace of her skin and the invitation of her lips and he begins to lose himself in exquisite sensation.

¢

After they've made love, and are lying in each other's arms, the light extinguished and sleep not far away, Lara, with her hand in David's hair at the back of his head, whispers, 'All the Young men, but not my Zak. Never Zak.'

'No, not Zak. I hope never Zak.'

¢

In the morning, things are hectic. Lara has the alarm set for 6.30 am. She's out of the shower in her royal blue terry towelling dressing gown by 6.50 am. David watches from the bed as she applies eyeliner. She's sitting at the dressing table which is against the wall at the foot of the bed. She has her back to him. Her hair is glossy from the shower, blue-black as a raven's wing. Lara can see him in the mirror watching her. She half-turns and says, 'G'day.' She offers him the use of her bathroom for a shower. Her make-up done, Lara doesn't stay long. She's off to get Zak up, dressed, breakfasted and ready for kindy.

David lies there awhile, coming to, unwilling to leave the warmth of the frowsty bed, his memories as stained as the sheets with desire. He thinks about the prospects for the coming day. In between struggling with his painting of the broken woman on the jungle track, he's primed two canvases for the second and third paintings in his triptych. Today, he could make a start on the second picture. He thinks maybe if he takes a break from the first he'll be able to go back to it with fresh eyes and bring it closer to realisation. To spend the day blocking out a blank canvas fills him with a sense of excitement and possibility. The only shadow darkening this prospect is the situation with Josie. There was the token apology at parting, but in retrospect she may be less forgiving, particularly if the relationship with Michael is ongoing.

In the shower, David tries to wash away such forebodings. He tells himself he doesn't have to act immediately. He can have the day painting. Maybe if he just leaves things alone for a while, the right way forward will suggest itself. Today, if he allows himself, he can escape into the private world of his art.

As David enters the kitchen, Zak is sitting at the counter with a bowl of porridge in front of him and a plastic spoon in his fist. In between mouthfuls he is singing and beating time with the spoon. Gluey gobs of milk and oats go flying. Lara points out coffee in the pot before disappearing to dress and put on her shoes. Zak continues with the musical accompaniment. The words are indistinct. It sounds like, 'smunchy wumsy slaverly blim/ramsy mamsy darla.'

David pours himself a coffee, doesn't bother with milk. He needs the astringent buzz of the bitter black liquid. He asks Zak what he's singing.

'A song, silly,' Zak replies.

'Did you hear it on TV?'

'No, Dawid. Seriously, it's a new song.'

'Seriously?'

'Yes. Smunchy wumsy slavery blim/ramsy mamsy darla.'

'All your own work, then.'

'Course. You're silly, Dawid.'

David experiences a lurch of affection for the little boy, the powerful charm of his creativity. Lara appears from the bedroom. Tells Zak to get a move on. David says he'd better be going. Lara and David embrace and kiss. Even in this brief and chaste exchange, David registers the luscious softness of her lips, their warmth and promise.

''isgusting,' says Zak.

'Pipe down, little guy,' Lara commands.

Before David leaves, Lara detains him for a moment with a hand to his sleeve. 'I think you should talk to Josie,' she says. 'Sooner rather than later. I don't think it's good to let things fester. Better to sort it and clear a way forward.'

'I'll think about it. Maybe see you later.'

'Maybe,' Lara says. 'It *is* only Monday.' Her smile looks to David like the light of the world.

XVI

David spends the day fighting with himself and his work. Indecision about how to handle his issues with Josie spills over into indecision with the soft charcoal pencil he's using to sketch out the scene on his next canvas. His lines waver with his vision. His drawing lacks boldness and resolve. Using his earlier sketches of the bar room in Vung Tau, he's trying to reproduce their promise on the larger space of the pristine canvas which both entices and threatens. He purposely avoids looking again at Manet's famous picture, *A bar at the Folies Bergère,* or at anything by Beckmann or Kirchner, which are closer to the style he wants to achieve. He doesn't look because he's scared of being overwhelmed by their brilliance and falling into the trap of simply trying to copy them. He needs the painting to be *his.* His style, his vision.

But the demands of the composition are severe and greater than anything in his previous work. It's the difficulty of capturing the angles and perspective so the reflections of the bar girls are partial in the gaze of the observer who stands outside the frame, looking at them in a mirror shattered into lozenges of light.

David doesn't want the bar counter horizontal across the picture as in Manet's work. Rather, he is intent on a diagonal from left to right leading from light to darkness. It will be another technical challenge to suggest the light from the street outside flooding into the foreground of the bar, then dimming into the interior and finally darkening towards the right edge, suggesting the exit where the girls took their customers.

The drawing doesn't go well. David sketches then erases the bar, the figures, the mirror, the reflections. Sometimes he thinks he's pretty close, but he can't convince himself. Periodically, his concentration is compromised by thoughts of Josie and Michael. In the end, he gives up and decides Lara was right. He has to deal with this.

So now, he's parked up outside Hawker College again. This time, though, there's going to be no shirking the task. He's already out of the cab, leaning with his back to the tray, facing towards the college gates and the bus stop. He's early so he figures he can allow himself the indulgence of a smoke without other parents thinking he's leading youth astray.

It's been one of those bright Canberra winter days which begin with frost, but mellow as the day goes on, the sky an outrageous pure blue, the light sharp and clear as cut glass. Now, as the sun starts to decline, David can feel the beginning of a chill reaching for him again. He's glad of his battered army-style camping jacket, with its quilted lining, which he wears over a thick green jumper.

When he sees the first kids emerging, he drops his cigarette onto the road and grinds the stub with the sole of his boot. Here we go, he thinks, clearing the air. That's what he'd really like to do. Clear the air.

David attracts a few curious stares as the youngsters move towards the bus stop, which is about thirty metres below him down the slightly sloping road. It's an anxious and awkward business standing exposed like this, trying to look nonchalant, trying not to look like some old perv. Yet he has to keep his eye on the crowd to make sure he doesn't miss Josie.

A first bus comes and goes before she emerges at last. Josie's with the same blond dude he saw her with last time and, just as on the previous occasion, she appears to be in earnest conversation with him. Something in the young man's attitude and address to his daughter makes David feel for the lad. He watches the way the boy inclines his head to look at Josie as they talk; the way he leans his body towards her. They're so close their sleeves are brushing. If David was a betting man, he'd say Dylan—David suddenly remembers his name—was besotted, head-over-heels, a goner. But Josie said they were just good friends. Go figure. Another bet David would put on is that Michael has never looked at Josie with the same mixture of reverence and respect.

David waves at the couple. Dylan gives Josie a nudge. She looks up. There's no smile or salute. She doesn't seem pleased to see him. Her face settles into a thin-lipped sulk. Pushing himself forward from his recline against the truck, David begins to walk down the road. Josie parts with Dylan and walks up to meet him, her head down. They exchange a perfunctory greeting before

David says more tersely than he intended, 'We need to talk. Get in the car. We'll take a drive.'

Josie says nothing. Does as she's told. David fires up the truck. 'We'll have a coffee,' he says. 'I know a quiet place.'

They drive in silence towards Belconnen Town Centre.

'We're not going to the mall, are we?' Josie says. 'All my mates will be hanging out there.'

'Ashamed to be seen with me, are you?'

When Josie doesn't reply, David modifies his tone a little. 'No need to worry. We're not going to the mall.'

They drive to Emu Bank in silence. David pulls into a car park where bars, cafes and restaurants are situated on the shores of Lake Ginninderra. He leads Josie to a small café opposite a burger joint and next to a chicken shack. It's about as down-market as you can get. All the furniture is flimsy white plastic. There's one table outside with a faded umbrella. It's too cold for outdoors. They go inside. David orders two coffees, one black, one white. No fancy cappuccinos here.

'Sorry it's not posh,' David says.

Josie shrugs. 'Whatever.'

She takes a seat against the wall opposite the counter. David joins her, carrying the coffee served in mugs. It's cheap and nasty with the colour and taste of mud. He notes Josie's grimace as she takes a sip. Given the coffee Lara keeps serving him, David thinks maybe he needs to revise his opinion about expensive varieties. The brew at the *Force Majeure* wasn't bad either. But this isn't the time to be admitting temptations to sophistication.

There's no offer of conversation from Josie. Now he's here with her, David experiences a familiar sense of bafflement. He keeps imagining he's getting better at communicating with his daughter, yet confronted with the reality of her glum presence he doesn't know where to start.

The silence is long and uncomfortable. Josie keeps her eyes down most of the time, occasionally scowling at him over the rim of her mug. Since he can't smoke inside, David takes to fiddling with the cylindrical paper sachet from which he's poured his sugar. He folds and rolls it, holds it like a cigarette.

This is fucking ridiculous he thinks to himself. 'Look,' he says. 'I'm sorry this business with Michael has made things difficult. But he was out of order.'

Josie glances up. 'Yeah,' she says, her voice dead, expressionless.

'You didn't put him up to that stunt, did you?'

'No.'

'But you obviously told him quite a lot about me?'

'Obviously.'

David scratches his cheek with one hand, holding his imaginary smoke in the other. 'Well, I wish you hadn't,' he says. 'I'm not keen on advertising my PTSD. It's not something I'm proud of. Not something I'm comfortable discussing as if we're talking about the flu. You know what I mean? It's *personal*. And anyway, I'm nearly over it.'

'So am I,' Josie says, giving him an icy look.

David takes a breath before he says, 'I'm not looking for another row.'

'What *are* you looking for?' Josie asks. 'I said I was sorry. I don't think it was my fault. I couldn't control what Michael said or the way he said it.'

'I know that. But the point is he wouldn't have been able to ask those questions if you hadn't given him the Vietnam Vet briefing.'

Josie looks at David, hurt and defiance in her eyes. 'You still don't get it, do you? I'm proud of you, of what you did.' Her bottom lip wobbles. She's working hard to contain the tremble in her voice. 'I want to be proud of you, but you won't let me.'

David is moved. 'It's not that I won't let you. I want you to be proud of me, but I want to earn it for the right reasons. I was in Vietnam for a year. I'm forty-four years old. I don't want that one year to define everything I am—my past, present and future. Do you understand?'

'I do understand. But do *you* see how your one year in Vietnam has defined *my* life? You never seem to consider that. The way my childhood and everything now is defined by the strife at home which everybody says was caused by your PTSD. Grandma says so. Mum says so. My memory and experience of you says so. So excuse me for talking about it. But, you know, I can't like bottle it up all the time. I'll go mad if I do.'

Josie pauses for a breath. David can't say anything. He's chastened. He feels empty, eviscerated. Josie hasn't finished. She goes on.

'And everything that happened with Michael turns out to be about you and Vietnam as well.'

‘How do you mean?’ David is genuinely surprised by Josie’s assertion.

Josie winds an errant curl of hair round her finger and rocks slightly as she speaks. ‘He’s only interested in me because someone told him you were a Vietnam Vet. He used me to get at you. To try to interview you. He thought it would be great for his uni project. He also thought he might get an article out of it for the student newspaper. So he cosied up to me.’ Josie stops. She takes a shuddering breath and wraps her arms around herself, fighting to control her evident distress. ‘As soon as it didn’t go to plan, instead of being pissed off with you he was pissed off with me. Accused me of not helping him out, not standing up for him against you. He was horrible to me and now I don’t know if I’ll ever see him again and everything’s ruined.’

Anger and relief collide in David. He’d like to teach the little shit a lesson but he’s so glad Josie might be free of him it makes him blurt, ‘Not everything, surely?’

David’s instinctive rejoinder proves the breaking point for Josie. To his alarm and chagrin, she begins to weep and swear simultaneously. ‘Fuck, fuck, fuck,’ she mutters as she sobs.

He can’t tell if she’s angry or sad. Both probably. He searches in his pockets for a handkerchief. Finds himself bereft. Josie is brushing tears off her face with the back of her hand. David fights with the spring-loaded metal container of paper serviettes which is on the table. Getting one out is impossible. He ends up with a great fistful which he proffers to Josie. She takes them from him.

Between blowing her nose and smearing tears from her face, Josie gasps, 'I hate crying. I'm *not* weak.'

'I'd better get you home,' David says, trying to hide his desolation, the consciousness of how inadequate his response is. 'I'm sorry, Josie,' he says. 'Sorry I've been no good.'

This only provokes another storm of tears. The rotund guy behind the counter is pretending not to look or listen, cleaning surfaces assiduously with an insouciant nonchalance. David is glad they're the only ones in the joint.

'I don't want to go home,' Josie sniffles. 'I *hate* it at home. And when we move to Red Hill, I won't have a home. It won't be *my* home. All Mum cares about is Barry. And all you care about is that chicky babe next door. Then, when I thought I had a chance with Michael and I'm like falling in love with him, it all goes to shit.'

David resists the temptation to point out that Michael is a first-class prick and that Josie is better off without him. He realises the wrong response will spell disaster. A swirl of panic threatens to confuse his thinking. He considers clichés concerning fish and sea. They seem horribly lame. He walks down other avenues of consolation, but they all turn into cul-de-sacs. He knows he's perilously close to the question of Josie moving in with him. He can't go there. He can't see how it could work. He can't promise things that won't come to fruition. He's got nothing. Only desperation makes him say, 'That guy Dylan I keep seeing you with seems pretty keen.'

The remark earns David a withering look. 'I told you before, we're *friends*. He's keen on this girl, Kat, but she's with Joel. It's just another load of heavy shit to deal with. Dyl's on antidepressants.'

'You're kidding.'

'I wish I was.'

'He doesn't look the type.'

'Is there a *type*? Do you reckon you *look* the type to have PTSD?'

'I hope not,' David says.

'Well, there you go.'

Josie looks as if she might succumb to tears again. David can't stand it.

'Come on, Jo-Jo. Things can't be that bad. Tomorrow's another day.'

'Unfortunately.'

'Don't be daft, Josie. I know it's hard sometimes, bloody hard, but you have to do the best you can with every day. Life's a gift. You can make it bitter or throw it away, but it *is* a gift. Best to try and make the most of it. I had a mate in Vietnam. Twenty years old. He was killed. I grieve for him and sometimes feel guilty because I survived and he didn't come home. But there's nothing I can do for him except try to honour his memory by making the most I can of every day. It's one of the reasons my painting is important to me.'

Josie blows her nose and cleans her face with another serviette. She doesn't say anything, just looks at David as if he's someone she doesn't know. He can't read her expression. He feels embarrassed, exposed. He realises he's shared something about Vietnam. Only a little, but something. He's not sure what impression it's made on Josie.

Seeing she isn't going to respond, David says, 'We should get going. Your mother will be worried about you.'

'She won't,' Josie replies. 'She doesn't get home until six-thirty or seven. Barry's the same. They're always going on about how important they are. They make me sick.'

'Okay. Okay. I didn't mean to cause another upset.'

Josie pushes back her chair and stands up. 'We might as well go, though,' she says.

They drive to Margaret's place in Flynn (*upper* Flynn). Josie is utterly silent. David feels defeated. He wanted to smooth things over, make things right between them. When they draw up outside the smart double-storey, double-fronted, double-garage, double-brick place adjacent to the reserve at Mount Rogers, David tries to say as much.

Josie's response is, 'Yeah. Right. Thanks.'

David leans to kiss her, but she evades him. She's out of the truck. 'See you later,' she says, as she slams the door. He watches her walk away from him up the path and out of sight behind the screening shrubs and trees.

XVII

David wakes from a recurrent nightmare screaming *stop, stop, stop* and wrestling with an assailant's arm to prevent them firing. He sits up, drenched in sweat, still battling, until Lara's voice penetrates and he realises it's her arms he's struggling against. He lets go of her and sits there, feeling shattered, trembling and disoriented. He shakes his head as if to dislodge the images from his mind. It's been some time since this abomination has re-visited him. Each time the dream recurs, he prays it will be the last. He becomes aware of another voice crying. Lara switches the light on to reveal Zak, standing by the door, shouting, 'Mummy, Mummy!' through his tears.

'Mate, everything's okay.' David tries to reassure the little boy, though his heart's still battering his ribs, and a sinking despair hollows him.

Lara is out of bed and pulling a robe on as she coos to console Zak. Soon, she's holding the little boy and ushering him back to his own room. David sits there, listening to Zak quietening, as his own pulse returns to something like normal.

When Lara doesn't return immediately, David hauls himself

out of bed and begins to get dressed. He dreads the inevitable inquest into his night terror and fears how Lara will react. Such disturbances in the night proved another nail in the coffin of his marriage. Margaret hated them. She used to show sympathy at the moment of his waking, but in the aftermath seemed to punish him with a barrage of complaints and questions, which became increasingly aggravated as the years went by. It was as if she thought he should be able to switch the nightmares off and get over it; as if he suffered from some weakness that she couldn't fathom and resented.

It seems likely that Lara won't find it easy to cope either. She certainly won't appreciate the upset to Zak. Perhaps he isn't fit to have a relationship. Doesn't deserve love. He should go home and forget it. Can't face confrontation now. He feels sick and ashamed, as if he carries the contagion of war inside him, infecting everything and everybody he touches. There's no escape.

David is pulling on his jumper when Lara comes back into the room. She stands on her side of the bed, untying the belt of her robe, looking over at him. 'What are you up to?' she says. 'It's three in the morning. Let's get back into bed. It's freezing out here.'

David turns and meets her eyes. He shakes his head. 'Sorry, sorry, *sorry*. Is Zak okay?'

'Yes, stop worrying. He's good. I stayed with him till he went back to sleep. He sometimes has nightmares. I explained that you'd had one. He was fine with it.'

David isn't convinced. He feels horrible. 'How are *you*? Did I hurt you?'

Lara rubs her upper arm ruefully. 'I might have a couple of

bruises, but otherwise I'm all right. It was the shock more than anything.'

David moves towards the door. Lara intercepts him and puts her arms round him. He holds her, but his body is still tense and unyielding. 'I think I should go home,' he says.

'You needn't on my account.'

'I'm so sorry. It's the first time it's happened for months.'

'It must be me. You must secretly want to fight me. Maybe I should get lessons in unarmed combat.' She laughs lightly. But it's no laughing matter to David.

'It's not you. Nothing to do with you.'

'Come on. Come to bed. We can talk about it again tomorrow.' She unclasps him.

'I won't sleep. It's best if I go. I don't want to disturb you any more than I already have. I'll see you tomorrow.'

Lara shrugs. 'It's up to you. I don't mind.'

He kisses her on the forehead. 'Thank you. I just need to be alone for a while. I'll make myself a brew. Maybe do some work on my painting for a while, until I settle down. You have a good sleep. I'll see you tomorrow. I'll let myself out.'

'Whatever you say.' Lara sounds resigned.

As he leaves the room, David notices the look of disappointment on her face. He takes her parting words with him.

'You've got to stop fighting,' she says. 'Stop fighting people who love you.'

¢

Back in the sanctuary of his flat, David pours himself a whisky and waits for the kettle to boil. The familiar hushing sounds of jug and heater soothe David as he sips and feels the burning spirit steady him with its suffusing warmth. He stares out of the kitchen window. The streetlights make the walls of the arts complex shine a sickly yellow. Beyond, the quiet acres of suburbia are sound asleep.

He remembers the alienation when he came back from Vietnam.

The weirdness of the broad, ordered, silent streets, the neat houses with their trimmed lawns, the restraint, the politeness of it all. After a year in Phuoc Tuy province, it was like landing on Mars. The hostility of a few and indifference of many towards the war hadn't helped. But it was more the triviality of most people's concerns that irritated David. The raw simplicities of life at war gave way to the avid struggles of materialism. He found most people were obsessed by clawing their way up career ladders and progressing up the real estate league table into evermore fashionable suburbs. He remembers listening to Fast Eddie, the accountant, on how to fiddle the taxman and boost the savings. He couldn't stand it.

Before he went to Vietnam, he was just like all the other punters scrabbling around, trying to find a way to 'get on'. It used to amuse him the way people would dignify their pursuit of wealth, power and position with stories of idealism. They would define themselves by conflict and competition. Everybody was fighting for something whether it was political advancement or market position and everybody needed to believe they were fighting for what was right and good and true. Everybody told themselves a story. Just like he'd spun himself a yarn about going to fight in Vietnam. It had seemed more exciting, more noble, more romantic than working in an insurance office. He'd not known much then about friendly fire.

With a cigarette between his lips, he carries his drinks to the occasional table and slumps onto the sofa. He cradles his cup of tea for a while, letting the heat thaw his hands, trying to dispel the gloom and anxiety which is the legacy of his nightmare. He thinks about Lara telling him to stop fighting.

It's easier said than done.

The only person he really wants to struggle with is himself. Yet he's at loggerheads with Josie. A great wave of shame washes over him. He realises where the dream has come from, the connection. The horror of the nightmare always leaves him with a nauseous extract of shame. Shame is what he feels about Josie. And shame is what he feels when he thinks about Lara and Zak having to deal with his brittle equanimity, his damaged soul.

David knows he can't change the past. He can only change his attitude to it, his angle of vision. Donna has spoken to him about this. He has to learn to forgive himself, not only for what happened in Vietnam but for everything before and afterwards as well. But how? That's the question. You can't apologise or make reparations to the dead. Jez, his father, the Vietnamese girl on the jungle track are gone beyond recall. You have to look to the living, find a way to break the glass panes of separation and express your love and longing, the better parts of yourself. He thought he was making headway with Lara and Zak, but perhaps his nightmare and his refusal to stay afterwards will have stuffed that up. Maybe he's not ready for a real relationship.

Maybe he doesn't deserve it.

Maybe he doesn't deserve it because of his failure with Josie—his inability to communicate, to make things right with her. It isn't a failure of love. He knows his love for his daughter burns with a pure flame. But it is inexpressible. Josie might *not* know it. That's the problem. How does he make it clear? How does he show his love? The obvious way is to say *yes* to her request to come and live with him. But how can that work? The thought makes him quail. It's not just the responsibility that's daunting; it's more the day-to-day logistics and practicalities. He can't give up his painting. And the idea of ending his relationship with Lara fills him with desolation. He can't see how that could continue if Josie were living with him. How could he say, *Righto, just off next door, love, see you in the morning?* It wouldn't be right. It wouldn't work. He'd feel guilty.

There must be another way. David can't see what it might be. He hauls himself to his feet and goes to his painting room. To do some work is the only way he knows to allay his distress. To bring back a measure of balance. He sits with the whisky bottle and his cigarettes, sketching some drawings for the third painting in his triptych. The woman kneeling side-on, her head turning towards the viewer. He wants to paint her in a halo of light, as if illuminated by candles against the enveloping darkness. Like the first painting, the black surround will be punctuated by streaks of white and vermilion. David wants to paint a picture of prayer and praise, a figure of light suggesting the possibility of redemption.

XVIII

Late on Saturday afternoon, David walks home through the rain from the City Markets, hefting his provisions in two plastic carrier bags. Head down, he trudges against the blustering wind, relishing the scouring quality of the elements. He's spent the last few days and nights working obsessively on the triptych of paintings. In a sustained burst of energy, he's brought them close to completion. But his labour has meant he's been insular and hasn't spent much time beyond the confines of his flat. He's been living his work, so to be out in the weather in the middle of the day feels like a blessing, despite the discomforts of the wet.

When he reaches the flats, he can see all kinds of garbage sticking out of the mailboxes, which stand in a brick phalanx out the front. Instead of making a separate journey, David dumps his bags and quickly retrieves the bundle of bills, circulars and junk mail which is clogging the box. He stuffs them into one of his shopping bags and hurries up the stairs, beginning to feel cold now and anxious to get out of the rain.

David gets the heater going and changes out of his wet clothes. He sticks the kettle on and begins to unpack his shopping;

nothing exciting, just the staples: bread, milk, cheese, canned soup, eggs, tomatoes, beans. There's no order to his stocking of the cupboards. He completes the tedious chore as quickly as possible, brews a cup of tea and shoves a couple of pieces of bread and cheese under the griller to toast.

He's eating alone tonight. Lara has taken Zak to her brother's place where they are having dinner with her dad. Lara says the old bloke is doing okay now, but she's worried about how frail he seems. She said she might stay over in Queanbeyan, invited David to go with her, but he couldn't face it. He cited the demands of his work, his need to concentrate while he has the spell on him. He's been saying the same to her all week, explaining as best he can the necessity of his compulsion.

He hasn't slept with Lara since his nightmare. She has accepted his excuses and justifications, at least outwardly. But David has seen the doubt in her eyes, the perplexity. And today, before she left, she said, 'You're not going off me, are you?' David was effusive in his reassurances. He held her and kissed her and told her there was no chance of him 'going off' her. It was just that he needed to work. He promised to meet her family sometime soon. He didn't say how frightened he was of having another night terror in her bed, of alienating her through the violence of his dreams.

While he's waiting for the food, David goes through his mail. It doesn't take long—he throws as he goes. Most of it is rubbish, as usual. The adverts irritate him—the waste of paper. The smell of singed toast interrupts his indignation. He snatches the grill pan from under the heat. Toast and cheese are both well done. He opens the kitchen window to let out the whiffs of smoke, then prepares a plate and takes it into his painting room.

He contemplates his work while he chews. He had thought of taking a break this evening, but his impulse is to work. Thinking about Lara has made him wonder if there isn't an element of self-punishment in the drive to perfection which fuels his art. There is certainly pain as well as pleasure in the struggle to channel his grief and anger into the three pictures which have been his focus for the last few days. But at least it is pain and pleasure which isn't directly inflicted on anybody else. In his strife with colour, detail, and perspective he can forget his troubles with Josie and his insecurities with Lara. He can lose himself by stepping out of time into the magic of his art. The dead girl on the track, the bar girls of Vung Tau, and the kneeling figure, which is a disguised portrait of Lara, command his attention and commitment.

From the moment he takes up his brush and palette, nothing else exists.

¢

When David is woken by the insistent clamour of the telephone, it takes him a few moments to realise where he is and what time it is. He's fallen asleep in the chair in his painting room, an unfinished cup of tea and glass of whisky on the floor by his side. He stumbles to his feet, feeling old, cold and stiff in his joints. He glances at his watch—12.40 am—the wrong time for the phone to be ringing. Possible disasters accelerate through his mind as he rushes towards the kitchen.

He snatches the receiver from the cradle and senses a strange gulping pause before a torrent of speech begins. Josie's voice sounds high, manic, slightly slurred.

'Dad, thank God, can you come and get me? I'm at the police station in Civic. There's been some trouble. It's terrible. I can't face Mum and Barry. Please come and get me. They say I can go home now.'

David's heart is bouncing. He feels as if he needs extra air. 'What kind of trouble? Are you all right?'

'There was a fight in a nightclub. It was awful. Someone got hurt. It's really bad. I'm okay. A bit pissed. I'm all right. Please come and get me. I have to get out of here.'

'Okay, okay. Settle down. I'm on my way. Does your mum know where you are?'

'No. I'm supposed to be staying at Kat's. But I can't now. I'll explain. Don't ring Mum. I can't deal with her and Barry right now. You've got to help me. *Please.*'

'Sit tight, Jo-Jo. I'll be there in a few minutes. You're at the main cop shop on London Circuit?'

'Yes.'

'Try and calm down. It won't take me long.'

As he searches for his keys, David is glad he fell asleep dressed. He grabs his padded rain jacket and, leaving the lights and heater on, closes the front door behind him. The night is still, cold and clear, the sky freckled with stars. It feels as if he's breathing shards of ice. As he emerges into the car park, the tarmac glitters with frost, the air knitting moisture together into a sparkling gauze. The windscreen of the truck likewise wears a thin coat.

The truck refuses to start. It takes four turns of the ignition before it coughs into life with a great belch of diesel cloud which David sees and smells through his open window. He allows the motor to run while he gets out and gives the windscreen a going over with an ice-scraper. It's a rough job, but he doesn't want to delay.

He's soon on the move, hunched forward over the wheel, peering ahead through the orange lit city streets. He regrets not rolling a smoke before he started. No opportunity now, despite the four sets of traffic lights he has to navigate before he turns left onto Northbourne Avenue, the main drag. Another few minutes and a right into London Circuit and he's in the car park adjacent to the Police Station.

'Christ it's cold,' David mutters to himself. He jogs from the truck into the unforgiving, fluorescent light of the station foyer. Josie is sitting on an upright chair against the wall opposite the counter. There are other young people on either side of her in various states of disarray. Josie leaps to her feet when she sees David and totters into his arms on her party heels. She's sobbing uncontrollably. David holds her, strokes her hair, tells her everything is going to be okay.

David's eyes go to the policeman on the desk.

'You're fine to go, sir,' the cop says, 'but the young lady knows she has to come back tomorrow to make a full statement. We've taken some preliminary details tonight, but we'd like to see her again when she's sober and has had chance to collect herself. We've cautioned her about the underage drinking. If there's a next time, she'll be up on a charge. Understood?'

'Absolutely, officer. Thanks,' David says. 'I'll be having a word.' And to Josie, 'Come on, let's get out of here.'

David takes his jacket off and wraps it round Josie as they venture into the night. She's dressed for pub and club, not the weather, wearing only a denim jacket over a short black miniskirt. Her flimsy matching top only reaches to her belly, leaving a band of midriff exposed to the icy air. He bundles her into the truck. Josie is crying again, sobbing and trembling. David doesn't bother trying to interrogate her. Concentrates on getting them back to the flat, out of the cold.

Even though the place is shabby, there's a wonderful comfort in the warmth and familiarity of the flat. It smells of paint and turpentine. The subdued orange light thrown from an old standard lamp is like a caress after the garish assault of the police station fluoros. With the kettle on, David settles Josie on the couch with the doona from his bed wrapped round her shoulders. He reckons she might be in shock. He puts plenty of sugar in her tea. Josie leans forward cradling her mug in both hands, absorbing the warmth as if her life depends on it.

David pulls up a chair opposite and rolls a smoke. He takes a sip of the scalding brew. 'So, let's have it,' he says. 'What's gone on?'

Josie looks at him. She sniffles and shudders. 'Everything is *so* shitty, Dad. *Everything*. Nothing went right. It was supposed to be a fun night. We all met up in Civic—a bunch of us from college. We had some drinks then Joel suggested we go to this nightclub place. He reckoned he'd been before and it was cool. He knew the bouncers. They'd let us in. So, we all partied on down there. We had some more drinks. There was dancing. Everyone seemed fine. There were lots of people there, including this bunch of guys from Duntroon or the Defence Force Academy or whatever you call it. You can tell them by their haircuts. Anyway, Kat and Joel have some sort of row, so she's dancing with us while Joel's sulking with Cam, Pete and some of the other guys. Kat's really putting on some moves on the dance floor and this other guy, one of the cadets, comes over and starts cracking on to her. She's, like, all over this dude, trying to make Joel jealous. At first, we all thought it was funny, but then it worked—Joel *did* get jealous and he comes onto the dance floor and gets hold of Kat while she's still smooching with this other bloke. I don't even know his name. Anyway, Kat refuses to stop. So Joel starts shoving this guy about and telling him to fuck off and that. Then, suddenly it's on. The bloke takes a swing at Joel and Joel fights back. The bloke's mates pile in. Pete, Cam and some of the others run over to help Joel out. Joel's going mad. There's lots of pushing and shoving and fists flying. It's really chaotic and we're, like, just getting out of the way. I pulled Kat out of it, but then I saw the cadet, the one who fancied her on the floor, and Joel …'

Josie stops and breathes, shakes her head. 'Joel *kicked* him. Kicked him in the head. The guy spasms a bit and goes still.

Everything stops. The cadet's mates are kneeling by him, there are calls for help, an ambulance, the bouncers turn up, grab Joel. It's mayhem. Girls are screaming. I'm just, like, trying to comfort Kat, who's a complete mess. It was *awful*, Dad. The police turned up. The ambos were with the bloke for ages, giving him oxygen, someone said. I don't think he'd come round by the time they carted him off. The police shoved us all in paddy wagons, said they needed statements and that. Joel was hauled off on his own. I think they arrested him. Kat was hysterical.'

Josie runs out of steam. She looks a mess, her make-up smeared, black mascara tears staining her cheeks. She rocks backwards and forwards.

David says, 'And your man Michael, Mickey, whatever it is, he's not part of this show?'

It's the wrong question. Josie gives him a scathing look. 'He's not my man. That's all over. Gone. History. I was out trying to forget about all that. And then this happens. It's like I'm cursed. What if the guy *dies?* Joel will get done for murder. He'll go to prison. I can't—it's just too horrible. What if I'm asked to give evidence against him? I've already told them I saw it. I couldn't lie.'

'Whoa. Let's not get too far ahead of ourselves here. Maybe the guy wakes up with a headache. Let's not rush to the total disaster scenario. The main thing right now is to get you cleaned up and into bed.'

David fetches her a towel. 'You have a shower while I get some clean sheets on the bed. You can have a nice long sleep. You'd better drink a glass of water. Have some Panadol as well. Things will look better in the morning.'

Josie looks completely unconvinced, but is biddable. There's no fight left in her. She gets up and goes to the bathroom.

Once David has tucked Josie in, kissed her, told her everything will be fine, he retreats to his painting room and collapses back into the chair. He drinks the cold tea and whisky which are still there on the floor. He's exhausted. Tomorrow there will be the police station again, Margaret and Barry to deal with.

What a fucking mess.

XIX

Sunday mid-morning. David sits in the same chair Josie occupied in the police station only a few hours earlier. He is dishevelled and unshaven. His head feels as if it's full of cement. They've taken Josie through the security door to an interview room. He asked if he should go in with her, but the policemen said there was no need. Given the gravity of the incident and the number of pupils involved, they'd brought in the college counsellor to act as the responsible adult present. Though she looked pale and shrivelled with anxiety, Josie said, 'It's okay, Pa,' as she disappeared to face her ordeal.

There's nothing for David to do but wait. The fluorescent glare of the strip light probes his headache. He has the arrival of Margaret and possibly Barry to look forward to. It's not promising. He's already had an aggravated conversation with his ex-wife as he outlined the situation to her. Despite David offering to drop Josie home when they'd finished, Margaret insisted she'd meet them at the police station. She said she needed to be there to support Josie. But she's late, hasn't shown up yet. David doesn't know what this portends. He wishes he could roll a smoke. No point. He sits and watches the second hand of the large, plain-faced wall clock.

The presence of other mums and dads with their teenagers, who are presumably Josie's mates from school, is a further source of worry. He feels as if he should say something to them, but he doesn't know them and has nothing to say. To be fair, they are mostly silent as well. It's as sickly and tense as a doctor's waiting room. David begins to have the hallucinatory feeling they've been here all night and they're all trapped in some horrible circle of hell. He closes his eyes and tries to relax his breathing, tame his bouncing knee.

When he opens them again, Margaret is pushing through the swing door with its opaque shatterproof glass pane. There's nowhere for her to sit. Despite her immaculately fitted black trousers, carmine roll-neck sweater and tweed jacket, she looks flustered and red in the face. Margaret sees David, but for the moment ignores him as she greets the other parents. They are all on first name terms and commiserate with each other over the terrible events of the previous evening.

David stands and moves to Margaret's side. He gestures towards the seat he's vacated.

'Perhaps we should have a word outside,' Margaret suggests, her face and demeanour stony.

They convene on the pavement. The day is grey and there's a bitter wind blowing down the concrete canyons of the city streets from the Brindabellas with its intimations of the snowfields beyond.

There are no preliminaries. 'You should have rung us last night and told us what was going on.' Margaret's opening gambit isn't helpful.

David holds his hands up, tries to placate her. 'I didn't see the point in disturbing you.'

'The point is, I'm her mother. I have a right to know where she is and what's going on.'

'Which is why I rang you first thing this morning to tell you. If you'd been here on time, you could have given Jo-Jo a hug before she went in there.' David knows he should have resisted the barb, but he couldn't.

Margaret squares up to him, so she's seething into his face. 'I was late because I had to work very hard to dissuade Barry from coming down here with me. I didn't want there to be any more of a scene than there needs to be.'

'I don't understand why we need a scene at all,' David replies. 'All I've done is look after Josie when she asked for help as any father would.'

'The *point* is Josie spent the night at your place when she was supposed to be at her friend's and we weren't informed. I want to make it plain right now this is *not* going to be the thin end of the custody wedge. You needn't even begin to think about Josie moving in with you either permanently or part-time.'

'It was one night, Margaret. In an emergency. Don't you think you might be overreacting?'

'I'm just letting you know where things stand. Josie is being difficult about the idea of moving to Red Hill, as if you didn't know, and she's already screaming at us about wanting to live with you.'

David scratches his cheek. Shakes his head. 'Look,' he says. 'I've already talked about this with Josie and told her it isn't on. But I do think you and Barry could hold your horses until Josie's finished college. When she's at uni, there'll be no problem living in Red Hill or wherever. Once she's eighteen, she can sort herself out.'

'If you think Barry and I are going to pay for her to live in a hall of residence you've got another thing coming. We'll have to bear the cost of her going to uni anyway. That's if she gets there. The way she's going at the moment she'll be lucky to get a decent TER score.'

'Jesus, Margaret, could you just ease up a little?'

The unlikelihood of Margaret calming down isn't tested further as Josie emerges onto the pavement.

'Darling,' Margaret says, and moves to embrace her daughter. Josie allows herself to be hugged. 'Are you all right?'

Josie stiffens and disengages from her mother.

'Was everything okay in there?' David asks.

'They questioned me some more, then I had to write down what I saw and sign it. It felt like I was dobbing on Joel. Betraying him. But I couldn't lie. I'd already told them last night. They wouldn't say how the guy is or what will happen to Joel.'

Josie is on the brink of tears.

'Come on,' Margaret says, 'Let's get you home.'

Josie looks towards David, as if he's her accomplice. 'I don't want to go home. I want to stay with Dad.'

'You know that isn't possible, love,' Margaret says, cajoling. 'You have to come home.'

'It doesn't feel like home. I'm not sure where home is anymore. If we move to Red Hill, it won't be my home at all.'

'We're not having this discussion here. We're going. *Now.* And when the time is right and you're not in a state, we can talk about this calmly and sensibly.'

David regards this stand-off with dismay. He can see Margaret winding herself up. A screaming match on the pavement isn't going to help anyone. 'Jo-Jo,' he says, 'I reckon it's for the best right now if you do as your mother says. Maybe we can all have a sit-down in the next little while—I mean all of us, you and me and Barry and your mum—and we can work out a way forward.'

Margaret raises her eyebrows. She gives David a baleful look but is wise enough to say nothing. David can almost see the cogs turning. She's thinking if she gets her way now, she'll be able to scotch or manipulate any further negotiations. She'll have time to prepare, work out a strategy. She's not a senior public servant for nothing.

Josie shrugs. 'Whatever.' She looks washed out and sounds defeated. The trauma of the last twelve hours catching up with her.

David holds out his arms to her. She doesn't move. The tense family triangle, standing together but manifestly apart, is broken by the appearance of one of Josie's mates with his father. It's the blond boy, Dylan, David has seen with Josie before. Now she runs to him and they hug each other, talking low. David finds the sight of them unutterably moving—their evident closeness, the comfort and support they give and take from each other.

Margaret greets Mr Rose and introduces David. They shake hands.

'Terrible business, this,' Mr Rose says.

David and Margaret agree.

'I'd better get on and take Dylan to face the music.'

'That's right. We're done now,' says Margaret.

As if she's been fortified by the appearance of her friend, Josie capitulates without demur to her mother's move to leave.

'See you later,' Josie says to David. She leans up and kisses him on the cheek while he hugs her, his chin resting on her auburn curls.

'Hang in there, love,' he whispers. And then she's gone, walking head down beside her mother, who is striding briskly away.

David watches them go. He kicks a stone that lies in the middle of the pavement onto the road, before he turns and makes his way back to his truck.

¢

That night, David takes comfort in Lara's arms. They have dinner together after David has played robots with Zak and the little boy is safely tucked up in bed. The fight at the nightclub makes the local news. The young bloke in hospital is in a bad way. He's in a coma and described as 'critical'. Since he's a minor, Joel isn't named as the assailant, but the report says he's been bailed and will appear before a magistrate on Monday charged with grievous bodily harm.

Anxiety about this and Josie's situation, together with their few days of abstinence, gives an extra edge to David and Lara's lovemaking. There is an abandoned hunger in the way they explore each other with a frenetic exchange of tongues, palms, fingers. They cling to each other as survivors to a life raft, pulling each other into the deepest exchange before the ecstatic release.

Afterwards, breathless, they share the secret smile of lovers who in that moment believe that only they, in the long history of the world, could have achieved such bliss together. As their heartbeats slow, the silence and stillness of the night seem exaggerated by contrast with the sighs and cries of their passion. They lie quiet for a long time. Lara's head is on David's shoulder, her hand resting on his stomach as if to calm any resumption of anxious turbulence there.

David wants to perpetuate these moments of peace but can't help thoughts of Josie intruding. He desperately wants to help his daughter, particularly given his derelictions when she was young. But he can't see how.

Lara glances up at him. 'That was a big sigh,' she says.

'Of contentment.' The white lie a reflex response.

'Mmm. Didn't sound like that to me. You're worrying about Josie?'

'Yes.'

'There's nothing to be done tonight. Let it go. Have a sleep. Tomorrow's another day.'

David strokes the back of Lara's head, his fingers feeling the lush softness of her hair. He's grateful for her attempt at wisdom.

‘She wants to move in with me,’ David whispers. ‘But I can’t see how to make it work. And I *can’t, I can’t* give this … I can’t give you up. I just can’t.’

Lara turns onto her side, leaning up on one elbow so she’s looking at David.

‘I don’t want to give this up either. But it won’t work if I come between you and Josie.’

‘It’s not just about you and me. There’s my painting as well. The flat’s not big enough. And anyway, Josie needs her mother.’

‘I can’t do that,’ Lara says. ‘I can’t play the wicked step-mum. I’m too young and it doesn’t feel right. Maybe I could be her friend.’

‘I’d like you to meet each other. But things are so fraught right now. I dunno.’

Lara smooths her free hand over David’s brow trying to iron out the wrinkles. Her fingers and palm move to his cheek. ‘We’re not going to solve anything tonight,’ she says. ‘We need to sleep. We’ll talk some more, work something out. The great thing is we both want to—that’s what really matters.’

David arches his neck to kiss her. The touch of her lips, their warm, ripe fullness is intoxicating.

‘I’m falling in love with you,’ David whispers.

‘Shhh,’ Lara says. ‘It’s wonderful, but let’s not spoil it with words. We’re meant to be going slowly, remember?’

‘Oh yes, I remember. We’re having a casual affair, right?’

Lara doesn’t smile. Her eyes are intense as she leans in to kiss him again.

XX

David spends the following days fiddling with fine details in his paintings; touching here, rubbing back, touching again in painstaking pursuit of perfection. It's not the same kind of work as the initial bursts of energy when the picture is in the process of composition, being brought to life through instinctive gestures. This is more considered, more cerebral—a standing back to evaluate and eradicate any weaknesses. It's the final application with a fine round brush to make sure the paintings shine with a life of their own. This intricate labour, more technique than inspiration, suits David's short concentration span and sporadic commitment. He's distracted by everything else going on in his life, his attention divided between worry over Josie and the effervescent excitement which fizzes in response to his developing relationship with Lara.

Seeing Lara and Zak is easy. Too easy. David has to fight the temptation to be with them whenever they're home. He makes himself stay put. He makes himself work. He doesn't want to ruin things with Lara. He's convinced he must step lightly and delicately.

It's even harder to gauge his approach to Josie. He tries ringing her in the late afternoon or early evening, attempting to reach her before Margaret and Barry are home from work. Several times there's no response. David guesses Josie is with her friends. He imagines the young people comforting each other as the drama following the nightclub incident refuses to resolve itself. News coverage continues. It's clear the young man in hospital is very seriously injured. Reports suggest he is now in an induced coma. Joel, meanwhile, has been remanded in juvenile custody due to the seriousness of the charges he's facing.

When David does eventually manage to talk to Josie, she is morose and monosyllabic at first. David doesn't know how to cheer her up. She's fixated on Joel's calamity and the fate of the guy he's attacked. She blames herself for doing nothing. David tries to persuade her none of it is her fault.

'I should have done *something*,' she says. 'I should have stopped Kat from messing about. I should have stepped in when Joel started acting up. Dylan feels the same. He'd been talking to the guys from Duntroon, so when it all kicked off he was on the wrong side. Now the boys at school are calling him a coward and a wuss for not wading into it.'

'You can't be responsible for other people's actions,' David offers, feeling how lame his remark must sound.

'It all sucks, Dad.'

The conversation ends with David suggesting she should come round at the weekend. She says she might see him on Sunday arvo. There is no enthusiasm in her voice.

¢

When Sunday morning arrives, the weather is a distinct improvement on last week. The day's too good to miss. David and Lara decide to take Zak to the park. For David, it's a way of trying to banish the worries of the week, the shadows cast by the nightclub fracas, the knowledge of the young men suffering, one in a hospital bed, the other in a cell, the result of a moment's testosterone and alcohol-fuelled rage. A way, too, of trying to forget Josie's reaction to these circumstances and her other troubles for a while. If she comes round this afternoon, he'll have to find words of comfort for her, though there's no mistaking her classmate, Joel, is in plenty of trouble. No amount of talking is going to change that.

But for now, there are a few lighter moments to enjoy. As David walks into Glebe Park with Lara and Zak, there's a towering blue sky, the air brittle and the light like glass. His earlier lovemaking with Lara has made the natural world gleam, polished, clean and bright. David punts the junior footy he carries high into the air in an exuberant release of energy. Zak stops to watch its trajectory and Lara puts her hands to her head in alarm as it looks as if the ball might bomb another family group walking on the path with a stroller. David begins running towards the ball. Zak follows, struggling along as fast as he can in his new Wellington boots. When the ball lands, bouncing safely on the grass, David turns and grins at Lara, arms outspread, palms up, as if to say, 'never in doubt.' He lets Zak reach the footy first, and then mock tackles him, rolling the little boy into a laughing hug on the cold grass.

Lara catches up and the three of them play. Zak finds it difficult to kick in his boots, which he insisted on wearing, so they toss the footy to each other in an anarchic version of piggy-in-the-middle. David notices how adept Lara is with the ball. Occasionally when it's spilt, she kicks it to him, straight and true, her long elegant legs balletic in the follow through.

'My brother's training,' she says, when she sees his glance of admiration.

David's lack of fitness soon begins to show. He's breathing hard and thinking ruefully of the booze and smokes. The romp continues until he's lying flat on his back, arms akimbo in an attitude of comic and exhausted surrender. He glances at his watch. Maybe they should be getting back. He doesn't know exactly if or when Josie will turn up. But he doesn't want to miss her. Though he's left a 'back soon' note on his front door and a key under the mat, he still experiences a stirring of disquiet. He doesn't want to stuff-up and upset Josie again. He needs to show he's there for her.

He begins to struggle to his feet but hasn't counted on Zak, who launches himself at David in a manic hug, or tackle, knocking him back down. Lara arrives as well, laughing as she too collapses close beside them. The three of them roll around together in an ungainly embrace until they're exhausted and come to rest in a clumsy bundle, Zak with his arms round David, sandwiched between the adults, who lie on their sides, looking breathlessly into one another's smiling eyes.

'We should get back,' David says. Lara nods.

'I'm sorry, I do not want to do that,' Zak declares.

David sits up and sets the boy on his feet. Zak immediately grabs the football and runs off in the opposite direction from home. Lara stands and offers her hand to David. She hauls him up and into her arms. They kiss. She's wearing a blue beanie from which strands of her dark hair escape, giving her a ragamuffin demeanour. David sees the delight in her eyes and can't believe his luck. He stands looking at her with a foolish grin on his face. He hasn't spoken of love again. He daren't. He's afraid of breaking the spell, afraid of frightening her off.

Instead, he breaks the embrace and turns to face in the same direction as Lara, who is regarding her son, standing in the middle distance looking back at them with the ball in his hands. David puts his arm round Lara and they both shout for Zak. The little boy stands for a moment, evidently deciding whether to defy them or not. David begins to turn away, thinking that Zak will follow if he sees the adults moving in the opposite direction. Lara half resists, unwilling to let the boy out of her sight. For a moment they are facing in different directions. It's then David sees his ex-wife and Barry. They've left the path and are about a hundred metres away, walking towards him, their stride purposeful, faces serious.

David's stomach dips. What's this about? He moves away from Lara, who turns to see what's happening.

David begins to stride towards the approaching couple. Lara calls Zak and tells him to hurry. David glances behind him and sees Lara running to meet her son. David is soon breathing hard again as he pounds across the grass towards Margaret and Barry, something in their manner making him rush. It seems to take an age before he comes up to them.

'I didn't expect such a cosy domestic scene,' Margaret says, as soon as David is within earshot.

'What's happened?' David ignores the jibe.

The three of them come to a halt. Barry's hands remain buried in the pockets of his expensive charcoal-grey overcoat. David ignores him and searches Margaret's face, which he recognises as tense with the effort of control.

'Josie's gone missing,' she says. 'We've been trying to ring you since late last night. True to form, you weren't there.' She glances over his shoulder at Lara and Zak. 'Obviously, you've been busy elsewhere.'

'What do you mean *missing*? Jesus Christ. Since when? You saying she's been gone since last night? Shit, Margaret.'

Barry shifts the weight on his feet. 'I think it'll be best if we all try and stay calm.'

David looks at him. Breathes. Refrains from telling him to piss off. Says nothing.

'We haven't seen her since Friday morning,' Margaret says quietly.

'*Friday?* But it's *Sunday* bloody lunchtime. What the fuck's going on?'

Margaret looks at her feet for a moment. Barry regards David with a mild grimace of distaste on his face, as if he's detected a bad smell.

'We're pretty sure she's all right,' Margaret resumes. 'We've checked with the police and the hospitals.'

'*Pretty sure?* Fuck me.'

'There's no reason to believe otherwise,' says Barry. 'As I say, we all need to stay calm.'

David sees Lara giving them a wide berth, pulling Zak along by the hand, while the kid tugs back, yelling 'Dawid! Dawid!'

'I'll see you at the flats,' Lara shouts.

David waves back, before his eyes meet Margaret's again, and he sees both fear and anger. When she begins to speak, he can hear the defensive aggression, despite her efforts to remain cool and deliberate.

'There was supposed to be a sleepover at Kat's on Friday night. A group of girls were going to go round to support Kat after what happened last week. Josie said she'd go straight from there to her shift at the supermarket, said she'd be home round teatime on Saturday. Barry and I were due at a barbecue. Josie said she'd be all right, she'd fix her own meal. We didn't get home until after midnight. When we looked into her room she wasn't there.'

Margaret glances at Barry, as if for reassurance. He takes up the tale.

'There were no phone messages. We thought if anything had happened we'd have heard. We rang the police and hospitals. Nothing. The cops asked if she had a boyfriend. Said she'd probably show up in the morning. That's what we thought too. Guessed perhaps she'd got it back together with this Michael character. She's been pretty spiky since all the trouble at the nightclub, so we thought maybe she was, you know, just trying it on with us.'

'Brilliant,' says David.

'Well, you're not exactly a candidate for parent of the year are you?' Margaret says. 'We've done our best, with very little help from you.' She grabs Barry's hand. David knows Margaret is gearing up for tears. But he needs the full story.

'Go on,' he says.

Margaret takes a breath. 'It turns out there was no sleepover. We've spoken to Kat this morning. The last time she saw Josie was Friday lunchtime. Apparently, she bunked off with Dylan Rose. We've spoken to his parents this morning. Dylan's borrowed his brother's car. Told his mum and dad he was going camping with his mates for the weekend.'

'Camping? In June? Where?'

Margaret shrugs. 'They think maybe down the coast.'

'They *think, maybe.* Jesus Christ.'

'Josie and Dylan are nearly adults. What can you do? The police said the same thing. Once they're seventeen they can do what they like, more or less.'

'She's not seventeen for a few weeks yet.'

'I know when her birthday is.'

'So you think she's with him?'

'Seems the most likely scenario.' Barry answers, while Margaret reaches for her tissues. 'Though we had thought perhaps she was with you. But obviously not.'

'And when's this Dylan due back?'

'Tonight.'

'Do we know if there *are* other mates involved?'

'We haven't got that far.'

He turns away, while Barry comforts Margaret. David takes some deep breaths. He's filled with fear. Thinks about the morning's fun. Ruined now. Perhaps he doesn't deserve anything good in his life. All he knows is that he'd give anything and everything to have Josie safely with him again.

He turns back. 'Where do we go from here?'

'Not much we can do,' Barry says, 'except wait. See if they come back this evening, then read them the riot act. No percentage in setting off on wild goose chases.'

'Can I have Kat and Dylan's phone numbers?'

'They're in the book,' Margaret says. 'But I can't see the point of you meddling. We've already done what we can.'

'I'm surprised you even bothered to tell me.'

'Courtesy,' says Barry. 'And the off chance she was with you.'

'*Courtesy.*' He shakes his head. She's my *daughter,* for Christ's sake.'

'A pity you didn't take more notice of her when she was little.' Margaret turns to Barry. 'I think we should go home now, in case Josie rings.'

'Good on you.'

Margaret and Barry turn and begin to walk away.

'What's Kat's surname? Where does she live?' David shouts to their retreating backs.

'McNamara. Weetangera.'

'Keep me in the loop. We have to be together on this.'

Barry raises a hand in acknowledgement, as they walk off.

David stands and watches them go wondering how the bright, sparky, warm, fun-loving girl he'd known at eighteen had become this bitter, uptight, conventional, middle-class woman. Was it him and Vietnam that had done it to her? Made her afraid of life, afraid of everything that lay outside the confines of suburbia? And is it really Vietnam that lies behind Josie's problems too? Is it a failure of his parenting that has made her run, rather than facing things directly?

David half runs, half walks back to the flats. He needs to expend energy, his mind in overdrive. Irrationally, the idea Josie might be at his place propels his feet. Approaching the stairs, David notices his letterbox is stuffed with the usual weekend junk mail. He grabs it in a fury. The he grabs at another thought. Maybe Josie has left him a note, a message of some kind. There's some real mail amongst the advertising pamphlets. The volume of rubbish makes it impossible to handle without dropping the stuff all over the pavement. He rushes up the stairs. His note is still on the door. He fumbles with the key in the lock, drops some of the mail as he pushes open the door.

'Josie,' he shouts.

There's no reply. He dumps the clutch of paper onto the kitchen counter. He rifles through it. A couple of bills, nothing else but adverts. Nothing. Silence. The emptiness is awful.

David can't bear it. He stumbles next door. When Lara answers he tells her about Josie's disappearance.

'I'm scared, Lara. Scared of what she might do.'

XXI

Lara makes coffee in her kitchen while David paces up and down. Zak wants their attention. He's round David's feet with his robot, asking him to play. It tests David's patience.

'Not right now, buddy,' David says, 'I have to make some calls.'

Zak looks disappointed. Lara steps in. She soothes the little boy and settles him with his Lego in the lounge room. She puts a mug of coffee in David's hands.

'It's probably just a cry for help,' Lara says. 'You know how dramatic teenagers can be. Maybe no news is good news.'

'I'm not sure I want to gamble on that. I have to *do* something.'

Lara strokes his upper arm: a gesture of comfort and support. 'Make your calls then decide. It might be better to wait and see if they do show up this evening.'

David continues to pace. He can't drink his coffee. He's only just controlling the ball of panic spinning in his stomach, threatening to make him sick. An idea occurs to him. He has a sudden rush of hope. He apologises to Lara, kisses her, says he'll come back later. He needs to go next door to use his phone. He doesn't want Zak to overhear his distress.

David's hand is trembling as he dials. 'Come on, come *on*,' he mutters as he hears the ring tone's insistent repetition. He counts to nine before the receiver is picked up. His mother sounds breathless. She barely has time to gasp an interrogative, 'Hello,' before David blurts out, 'Ma, is Josie there?'

'I'm sorry, love. I was just out the back. No, Josie isn't here. Should she be?'

'I was hoping …' David's voice tails away as he experiences the thump of deflation.

'Why, what's going on, Davey? What's the matter?'

Reluctantly, he outlines the circumstances, trying to put the most benign interpretation on Josie's disappearance.

'I told you, didn't I? You need to go easy with her. She wants understanding. An arm round her shoulder. Not you being aloof and bad-tempered. Now, look what's happened. What has Margaret got to say?'

'Margaret and Barry don't seem that worried. They reckon Josie'll be back tonight with this Dylan character.'

'Well, I hope for all our sakes they're right.'

'Try not to fret, Ma. I'll let you know as soon as we hear anything.'

David hears his mother *tsk* on an indrawn breath, before she replies.

'How can I *not* worry? I've always thought Margaret has done a good job with Josie, but now she seems to have her mind on this Barry fellow, and I'm not sure where your head is. I thought you were getting on top of things and beginning to sort things out. But I don't know. You need to get a grip. Josie needs you.'

The last thing David needs is a ticking-off from his mother. He has a struggle to keep his tone even. 'Thanks for the advice,' he says. 'Maybe she needs you, too.'

'I'm always here for her. Josie knows that.'

'Yeah. Well. That's why I rang. I've got to go. I've another few calls to make. I'll keep you posted.'

'You make sure you do.'

'Try not to worry,' David says, relenting a little before he hangs up and punches the wall by the phone so hard it cracks the plasterboard and takes some skin off his knuckles. He sucks his fist, then lights a cigarette with shaking hands.

When he's calmed down a little, David searches for the phonebook. After rifling through several unpacked boxes and peering into his kitchen cupboards, he eventually discovers it slung in the bottom of the old wardrobe in his bedroom. He looks up the McNamara and Rose numbers. David braces himself and dials.

The conversations don't help. Kat McNamara repeats what she's already told Margaret: she last saw Josie with Dylan on Friday lunchtime. She had no idea they were planning to run away and doesn't know where they've gone. She was expecting to see Josie that evening. When David asks if she thinks they might harm themselves, Kat seems genuinely shocked.

'Oh,' she says. 'I never thought of that. No, no, I don't think so.'

David backpedals. Feeling guilty for even raising the possibility, he tries to reassure Kat, telling her he had to ask, but he's sure there's nothing to worry about. He expects Josie and Dylan will be back this evening, ready for college in the morning.

By the end of the call, David is sweating with the strain, trying not to betray the knife-edge of fear which might slip into anger and recrimination. When Mr Rose answers the phone, his attitude baffles David. Dylan's father doesn't seem perturbed at all. He talks about 'boys being boys'. Says Dylan and his brothers are used to camping at the coast. There's nothing to worry about. David wonders if the guy even *knows* about his son's depression. Maybe not. Or maybe he thinks depression is some kind of bullshit condition.

In answer to David's further enquiries, Mr Rose says they might have chosen anywhere north or south of Bateman's Bay to camp. Dylan is familiar with the beaches down the coast to Broulee, or north to Depot Beach and Pebbly. There's plenty of good spots to camp.

David thanks Mr Rose for the information.

'No worries,' he says. 'I reckon it will have done them good to get away for a bit, after all the trouble. I expect they'll be back later. No worries.'

David doesn't bother to argue. There seems little point. He spends the rest of the day at Lara's place, pacing up and down, ducking out for a smoke, intermittently playing with Zak, intermittently discussing with Lara what he should do, rehearsing the possibilities. Time seems to move at a sepulchral pace. All the while, David is wondering if Josie and Dylan are moving steadily away from Canberra. They could be in Sydney or Melbourne or beyond by now. The only good thing to come out of his phone calls is the lack of concern for their safety shown by Kat and Mr Rose. It doesn't necessarily make them right though.

By half-past four, with the light beginning to fail, David is loading his truck. He flings in his swag, some camping gear. He rings his old army mate, Glen, in Bateman's Bay and gives him the drum, says he's going to drive down, can he have a bed for the night? David speaks to Margaret again. There's no sign of Josie, but it's early yet, she says. He tells her he's driving down to the Bay to look for them. Margaret says he's mad. It's a fool's errand.

David doesn't care. He's not going to sit around any longer. He can't. It's intolerable. He has to do something. Lara suggests he should wait until morning—it's going dark, there's some weather on the way. Josie and Dylan might still arrive home. David agrees to wait until evening. He'll check again with Margaret. If they're not back by then, he's off. There's nothing else he can do. He has to try and find them.

¢

David leans forward, peering through the windscreen, which is dashed and puddled by torrential rain. The wipers are on high, their manic slap grating on his nerves and adding to the tension. When he set out from Canberra, he hadn't counted on the weather turning this shitful, landing him on the switchback of Clyde Mountain in a terrific electrical storm. The road is treacherous and visibility poor. What began as a relief and a release of energy is rapidly turning into an exhausting ordeal. The forest rears up on both sides, seeming to crowd the car and further confound the light. Between dramatic flashes of lightning, which illuminate the immediate vista with a ghastly pallor, the mottled darkness is profound, the headlights' beam rendered uncertain by the downpour and the lowering canopy of cloud and trees.

There's little traffic on the road, which is a blessing, but it increases David's sense of isolation and the illusion he has of proceeding along some winding subaqueous tunnel. Occasionally, he sees a reflected gleam in his lights and imagines creatures hesitating on the margins of the road. The threat of hitting a roo is nerve-wracking and the sight of roadkill littering the verges only serves to heighten his unease.

Flooded with fear that Josie's disappearance is some kind of punishment, David squeezes his knuckles round the steering wheel. A black abyss opens in him. He knows there are grim statistics about self-harm among children of Vietnam Vets. Surely she wouldn't, she couldn't? He can't bear to name the possibility. Everything would be over then.

Eviscerated creatures by the side of the road don't help. They take David's mind back to his recent night terror in which he was trying to stop his mates shooting and shooting at an animal that refused to die. He remembers the horror in Vietnam which his recurrent nightmare commemorates.

It was at a feature called The Horseshoe, a defended encampment on the top of an extinct volcano looking over the rice paddies around Dat Do. The company had been deployed to conduct patrols from there into the surrounding countryside. Though the Horseshoe itself was a safe haven, the ops beyond their base were difficult, not least because of the minefields in the area.

It was late in the afternoon before Anzac Day. A yippee shoot was ordered to clear their weapons. Feelings were running high because David's mob had lost two blokes on the last patrol, one dead, one with his legs blown off. The forward scout had kicked a jumping jack mine. He was killed outright and the second scout just behind him was hit by the shrapnel from the explosion. It was a bastard of an incident.

When the yippee shoot began at stand-to, some water buffalo wandered across their position. A kind of madness took hold of the platoon. Suddenly they were firing with savage abandon at the creatures which sank to their knees, great chunks of flesh flying off them. All the anger, fear and frustration of the previous days was levelled at the defenceless creatures. Some of the lads thought it was fun. Others fired away, grim-faced and passionate. David was horrified but continued to fire, caught up in the contagion of fury.

Not all the beasts died. That was the worst thing. Some of them escaped wounded into the paddies. All night they moaned and bellowed. The following day, after the parades and bugles and fine words to mark Anzac Day, David and his mates were sent out to finish the job. Slaughter the beasts and burn the carcasses.

How could you tell anyone stories like that?

How could you explain that at the time, horrible as it was, it seemed understandable—the soldiers made brutal by the necessary brutality of their situation. A familiar flare of rage ignites. David hammers the flat of his palm against the wheel making it judder under the impact. How could you explain what it felt like to lose your mates or to kill other human beings who were designated 'the enemy'? How could you explain all that was taken from you in the ecstasy of combat?

Yet he sees now his silence has been met by Josie's. She's gone without a word. Her disappearance *is* a rebuke. As he steers the hairpins and other tight corners on the mountain, David interrogates himself without mercy, wondering what he could and should have said and done to prevent Josie running away. A further test is provided by the gruelling puzzle of what he is to say to her, should he find her. It's not as if he can persuade her to return home by force. He will have to try and talk to her. But as ever, David can't think of any words. That's why he paints. He has no voice for his deepest thoughts and feelings.

Unbidden, the idea for a picture comes into his mind. He has a vision of another black and red canvas, this time with the head of a water buffalo emerging in umber and white like a totem. He wants to paint a homage to the animals which he helped to kill. He wants to capture the power and strength of the creatures, as well as commemorating their docile suffering. He wants to assuage his guilt.

The terrifying sensation of the back wheels of the ute drifting out on a bend slick with rain and mud, brings David back to immediate concerns. He pulls the wheel onto the opposite lock and brings the ute back on track. He only has to survive a few more kilometres and he'll be at Glen's place. David comforts himself with the thought of the welcome he'll get from his old mate and the drink they'll have together before turning in.

Tomorrow, he'll start the search for Josie in earnest. For tonight, he's determined to concentrate on surviving what's left of the mountain unscathed.

XXII

David spends all day Monday touring the beaches and camp sites south of the Bay. The day is bright and mild with sunshine and cobalt skies. In other circumstances it would have been an ideal pleasure trip through Batehaven, Sunshine Bay, Malua, Rosedale, Guerilla Bay, Tomakin and Broulee. The absence of high-rise, the unspoilt beauty of beach and forest are treasures David hopes the developers, the greed merchants, the men of dangerous visions won't destroy.

He doesn't dwell on this. He has more than enough dark thoughts to fill his mind as he drives from place to place, asking at camp sites, newsagents, motels, service stations and shops if anyone has seen the runaways. He flashes a photo of Josie whenever he can, explains his search. People are variously kind or suspicious. The only thing they have in common is they haven't seen Josie or Dylan. At least they say they haven't.

When he finishes scouring Broulee, there are maybe a couple of hours of daylight left. The longer he drives, the further he travels, the more futile his search seems to be. Still, he puts in the extra kilometres to Moruya, even though this seems counter-intuitive. If the kids want to keep a low profile, why drive to the next large town? Unless Dylan knows of somewhere to camp by the riverside or near the beach.

As he approaches, David clocks black swans cruising on the river between the moored yachts and pleasure boats. Pelicans come in to land like miniature flying boats. He drives through the town and out to the deserted beach where he walks for a while and stops to observe a pod of dolphins making their elegant arcs through the waves, one after another, about a dozen of them, sleek, mysterious and fine, creatures of the sea who also seem to seek the air and sky. How at home and peaceful in nature they seem. Not like humans, always fighting themselves and their environment.

But there is no sign of his daughter. None at all. David drives back to Bateman's Bay depressed and defeated, the falling light in keeping with his sombre mood. He tries to cheer himself up with the idea that Josie and Dylan have driven north. He'll go that way tomorrow. There's no need to give up hope just yet.

At Glen's place, he phones Margaret, his mum, then Lara.

Josie hasn't turned up. There's no news.

Lara is fine but says she's worried about him. She misses him. David chokes up. He tells Lara he has to keep looking for Josie, but the thought of her and Zak is keeping him going, making him feel there's the possibility of a future. When he puts the phone down, though, he knows that if anything has happened to Josie, he has no real future. It will destroy him.

This bleak reflection is interrupted by the irrepressible Glen, who outlines a plan for the evening's entertainment. On Monday nights he meets at group of mates at the Soldiers Club. There's a meat raffle. Glen reckons if Josie and Dylan have been in the area, some of these blokes might have seen them. David isn't sure if this is just Glen's way of coercing him to indulge in a few beers. A jolly night at the bar is the last thing he needs. He says as much, but Glen is insistent. David complains he's got no decent shoes; he only brought his old boots. There are dress rules.

'No problem,' says, Glen, 'you can borrow a pair of mine.'

Soon, David and Glen are walking along Beach Road at Bateman's Bay towards the Soldiers Club. It's early evening, already lights are winking from the farther shore and the streetlamps are throwing their sodium reflections onto the inky water. A brisk breeze is making the halyards rattle on the yachts moored inshore. The air smells of salt and seaweed.

David is struggling in the borrowed shoes. They're a size too small. His pinched feet might have been comic in other circumstances. As it is, David experiences the discomfort as the ironic mockery of an absurd universe; a bad joke to add to the wire-tight, strung-out tension he feels about his missing daughter.

'Christ, I'm going to have blisters. This is bloody ridiculous.'

'Stop your moaning. It's all in a good cause.'

'You know I hate these fucking places.'

'I'd heard rumours.'

'And why these brothel creepers should be considered respectable, I've got no idea.'

'Hey, they're my best shoes! Italian leather, mate. Cost me a motzer.'

The Bateman's Bay Soldiers Club is a rather grand concrete and glass affair with a Second World War canon mounted outside. In the summer it's packed with holiday-makers and tourists, as well as the large number of locals who use it as their regular watering hole. Even in winter, it's always busy, its three bars and two restaurants doing healthy trade. As he enters, the first thing David sees is the Honour Board, recording the names of the dead from the region. The next board his eyes light upon advertises forthcoming attractions: the twice a week bingo, the Saturday dance, the quiz nights, and the raffles.

Glen signs him in as a guest, and they go up to the 'Sportsman's Lounge'. On the way they pass rows and rows of gaming machines, their electric beeps and chirrups greet the fall of coins and seem to mesmerise the solitary players who press or pull in a glaze of desire. They remind David of the bad times when he sat in a drunken stupor feeding the slots as if he were trying to feed his soul. Hoping to be a winner, while making sure he could do nothing but lose.

A bloke dressed in a tweed jacket, grey slacks, and striped tie passes and nods. Glen says, 'G'day.'

As they approach the bar, Glen leans into David's ear. 'That was the club president. He was a base-bludger in Vietnam. So far up himself he can't see daylight.'

'And you like coming here because ...'

'Of these blokes here.'

Glen introduces David to a group of four, before ordering a

couple of schooners of VB. They look an oddly assorted bunch. There's Laurie, who, like the club president, is dressed in a coat and tie and seems affluent in an overweight kind of a way. It turns out he's a real estate agent. Aaron is a younger man wearing the khaki and olive uniform of a Park Ranger. He's Indigenous, probably Yuin, one of the south coast mob. He reminds David of Jez—he was a proud Wiradjuri man. Gus is flashier than the others. He has a shock of well-groomed hair, too black to be natural, and wears a gold chain round his neck. His grey slacks have razor sharp creases in them, and his round-necked blue jumper is an attempt at cool fashion. He looks like a used car salesman, but in fact owns a servo on the Princes Highway a few clicks north of the Bay. The most down to earth of the quartet is Billy the bricklayer: square build, medium height, muscular, in jeans and a flannel shirt.

As Glen passes David a beer, he announces to his mates, 'This bloke was with me in the Funny Country, now he lives in Canberra.'

'From the funny country to a funny town. Some blokes have no luck at all,' says Aaron.

'Leave him alone,' says Gus. 'He's another fucking hero. Good on you.'

Billy offers David his hand again. 'I was 8 RAR, 1970. Me and Hooter have to keep these other blokes in order.'

David shakes, says nothing. The shoes are pinching. It's uncomfortable. He doesn't like the atmosphere of false camaraderie.

'So, what brings you to our little piece of paradise?' Laurie enquires. 'If you're looking for an investment property, I can help you out.'

'Aaron's right,' says Gus. 'She's a strange town, Canberra. No wonder youse all want to come down here when you get sick of the place.'

'Break it down, boys,' says Glen. 'The poor bastard's only been here five minutes, and you're already into him.' He turns to David, 'If she were alive today, Laurie would sell his grandmother a nice little fibro-majestic in Broulee, but apart from that, he isn't a bad little prick. Beneath the blue blazer beats a heart of gold.'

Billy snorts. Laurie raises his glass. 'You can't blame a bloke for trying,' he says.

There's more banter until the bottom of the first glass. David gets more beers in, a full round this time. As he hands over his cash, he hopes it's worth it. He doesn't relish having to share his private business with these blokes, but Glen reckons they're okay. He has to trust his mate. He's desperate for anything that might help in his search.

They're halfway through the next glass before there's a hiatus in the analysis of last weekend's footy. A bloke sells them tickets for the raffle: twenty meat trays and twenty slabs of beer are up for grabs. All the boys are shelling out. David knows the drill. If he doesn't buy any, he'll immediately be on the outer, look stuck-up. Without enthusiasm, he hands over ten bucks and takes the five pink tickets. It's a bloody good job it's pension day on Thursday. He's nearly out of dough. His spirits aren't lightened by the thought that he's now invested in the occasion. He'll have to stay until the end of the draw. Christ knows how many schooners he'll have had by then.

David's sullen reverie is brought to an end by Gus telling him to drink up and shoving another glass into his hand. Glen says, 'Now then, boys, Youngey here has a problem I reckon you might be able to help with. Off you go, matey, tell 'em the story.'

'I dunno,' David says, uncomfortable with all their eyes on him. 'It seems like a hell of a punt. The thing is my daughter's shot through with her boyfriend. I'm trying to find her. She's not turned seventeen yet. I think they may have come down here, but they could be miles away by now.'

There are sympathetic nods and murmurs.

'They're travelling in an old red Corolla wagon with ACT plates.' David fumbles for his wallet; takes out the photo. 'This is Josie. The bloke she's with is about 5'10", skinny with narrow hips, a mop of curly blond hair. They've got camping gear with them.'

'Whaddaya reckon, Gus? Aaron? Seen anything of 'em?'

The two men look at each other as if seeking inspiration. Gus looks at the photo again and shrugs. 'There's so many kids on the roads these days and with the place being self-serve, you know, I don't take much notice of the punters. Darlene's usually on the till, and I'm in the office most of the day doing the accounts.'

Aaron gestures for the photo. Gus passes it to him. He looks at it closely, then up at David, his eyes narrowed slightly. 'What are you going to do if you catch up with them?'

It's David's turn to shrug. 'Talk to them, I suppose. I mean they're nearly adults, I can't see what else I can do. Try and persuade them, you know, to come home and finish their schooling.'

Aaron nods, thoughtful, looking at David as if trying to gauge the sincerity of his intention. 'There can be a lot of trouble in families over love.'

'My oath,' says Gus, 'You should have heard the shit I had to put up with from Darlene when young Bradley got Cheryl Saunders up the duff.'

The others laugh, but Aaron remains solemn. 'I had a girlfriend when I was seventeen. Her parents didn't approve. Fucked it up in the end. She went off to uni in Sydney. Never seen her since.'

'Christ, don't tell me you haven't had a woman since then,' says Laurie with a lascivious grin.

Aaron doesn't respond to the joshing. David thinks of the Indigenous blokes in the army. There were several in the company; quiet, dignified men, with a wry sense of humour. Jez sometimes liked to have a lend of the white fellas. He was great in the J though—careful, meticulous, switched on. A hopeless irony the way he died.

'Have you seen them?' David addresses Aaron directly.

'I don't know.'

'*You don't know.* What the fuck does that mean?'

'Take it easy. No need to get excited. It means what I say. I don't know. There are a lot of camp sites up and down the coast. You see kids from Sydney and Canberra round the place all the time. I don't take much notice unless they're doing the wrong thing.'

'Even in winter?' David says. 'I've been to a few places down south today and they didn't seem that busy.'

Aaron doesn't reply immediately, but continues to look at David, appraising. David apologises for his impatience. He tries a different tack.

'I'm going north tomorrow,' he says. 'Where would you start? Where would you go if you wanted to lie low for a while?'

Aaron gives a little chuckle. 'If I wanted to lie low, mate, I'd go bush. I wouldn't be using a camp site. And I can promise you, you'd *never* find me. But your kids ... I dunno. Depot Beach is more out of the way than most. And you're right. It's pretty quiet in winter. I'd maybe give that a go first.' Aaron's face suddenly relaxes into a grin. 'Come to think of it,' he goes on, 'I reckon I saw a tent out there a couple of days ago. A wagon, too. Didn't see the plates, but. I didn't get that close. And I don't know if it was kids. It might be worth giving it a go, even so.'

David thanks him and looking round the group says, 'So how do I get there? I went to Depot once, years ago, but I don't remember the way.' He looks at his watch. The idea of getting out of the club and hitting the road seems very appealing. Better than another night wondering, agonising.

'You're not thinking of going out there tonight,' Aaron says. 'No point, mate. It's a difficult turn off the highway, and then dirt roads through the forest. It'll be pitch dark and you've had a few beers. Best wait till tomorrow. If they're there now, they won't be going anywhere tonight.'

'I'll be right. The high beam on my truck's good. I've only had a couple of beers.'

Glen intervenes. 'Listen to the man. You've had three and here comes number four.'

Laurie sticks a schooner in his hand. 'Yeah, mate. Get this into yer. No point ending up wrapped round a tree. Do nobody no good. Might as well relax. Get out there first thing tomorrow.'

'It's my daughter we're talking about here.'

'Too right,' says Glen. 'And she'd rather have a live donkey for a dad than a dead lion. Know what I mean? No need for heroics. Just settle down with us. Have a few cold ones and see what's what in the morning. I told you these blokes would come through.'

There's a general murmur of agreement. Billy claps him on the shoulder with a big square hand. 'She'll be right, mate. You'll find her tomorrow. No worries. And they're just about to start the draw. You might as well stick around, see if you win.'

David slugs down the schooner. He can see there's no use arguing. He has to either stay or walk out and find someone else to give him directions. However tempting that is, he can see how churlish, even childish, it might seem to Glen and his mates. And there's the small matter of drink driving. He's done it plenty of times in the past, but not since the bad old days when he was trying his best to destroy himself without quite admitting that's what he was up to.

So he gets a grip, talks himself down. Persuades himself to stick with the beers. It sounds as if Josie and her friend are okay. He'll set the alarm for first light and get out to this Depot Beach place. Surprise the kids for breakfast.

It takes the best part of another hour for the raffle numbers to be called. Glen wins a meat tray. David has no luck. When it's time to leave, there are handshakes all round. Fuelled by beer, Laurie launches into a slurred and florid speech, 'Fucking privilege to meet you,' he says to David. He gestures expansively at Hooter and Billy. 'Always telling these blokes it's a privilege to know them and drink with them. After what you've done for Australia. You're fucking heroes. What you done in Vietnam. Deserve the medals and that. Bloody good blokes.'

'That'll do, you old pisspot,' says Glen. 'See you next time.'

David shakes his hand. Embarrassed and anxious to get away. He thanks Aaron again for the advice, says cheerio to Billy and Gus.

As they walk home together, Glen is on a high. Pleased to think he's helped David and chuffed with his meat tray. When they get home, he reckons his missis will cook them a steak each. And they can have another beer or two. 'You bloody beauty.'

David hasn't the heart to reply. He limps on, feeling the blisters developing. He knows if he shares his fears about Josie, his mate, half-pissed and happy with it, will bluster and try to cheer him up with anodyne reassurances. Instead, David finds himself addressing the God he has no faith in, praying that Josie is safe and sound at Depot Beach, not on the road somewhere, driving away from him through the night, or worse still, gone from him altogether.

XXIII

David leaves Glen's place a few minutes before six the following morning. He grabs the pencilled map his mate made for him the previous night and creeps out, being careful not to clang the screen door. He doesn't want Glen to wake up. This is something he has to do alone. Though it's still dark and the stars are still bright in the sky, he's glad to be on the move. The night has been long and tedious, punctuated by bad dreams, pints of water and too many trips to the bathroom. For the last two hours, he's not slept at all.

The familiar smell of petrol and dirt in the cab of his ute is comforting, and there's an exhilaration as the ignition fires and he guides the truck onto the road. The streets are quiet as David heads through the town and across the bridge over the Clyde estuary, heading north on the Princes Highway. Glen's scribbled directions reckon it will take ten to fifteen minutes to the turn-off onto the track, known as Mount Agony Road, which apparently is marked by an old wooden signpost. David tries to ignore the portent of the name.

As he drives, he wonders how wise he's been to waste the hours of the night at Glen's. The idea that he might be too late haunts him. In the last few days, whenever thoughts of teenage suicide and suicide pacts have invaded his mind, he's told himself off for being a morbid bastard, and reminded himself of Josie's cheek, her temper, her resilience. The fact that she's run off with this boy surely means she's fighting back, showing off her independence, not throwing everything away in some terrible psychological meltdown. The main thing is to keep believing they're safe and that their escapade is nothing more than a radical attention-seeking ploy.

He clings to this story, as he looks out for the first landmark. When he passes Gus's garage on the left-hand side, not open yet, he knows he's about halfway to the turn off. He puts his foot down. The old crate rattles along, the needle on the speedo just edging over a hundred clicks an hour. David is watchful on the long sweeping bends. This stretch of the highway has a bad reputation for accidents. There are only two lanes and there's a nasty history of head-on collisions. It's about the time of the morning when the dozy bastards who've been driving all night might decide to nod-off.

There's forest on either side of the road now, and David hunches forward, peering ahead, anxious not to miss the sign. The sky has lightened a shade to indigo, but he's still dependent on his headlights. It's about five minutes since he passed Gus's place. For no reason, he imagines Darlene, blousy in a towelling wrap, putting a plate of greasy bacon and eggs in front of a dishevelled Gus. Domestic bliss. He wonders what the future holds with Lara.

What kind of a life could they have together?

Best to leave that on the backburner. Get Josie sorted first. He sees what looks like a right turn up ahead, slows the truck, but it's only a track leading to someone's property.

The road winds on. David begins to think he may have missed the turn-off somehow. It seems a long time since Gus's garage. He glances at his watch. Wonders how much further he should go before he turns round. Wishes his stomach would stop its laundromat churning. The over-ripe banana he wolfed in Glen's kitchen before he left is prompting little spikes of acid to burn his gut and oesophagus, but his antacids are in his pocket and he can't reach them without stopping. There's no way he's going to do that.

David is nearly on top of the signpost before he sees it—it's set further back from the road than he expected. He brakes hard and negotiates the turn onto the unsealed track in a plume of dust and slurry, relieved that he's located the route. Soon, the forest is dense on both sides and David has to switch on the high beams. Through his rear-view mirror, all he can see are the clouds his wheels are churning. He drops the speed right back to forty and winces as the truck hits a pothole. The boys in the club were right. The drive is hairy in the dark. The sight of a roo crossing the road some distance ahead does little to reassure him.

There's another five to ten minutes of this before the next unmarked junction where he has to bear right.

Speed isn't an issue now. David is happy to concentrate on the road, happy that his goal is getting closer. Though he's focussed on the way ahead, it's impossible not to register the magnificence of the huge eucalypts on either side and the lush ferns and palms that signal gullies of rainforest vegetation between them. When he was a young bloke, before he went to Vietnam, he liked the idea of bushwalking. Since patrolling in the Long Green, he doesn't fancy it much. For now, he concentrates on keeping the truck on course as it slews on the loose surface.

He navigates the necessary junctions which should take him to Depot Beach. Glen has told him to look out for a rough parking area to the left of the road situated before the camp site at one end of the beach. The approach is via a right-hand bend on a fairly steep slope. As it happens, in his excitement, he misses the entrance to the car park the first time and has to brake sharply and reverse before he safely comes to rest in what is little more than a clearing in the forest. It isn't paved, and there are some puddles still lingering from the rain earlier in the week. Though it's boggy in parts, he's managed to park on relatively solid ground.

David reaches for his antacids to sort out his heartburn, and then rolls himself a smoke. He remembers the doctor telling him that tobacco would only aggravate his stomach complaint, as well as doing him all kinds of other untold damage. One day, he'll give up.

Not today.

He winds the window down and hears the waves folding themselves onto the beach with what sounds like a lazy roll. It's a comforting sound somehow, suggesting with the increasing light in the sky and the bird cries that resonate through the forest, the cycles of nature's continuity. He feels strengthened by the solitary peacefulness.

It's still not quite 7.00 am. David walks back to the road and along the verge. The road slopes upwards and after a few minutes to his left through the trees he can see the pale glimmer of the sand and the white spume of the breakers down below him. To his right are wooden cabins on a few acres of cleared ground where a mob of kangaroos are busy feeding.

David walks along the frontage of the camp site, scoping the situation. There's no sign of life until he gets to the far end and the house where the proprietors live. There's a light showing there. But nothing else. He walks back a little way. There are two well-spaced rows of the wooden chalets, which look pretty basic. Aaron reckoned the area beyond was reserved for tents.

Cautiously, David makes his way through the chalets until he's on open ground, which stretches to the edge of the forest where the giant eucalypts rear thirty or forty metres into the air. His heart gives a mighty bounce, as he sees to his right about hundred metres away, a tent and a car and the smouldering remains of an open fire.

He stands still, watchful. There's no movement. Slowly, he moves towards the camp. When he gets closer, he sees the car is a Subaru wagon. It isn't them. Suddenly, he is light-headed, breathless. He should have eaten something more substantial. He stands still again, feeling the thudding of his heart, reminded of adrenalin-soaked moments in the Vietnamese jungle. He tries to breathe evenly. He had persuaded himself they'd be here. His foolishness waltzes with his disappointment. He wretches, then forces bile and half-digested banana back down his throat.

The sky is grey by now with orange streaks flaming from behind cloud. David trudges back to the car. He rolls a smoke, swigs some water. Lacerates himself for his lack of forethought—poor planning, poor preparation—then forces himself to think. He fires up the truck and eases down the road. He draws up opposite the neat weatherboard cottage with its tidy front garden and white picket fence. There are lights on.

He walks up the path and bangs on the flyscreen. A grey-haired woman in a floral apron with glasses on a faux-pearl chain round her neck answers. She's in her sixties, maybe, comfortably plump and with the brightest blue eyes David thinks he's ever seen. He finds himself startled by them as he says g'day.

After returning his greeting, she says, business-like, 'You looking for a cabin or to camp?'

'Neither,' David returns. He explains his search for his daughter and her friend in the red Corolla wagon, and he makes sure to mention Aaron's name. Shows her his photo of Josie.

'They was here, love, but they've gone. Cleared out a couple of days ago. Hang on a minute.' She turns and yells down the passage, 'Eh, Bert! Them kids that were here, blond lad and his girlfriend, did they say where they was going?'

David hears the reply. 'Nah. Just said they was moving on.'

The woman turns back to him, 'I'm sorry, love, not to be more help. It must be a worry. They looked like good kids. They was no bother. Seemed well-organised, had their fire going at night and that. But we don't watch too closely if everything is quiet. You know what I mean?'

Before he leaves, David asks her about other camp sites nearby.

'Oh, yes,' she says. 'Round the corner at Pebbly Beach or back towards Bateman's at Durras. But they're all up and down the coast. You'll have a long job searching them all. You might be better off going back to Canberra and waiting for them to come home. You know what kids are like. I expect they'll turn up when they've had enough of an adventure and they want a decent feed.'

David doesn't bother to explain the circumstances fuelling his anxiety. He says his farewells. He knows the old girl is probably right, but he's not giving in yet. He climbs back into the truck, starts it up and flings a u-turn. He'll check out Pebbly and Durras and then head north. If needs be, he'll go as far as Sydney. If he's not found them by then, he'll have to go back to Canberra. Or maybe they'll turn up back there before him. But searching is better than sitting. It makes him feel like he's doing something. The thought of being idle and just waiting for news is unbearable.

He drives back past the camp site. To his right, down the wooded slope, through the trees, he can see the perfect crescent of the bay, serene in the grey winter light, its beauty indifferent to human drama and strife. Soon, he's turning back onto Mount Agony Road, following the signs to Pebbly Beach.

The unsealed road winds through the forest. David has to keep his speed moderate and his concentration high. Hunger is an increasing problem. He has a bottle of water from which he sips occasionally and his smokes to keep him going. But he's all too aware of a wide spacey sensation which he has to combat by focusing on the road. He deliberately shifts his vision from long distance through middle to foreground in a repeated sequence. It's a way of looking out for creatures and other hazards. It's a method for keeping his mind from straying to the everlasting problem of the whereabouts of the kids. It's also a way of making sure he doesn't miss a red Corolla station wagon with ACT plates parked by the side of the road. It's occurred to David that maybe they've moved from Depot Beach because they can't afford to keep paying the camping fees. The idea isn't comforting. It might make them harder to find. It might induce them to do something stupid.

David banishes the thought. Grips the steering wheel. Tells himself to stick to the task at hand. It takes longer than he thought it would to reach Pebbly Beach. It's another twenty-five minutes before he's pulling into the car park. There are a couple of other vehicles parked up but no red Corolla. David walks through the camp site, which turns out to be adjacent to the car park. There are a couple of tents, but no red car and no sign of Josie and Dylan.

A slender track leads to the beach. David disturbs a huge goanna, which scuttles across and into the scrub. A grassy clearing leads down to the sand and the ocean beyond. There's not a soul in sight, only a mob of roos feeding and the sound of the surf providing its rhythmic susurration. David walks to where the beach begins. He has a view of the whole bay and of the acres of grass which skirt the forest. A heaviness descends on him. The emptiness is vast, his mission hopeless. He needs to regroup and have something to eat.

David asks directions from a guy at the camp site and drives the shortest way back onto the highway. He puts his foot down and keeps going until he sees Gus and Darlene's servo on the opposite side of the road. He pulls in. Fills the truck with diesel before entering the roadhouse. He's lucky. Darlene is there behind the till, bold and blonde and blousy, just as he'd imagined her, in an electric blue jumper and violent red lipstick. Gus is there as well, filling shelves with chocolate bars and crisps. And, thank God, there's a warming oven full of pies.

Gus says g'day and introduces David to Darlene. David pays for his diesel and two pies with sauce. He buys a map of the local area and has a bit of a yarn with Darlene and Gus. Darlene reckons she might have seen Josie and Dylan the day before yesterday. She remembers because they only bought ten bucks worth of petrol. She gives a giggle. 'I asked them if they were trying to wean it. I don't think they knew what I meant. They were heading south.'

'There are camp sites and cabins at both North and South Durras,' Gus says. 'But why they'd go there after Depot or Pebbly beats me. I guess it depends how lonely they want to be. There are more folk about in Durras—beach shacks and holiday homes and that. Then again, there are lots of tracks and trails that lead away from the burbs by the sea. I dunno.'

'I'll have a look,' David says. 'It's all I can do.'

Gus and Darlene wish him good luck, if they can be of any

more help, they'd be glad. David's grateful for their friendliness but doesn't linger. He scoffs the pies as he drives to the Bay. He's not going to get caught out again. He'll buy some supplies, tucker, water and booze before he goes to Durras. He has a feeling he might be in the bush for a while.

XXIV

Entering the supermarket in Bateman's Bay, David realises he doesn't know what he's doing. He stands uncertain, wondering how much he needs—trolley or basket? He decides on a compromise, a small trolley. He doesn't need a dollar coin to liberate one. It's not like Canberra down here. But they do have the Canberra papers. It's the first thing he sees on the newsstand at the front of the store.

Nightclub Victim Dies.

The lurid headline smacks David in the face. He gets hold of the newspaper and reads. Sure enough, it's the guy Joel has assaulted. They've shut off life support. It's a story of broken-hearted parents, the perils of young men high on booze and drugs, the lifelong suffering caused by a moment's madness.

Joel will face murder charges.

Christ! What if Josie and Dylan have read or heard about this? What will it do to them? For the second time that morning, David thinks he might be sick. He has to stand and breathe. He replaces the paper. He doesn't need to read any more.

The artificial light and piped music serrate David's nerves as he wheels his trolley up and down the aisles, trying to concentrate on what he needs. He has a small camp stove, esky and his swag in the back of the ute. The makings for a brew are important, some bread and some tins that can be eaten hot or cold. He adds some ham and cheese, savoury biscuits, sweet biscuits, chocolate and energy bars. From the bottle shop he buys whisky, a slab of beer and a bag of ice. That'll do.

By the time he reaches South Durras it's early afternoon. After a careful drive through the forest on unsealed roads again, he pulls up in the car park opposite the cabins and the camp site. He has a sense of déjà vu. There's no sign of anyone, let alone Josie and Dylan. Despite the fibro shacks and weatherboard cabins, it seems even more deserted than Depot or Pebbly Beach, though the population of kangaroos may be greater.

David steps down from the truck, a weary sense of futility settling on him. He might as well have a scout around. A boardwalk path leads through some banksia and melaleuca over a grassy knoll and onto the beach. It's deserted. A bruised sky with scudding clouds lowers over the sea where white caps and heavy surf are punctuating the grey with seething white spume. He looks towards the light lead pencil line of the horizon. There's no ship or sail in sight. A few wind-blown gulls are strutting by the tideline and a sea eagle is on patrol out towards the distant headland. But otherwise, David is alone. Very alone.

There's no point staying here. There's no sign of the kids, no sign of their car. David makes his way back to the truck. He doesn't know how to proceed. There are a lot of unmade roads through the forest leading both north and south. Time is running and every minute might mean Josie and Dylan are taking the highway, moving further away from him. It's all a gamble.

David sits in the cab and tries to think straight, tries to put himself in their position. So much depends on what they are trying to *do*. Is it just a purposeless need to run away and have a few days' time-out together, or is there a more elaborate plan? And if it's the latter, what *is* it? If they were going to go to Sydney or Melbourne, there would seem little point in spending days at Depot Beach. They might also have thought through the possibility of the police being notified and on the lookout for them. Steering clear of the highway would make sense in those circumstances. On balance, David decides it's worth spending the afternoon having a drive round the forest to see if he can see any sign.

¢

The light is fading, as are David's hopes, when he pulls off the track into a firebreak. It's close to 5.00 pm and all he's seen are the seemingly endless pillars of trees, the pale gravel of the dirt roads, glimpses of the iron sky. His meandering drive further south has taken him up and down the steeply undulating track, slithering and sliding down to North Head and Honeysuckle Bay. As he bounced the truck over the rutted terrain, he couldn't imagine the Corolla wagon coping so well. Sure enough, when he reached the end of the road, he found both places deserted. He drove back north again. As far as he can tell he's nearly come full circle. He's ready to call it a day, tired from his early start and wrung out with the hum of anxiety and the melancholy news in the Canberra paper. The day started with hopeful energy which has drained into dull depression. He could drive back to Glen's place—spend another night in the Bay—but he doesn't want to be with people.

He wants to be alone with his fears.

Alone with his sense of failure.

If he'd been a better dad this wouldn't have happened. He deserves to be out here in the wilderness in this absurd position, deciding to bivouac where he is; unrolling his swag in the tray of the ute, unpacking his camp chair so he can sit on the margin of the forest with a beer and his truck for company.

The beer he sips tastes metallic and gassy. There's not much enjoyment in it. David thinks about food and wonders if he can be bothered with his camp stove. He could just eat a couple of cold cans; chunky beef soup, some beans maybe. It would be like being on ops in Vietnam. Sometimes they'd be allowed to use hexamine tablets to heat their tucker. But if there were enemy in the vicinity and the looey in charge was nervous, they ate their rations cold. The tablets were supposed to be odourless and smoke-free, but they emitted chemical fumes when they were ignited which risked giving away their presence and position. In the rainy season the hexamine tablets were difficult to light. They didn't like the wet.

David shivers. At least it's dry and he's not going to be surprised by VC. As the light begins to fade, he decides he might as well make the effort to get his stove going. It's a small cooking-ring powered by a gas cartridge, a more sophisticated affair than a hexamine cooker. Warm food and a brew will be good for morale. It will also pass some time. As he prepares his food, David has to fight the part of him he has to fight all the time—the part that wants to drink until all the pain goes away, until oblivion takes over. But it seems like blasphemy to go down that path of self-destruction, having heard about the boy who has died in a Canberra hospital and knowing that Josie and Dylan are still missing. He decides against another beer.

By the time he's eaten, it's dark and the stars are beginning their radiant sparkle. The forest around him is alive not just with the rustling of the trees but also with night sounds of insects, creatures, birds. At least he doesn't have to do picquet duty. Those awful hours peering into the scrub, hyper-alert, watching the fireflies dance, praying that you'll make the right decisions, not be fooled into firing at the movement of foliage caused by the breeze or creatures but still see the black pyjama-clad enemy moving stealthily towards you. The platoon relying on your judgement.

David finds the battery-driven industrial torch in the back of his ute and by its light he makes a brew to which he adds a drop of whisky. He rolls a smoke and sits awhile, thinking of Zak and Lara, wishing Josie was home and he was back at the flat with the promise of his painting tomorrow and lovemaking tonight.

Instead, he senses the brooding forest breathing behind him turning his solitude to loneliness.

He's had enough for one day. David packs up his gear and unrolls his swag in the tray of his ute. He has a last piss before removing his boots and crawling into his swag fully clothed. He pulls his beanie down over his forehead. He'll be warm enough. With the light extinguished, the darkness encroaches despite the intermittent star-shine. David watches clouds scudding across the sky, moving blots of ink on ink. He tries to think of the night as benign. On ops he always slept heavily clubbed by exhaustion. Now, though his mind is busy, he's not far off surrendering to his body's demands. Before he sleeps, he tells himself he will wake early and move on. He prays again to whatever mysterious powers energise the universe that Josie and Dylan are safe, that they've made good decisions, that they haven't succumbed to despair,

¢

David wakes to grey light and the manic chatter of kookaburras. As he stretches his stiff limbs, he registers their cackle as mockery of his situation. He scrambles up and out of his sleeping bag. He starts the truck up and leaves it idling while he has a piss, makes sure he's left no litter. It's not the same bash, burn and bury routine of soldiering, but not far off. It's about respect for the environment, not staining the weird beauty of the forest.

He stows his gear and consults the map, trying to work out

his way back to the beach. He reckons he might sneak a shower in the toilet block there. Clean himself up a bit. Then, head for the highway. Stop for some breakfast once he's on his way. Make some calls to Margaret and to Lara. See if Josie has turned up.

The shower is abrasive. No hot water. It's a case of bearing the needling assault of the icy cold, taking the cleansing chastisement, a masochistic delight in self-punishment. He towels himself as vigorously as he can and throws his clothes back on. In the truck he turns the heater up and takes another look at the map, trying to see if there's any track he's missed. David decides on a route northwards, which is not the same way he's come in from Bateman's Bay.

The problem with the roads through the forest is they all look the same. David takes his time. It's still early and the light low enough for roos to be on the move. He comes to a crossroads with no signposts. It doesn't look familiar. He punts on the right-hand turn, thinking it will take him towards North Durras and the lake. Though he feels better for his sleep and shower and is invigorated by being on the road again, he's also aware he's maybe behaving foolishly, clinging to the wild goose chase. But he's committed now. He has to go on.

The road is winding and the forest dense on both sides of the slender track. Still, David scans the margins of the road just in case.

It's only a few minutes later when he sees a glimpse of crimson behind the olive drab of the eucalypts and ferns.

He slams on the brakes and u-turns.

He drives back and draws off the road. He's out of the cab running to where the red Corolla has been parked in a small clearing at the beginning of a walking trail. Sure enough, under a coating of mud, the blue letters and numerals on a white background declare the vehicle's ACT identity.

David's heart is hammering, his breath short. He tries the doors and peers through the windows. The car is secure. He can't see anything in there to identify it with Josie. But then there's no reason why there should be if they've gone to camp nearby. He goes back to the truck and prepares to trek through the forest. He eats an energy bar and stuffs his pockets with chocolate and fruit. He doesn't want to carry anything with him. Keep things light.

Walking through the scrub, even though the flora is more familiar and very different from the Vietnamese jungle, there's enough to remind him of slow-stepping down tracks of fear. The sense of enclosure, the way the tree canopy changes and dapples the light, the noise of rustling leaves, singing insects, snuffling creatures, whooping birds. David moves his head through regular quadrants, scanning the bush through the trunks of spotted gum, blue gum, ironbark, peppermint gum. It reminds him of scanning his designated arc as the platoon moved single-file, stealthy, nerves stretched, waiting, fearing contact.

The difference here is David *wants* to hear or see something. He wants to detect movement, life. His greatest fear is of finding them but finding them too late. He banishes the idea and picks up his pace. He has to stop himself breaking into a jog, tells himself not to be stupid. He needs to preserve energy, stay focussed. The track seems interminable. And still no sign of Josie and Dylan.

David experiences the hallucinatory delusion that the forest is closing in on him. The trail seems narrower, less clearly demarcated, the trunks of the trees closer. He imagines the terrain opposing him, just as it seemed to work against them in Vietnam. He fights for rationality. Sweat is running down his neck and back and chest. A rising claustrophobic panic begins to coil, threatening to strike his mind and body. David thinks of Donna telling him to breathe, telling him to change the narrative, to remember present reality. He inhales deeply feeling the cool air expand his chest. He exhales and pushes himself forward, propelled by the wild hope he might find the teenagers safe and well.

It seems a long time, but maybe it's only fifteen minutes before David sees the track broaden into a clearing. He emerges onto a swathe of grass where to his left a mob of kangaroos are peacefully grazing. Away to his right is an expanse of water which he realises must be Durras Lake. There's no sign of anyone camping in the open. There's a ridge in front of him which must lead down to the lake shore. He makes for this, grateful to be out in the open, away from the pressing enclosure of the forest.

When he crests the ridge, David stops and scans the vista in front of him. The lake is a sheet of beaten pewter under the metallic sky. Away to his left, set back from the sand at the edge of the lake and close to the tree line, David spots a splash of royal blue.

A tent.

Their tent, perhaps. It's about eight hundred metres away. He can't see any sign of life. But then, it is still early in the morning.

David strides towards the tent. His heart is a piston, hammering. He's light-headed and sweat soaked. What an irony if he had a coronary—a cosmic sick joke. Other and worse circumstances flash through his mind. He imagines the tent sealed, the bodies inside, white and still and silent.

Panic and anger and dread clamour in him: No. No. No.

¢

David has to stop. He takes deep breaths. The vertiginous sensation provoked by his imagination of catastrophe needs to be stilled. He tells himself to get a grip. As he comes up to the simple two-person tent, more detail becomes clear. There is order and organisation around the camp site. An awning has been erected behind the tent to provide a sheltered space for food and gear. The ashes are still smouldering at an open fireplace made with a ring of stones. Two fold-out camp chairs together by the fire look quaintly middle-aged. Two beach fishing rods sitting in their holders point their tips to the sky, suggesting attempts to catch a feed.

There is reassurance in all of this. It doesn't look like a death scene. David steps towards the tent, treading slow and softly. His instinct is to be quiet. He doesn't want to alarm the kids, and anyway, the restraint helps him to quell the fear which is a chisel riving him.

The double-sided zip on the tent flap is closed. With a rush of recognition, David sees Josie's Doc Martens parked under the fly sheet. He has an impulse to hug them. He remembers ruefully when she first bought them, asking her why she wanted to wear such clumsy boots. Another moment of hopeless insensitivity on his part.

David straightens and listens. Not a sound comes from the tent. All he can hear is the faint caressing hush of the sea in the distance and the rough-tongued whisper of eucalypt leaves from the forest. The conflict between the desire to know they are safe and the unspeakable terror they are not paralyses him. He imagines taking the zip in his hand and slowly moving it down, the sudden distress it might cause the sleeping lovers—for surely that is part of this story—their rude awakening to the stern father's presence. The other possibility, which has already stained his mind, he doesn't wish to think of again.

David moves away. He mooches around and finds a stack of wood under the awning ready to feed the fire. This Dylan character shows signs of being a capable lad. Or is it Josie who has inspired the neat and practical organisation of their site? Maybe both of them contributed to the thoughtful competence. They've done well for a couple of sixteen-year-olds. David takes a stack of wood in his arms and livens up the fire. He slumps onto one of the camp chairs and rolls a smoke.

It's a grey day, but the cloud base is high. It doesn't look like rain. There's a breeze blowing from the sea. David pulls his coat tighter, feeling cool now after the sweat of his exertions. He sits and pretends to appreciate the view of the lake in the foreground and the sea beyond to the right. At his back is the forest handy for firewood. The camp is well positioned. He tries to distract himself by thinking of the palette he'd need to paint the scene in front of him.

When he's finished his cigarette and thrown the stub in the fire, David continues to sit, wondering how long he can bear not to act. He glances at his watch. It's just past 8.30 am. He's steels himself to approach the tent again. If only he could hear something from inside. A sniffle, a cough, even a snore, would make him happy to wait all day for the kids to emerge. He hunkers down by the entrance with its closed zip. He thinks maybe he *can* hear movement, a rustle as of limbs shifting in a sleeping bag. But then quietness descends again, and he wonders if he's imagined the noise.

David inhales deeply, mutters the word *please* under his breath. He grabs hold of the zipper and pulls it down quietly until there's enough room for him to look into the dim interior of the tent. He sees pale pillowed faces, two forms lying on their backs, no movement. They look rigid. He pulls the zip further and reaches inside. He grabs for a foot inside a sleeping bag. At the same time, he says, 'Hello?'

His voice is barely more than a croak, hoarse with tension.

There's a kick against his hand, a high scream.

Josie sits up with wild eyes. Dylan isn't far behind.

'Jo-Jo,' David gasps. The relief sucks the air out of him. He is light-headed, giddy. He drops onto all fours for a moment, his forehead to the cool earth.

'Oh my God, Pa,' she gasps. 'What are you *doing*? You nearly frightened us to death! We thought you were like some axe murderer or something, creeping around.'

'I came to find you,' he gasps, still overwhelmed.

'Oh my God. Hang on a minute while we get up.' Josie sounds as relieved as David feels.

'Okay,' he says. David has to brace, concentrate on standing, his legs boneless. He goes back to the fire, collapses into the chair. It takes some time for the riot in him to subside. He's settling a little when he hears an odd noise some way behind him. He turns just in time to see three kangaroos moving along the tree line. He follows their progress and notices the rest of the mob grazing at the margin of the forest. One of the roos scents him, stops, and straightening, looks back towards him, ears alert, the eyes in its beautiful, pointed face alive with intelligence. Seeing David is still and quiet, the roo hunches again and lopes to join the others.

Watching the creatures calms David. He experiences an odd envy for the simplicity of their lives. He thinks of the simple things the human animal needs. Fire, food, shelter ... then love. Maybe that's what Josie and Dylan have escaped here to find. Maybe it's their way of learning the importance of simplicity. David experiences a rush of memories. The foolishness of his young manhood: the way he had to go to war to understand what is essential and in doing so learned more than he bargained for. He realises part of his anger is self-recrimination.

There's another rustling closer at hand. David stands in time to see a head of auburn curls emerge from the tent. Josie straightens and completes the action of pulling a sweater over her head and then she's hopping about pulling her boots on, tucking her jeans in. David fights for composure as he waits for her to finish her inelegant ballet. He thought if it came to this moment, he might experience fury for all the stress Josie has caused. But he doesn't. Instead, he's aware of a heady lightness, the expansion of deliverance through his body.

They move to hug each other. Josie is more than ready. She clings to him, tight.

David is glad his chin is resting on her curls. She can't see the water that brims in his eyes, nor see the clenched jaw, the tongue pressed to his upper palate, so the tears won't spill.

XXV

David is still holding Josie as he watches Dylan emerge into the day. The boy looks pale, tousled, wary, expecting a difficult reception. He's dressed in jeans, a round-necked sweat-shirt, a pair of trainers. David breaks his embrace with Josie.

G'day, Dylan, is it?' he says, and moves to shake the boy's hand, anxious to reassure him.

Dylan's handshake is tentative, reluctant even, as if the gesture is uncool. He seems embarrassed. David looks between the young people. Josie is pale as well. There are dark shadows under her eyes. Maybe they've been hitting the booze. David refrains from asking. Instead, he says, 'Looks as if you're well set-up. You've done a good job.'

His remark is met with grunts of assent. Both Dylan and Josie are unsettled, not quite knowing what's coming next or how to react. David wonders if they've heard the news from Canberra. Maybe not.

'You got any tucker?' David asks. 'I'm starving. I could do with some breakfast.'

'Er, yeah. Okay,' Dylan says.

The kids look at each other.

'I'll see to the fire,' David says.

Josie and Dylan sort themselves out. They have eggs, bacon, baked beans. Dylan gets his camp stove going while Josie opens a can of beans. David toasts bread over the open fire. Nobody says much. They're concentrating on tasks and there is still strain in the situation.

The preparation and eating of breakfast gives David time to think. He knows he has to broach the difficult news from Canberra, as well as trying to glean what's going on with them both. What their thinking is, their plans.

Dylan sits cross-legged on the ground to eat while David and Josie have the chairs. The food tastes extra fine as all camp cooking does if it's well done. David relishes it all the more because he's found Josie. She's safe. It's the first time he's actually *tasted* a meal since she went missing. He's been fuelling rather than eating. Now, under a luminous grey sky with the sound of the sea and the crackle of the fire close by, it's as if he's come alive again.

With David's encouragement, Dylan makes a brew. They sit nursing mugs of tea, Dylan rocking slightly, Josie head down, quiet and thoughtful. At last David says, 'I reckon it'd be good to have a bash putting a line in, try to catch a feed of flathead for tea.'

Josie and Dylan look a little surprised by his suggestion but shrug their assent.

'Do you know a good spot, Dylan?'

'Yeah, there's the lake or the rocks at the far end of the beach. You can cast into deep water from there.'

'Sounds good.'

'Before we get started,' David says, rolling a smoke, 'we should maybe try to get a couple of things straight.' He glances at them as he runs his tongue along the edge of the cigarette paper. He can see them bracing.

Here we go, they're thinking. *Here comes the lecture.*

If only that's all it was.

'Have you heard anything about Joel and the guy in hospital?' David asks.

Dylan shakes his head. Josie whispers, 'No. We were trying to get away from all that.'

David draws on his cigarette. 'There's no easy way to say this,' he says, 'the guy died. They switched off life support.'

Dylan jumps to his feet and shouts, 'No!' at the top of his voice, the 'o' echoing on and on like an infinite zero. He flings his cup with its contents aside and stomps off towards the beach.

'Dyl, wait!' Josie says.

But he starts running then, letting out a wild scream of frustration.

Josie makes as if to follow him. David lays a restraining hand on her arm. 'Let him be for a bit,' he suggests. 'Let him get it out of his system.'

'You don't understand,' Josie says, 'he's been talking about killing himself.'

'Have you been talking about that too?'

Josie's voice is small as she replies. 'No. I've thought about it. Who hasn't? I mean we're doing *Romeo and Juliet* in English. But

I don't want to. I've been talking Dylan down. I think he feels kind of trapped. I felt trapped as well. But now, since we've come away, I've just been trying to, like, help Dyl and find another way out. But what Joel's done and now hearing the guy's died, it's like so awful. I dunno ...'

It seems words have failed her. David knows the feeling. He stands, moves to hug her again. Josie collapses into his arms. After a moment or two, David suggests they take the rods and the rest of the fishing gear to the beach, see if they can catch up with Dylan there. Not make a big deal of his reaction. Stay cool. But Josie is adamant. She must follow Dylan. Be with him. Make sure he's all right.

David watches her go. Maybe he can carry the fishing gear on his own. Maybe he should sit down and wait. Leave them alone to comfort each other. He thinks about Lara. What advice might she give?

¢

David stands on the rocks, casting into deep water. It's a long time since he's been fishing and he's still struggling to get a feel for the rig. He's clumsy and maladroit. He's also keeping an eye on Dylan, ten metres to his right. David had to work hard to persuade the young man to put a line in. Now, it looks as if Dylan has only complied in deference to David's adult authority. David thought it would be good for the boy, but if it's possible to fish angrily, resentfully, then Dylan is making a good fist of it. He's casting with a wild fling, then pulling and tugging the line in a welter of impatience for a minute or two before reeling in and trying again. His features are set in a stern grimace and in his eyes there's a world of hurt.

Josie sits hunched on the sand, looking out to sea. She's wearing her torn black jeans, a purple sweater over a charcoal t-shirt. There's not a lot of light in her clothes. Occasionally, she glances towards David and Dylan. She seems in better shape than her boyfriend, but both of them are clearly shaken by events in Canberra.

David had given them a few minutes before following them to the beach. He carried a fishing rod in each hand and found and hefted a backpack of Dylan's, which was full of bait and tackle. He found them sitting huddled together, Josie's arm round Dylan's shoulder, his head hanging. David urged them to join his expedition. Dylan mumbled he didn't feel like it.

Though he felt sorry for the young man, David had been brusque. 'Come on,' he said, 'no use moping, feeling sorry for yourselves. You're not responsible for Joel's actions.'

Neither Josie nor Dylan looked particularly convinced by this advice, but at last Dylan clambered to his feet and led the way to the fishing spot. Now they are here, the endeavour David hoped would be soothing seems to be having the opposite effect on his young companion. It's not helping that the fish aren't biting. It's a day that requires quiet persistence which clearly is in conflict with Dylan's mood.

Despite Josie and Dylan's troubles, and despite the difficulties ahead, David is aware of gusts of elation blowing through him on the seaborne breeze. That he's found his daughter safe and well means hope is restored in him, a hope he must communicate to Josie and Dylan as well, if he can. So as he casts, using his wrist to get some whip, sending the unravelling line snaking its slender graphite-line against the horizon, he senses an invigorating energy, gathering and expanding, which makes him glad to be alive. All his senses are heightened in the scouring breeze, which makes David feel with every breath he's being scrubbed clean. His painterly eye appreciates the shifting greys of sea and sky, pearl, oyster and gull. He enjoys composing the seascape, with the idea of transforming grey from dull indeterminacy into the shifting beauty of shades between extremes—the colours of compromise and understanding.

With a wry smile, David realises that Dylan is a long way from sharing such abstract enthusiasm. Dylan looks ready to hurl rod and tackle into the drink. There's a violence in the way he's flinging the line as he casts; an irony given the source of his distress. David searches his mind for something he might say to help. He comes up blank.

They toil away for another half-hour or so, Dylan becoming increasingly agitated, muttering to himself, though he's too far away for David to catch the words. At last, David suggests they pack it in. Go back to camp for some lunch. Dylan complies. They walk back to Josie who hasn't moved. She's sitting hugging her knees, staring at the strict line of the horizon. She clambers to her feet as they approach.

'How did you go?' she asks.

'No good,' David says.

'Futile,' Dylan adds. 'Like everything else. *Futile.*'

'Break it down a tad, mate,' David advises. 'Another day the fish will dance onto your hook.'

The boy says nothing, looks unconvinced, inclined to sulk.

Jesus, David thinks. *What am I going to do with this guy?*

Back at the camp site, they get busy with practical tasks—the reinvigoration of the fire; preparation of sandwiches, ham, cheese, tomato; boiling the billy for a brew.

While they're eating, David broaches delicate matters. He tells Josie and Dylan he thinks it only right that he should drive back into the Bay and phone Josie's mum and Dylan's parents to let them know all is well. He reassures the kids this doesn't mean they have to go home right away. He's happy to spend a few days with them while they work out the best way forward. He'll buy some more supplies so they can have a decent tea. They can come with him for the ride or stay here. But if they stay, David needs their solemn promise they won't do a bunk while he's off on the errands.

Josie is keen to agree. Dylan is less forthcoming. Eventually, following Josie's whispered urgings, he assents to the scheme.

'I'll tell your mum and dad you're okay,' David says to Dylan.

'Whatever. I doubt if they're worried. Probably enjoying me not being there.'

'Yeah, well, we'll see,' David replies, not willing to engage in a wrangle. All he needs at this stage is agreement.

Before he sets off, David gives Josie another hug. 'Don't run out on me again,' he says. 'I know I haven't been much of a dad to you, but I love you, right? We'll sort things out. Okay? Don't let Dylan persuade you to do anything daft.'

Josie looks up into his eyes. 'It's okay, Pa. I'm glad you're here. I'm really worried about Dyl. It's been hard work. I really care about him, though, you know. At least I've realised that. We're kind of soulmates.' She breaks the embrace, but still her eyes are locked on his, direct and earnest.

'We won't go anywhere, I promise,' she says.

¢

Later that evening, the three of them sit cosy round the camp fire. David has carried his swag and another camp chair from his truck as well as the provisions from Bateman's Bay. He's bought three decent sized flathead from a van by the road. He's dressed them with lemon juice, butter, salt and pepper, wrapped them in foil and placed them in a camp oven. Dylan has watched, showing an interest in proceedings, which David takes to be a good sign.

He offers the lad a beer. Dylan is inordinately grateful. He offers Josie wine. She refuses. 'I'll have orange juice,' she says, disappearing into the tent. She emerges with mug in hand.

David says, 'As long as you go easy, Jo-Jo. No need to be coy about the vodka.'

She pulls her tongue out at him, raises her mug. 'Cheers,' she says.

Under the purple velvet of the sky, the occasional glittering star visible behind the gusting clouds, the fish tastes wonderful. They eat it with their fingers, hot and sticky, the flesh melting off the bones and tasting of the sea. There are potatoes as well, baked in the ashes. David is pleased Josie and Dylan eat with a good appetite and evident enjoyment. He thinks Dylan's mood might be tempering a little.

When they've eaten and cleaned up, David opens a bottle of wine. He pours a little for the kids and some for himself. They sit nursing their enamel mugs mesmerised by the flames, the crackle of the burning logs, the scent of the wood smoke mingling with the salty breeze. Beyond them, the shadows of the forest look mysterious and magical, the canopy outlined against the sky. In the distance they can hear the rhythmic pummelling of surf on sand.

David loves the feeling of isolation. They are the only humans for miles around, huddled together, keeping themselves safe and warm against the dark.

David wonders if he should be talking to the kids, initiating dialogue. But he doesn't want to break the spell. He doesn't want to cajole or argue, much less to preach. Silence seems becoming.

It's Josie who speaks first. 'I can't stop thinking about Joel,' she says. 'What will happen to him?'

'He's fucked,' Dylan murmurs bitterly.

'I'm no legal expert,' David offers, 'but I think the best he can hope for is manslaughter. He'll do time, maybe in a juvenile prison at first.'

'It's all too horrible,' Josie says. 'It's not as if he's a bad person. He's always seemed okay. A bit arrogant, maybe. But *ordinary,* really. *Normal,* you know.'

'Violence *is* ordinary,' David says. 'We've all got the potential—the ancient animal brain. Given the right circumstances we're capable of anything. That's why I'm not a pacifist. Sometimes we have to fight. The point is about control, I guess. Learning not to lash out. Learning violence is a last resort. Learning to recognise anger and express it differently, if possible. That's the tragedy for Joel. He's lost it for a moment, acted impulsively, fuelled by booze, drugs maybe, and he's done a lifetime of damage in a second's madness.'

'It's fucked,' Dylan declares, disconsolate again. 'And I just stood there and let it happen. Maybe if I'd stepped in I could have stopped it.'

'Maybe,' David says. 'Maybe not. The point is you weren't rushing in to do more damage.'

'I was being a coward,' Dylan says with quiet finality.

Josie stretches out and places her hand on his arm.

'You're not a coward,' she says.

'There's a difference between care and cowardice,' David says. 'The situation seems to have got out of hand very quickly. You didn't have time to weigh things up. Nobody's blaming you for anything except yourself.'

'The guys at school gave him a hard time,' Josie says.

David has to attempt wisdom again. 'Oh yeah? And what were they doing? Wading into the ruck to make things worse.

Showing they were real men. Come on. You know that's nonsense.'

Dylan lapses into silence, unconvinced. David can think of nothing more useful to say. He remembers the power of the abstract nouns 'cowardice' and 'failure' when he was soldiering. Everyone was scared. It was about not showing it, not giving in to it, conquering it. But then there was the vicious circle: fear leading to anger, anger leading to the brutality and fierceness with which they fought. The fierceness and brutality leading to the grief and shame he's had to carry; the knowledge that damaging others means damaging yourself. David doesn't know how to say all this to Dylan. And anyway, the circumstances are different. Fighting the VC in the jungle wasn't much like a punch-up in a nightclub. Dylan and Josie's mate didn't mean to kill the guy. But there's no denying that's what he did. There aren't many consolations.

Josie says, 'I wish I'd stopped Kat messing about. I thought it was a bit of fun. How wrong can you be?'

'It should have been fun,' David says. 'Maybe one person's fun is another's cruelty. It's something to think about, not beat yourself up with. You guys need to go easy on yourselves.'

'The guy *died.*' Josie's voice is small and stricken.

'I know, Jo-Jo, I know. But there's nothing to be done. All of us, everyone, has their sack of grief to carry. We all have losses to bear. We have to learn to carry them the best way we can and try not to add to the load through our actions and attitudes. The bottom line is you and Dylan aren't to blame. You have to find a way to move on.'

'What about Joel?' Josie asks.

'We'll have to see what happens. Maybe you and Dyl and the rest of your mates can stand by him. Go to see him and try to support him. He'll need help to carry his grief. He's got to live with what he's done for the rest of his life. It won't be easy. He'll need all the friends he can get.'

Dylan has been quiet all this time, sitting forward in his chair, head down. He speaks to the floor. 'I just couldn't believe it, you know. Seeing Joel like that ... so furious, so out of control. It was so vicious. I dunno ...'

'What must he feel like now?' Josie says. 'That's what I can't get out of my mind. And how Kat feels. It's as if all of us have been given a sentence. It's why I wanted to get away. I felt imprisoned by all the negative thoughts and emotions. I thought coming down here would take the pressure off. And it has a bit, but it's like there's no escape.'

David says, 'Maybe there's no escape, but there is a way through. Maybe that's what this is about. Being out here in the quietness, in the dark. Maybe it's about finding a way.'

Josie nods uncertainly. The silence of the night descends. Somewhere in the forest an owl hoots, its hollow cry ethereal and strange.

'We'd better turn in,' David says. 'Tomorrow's another day.' He stands and begins to unroll his swag by the fire. Josie looks up at him hesitant, a question in her eyes.

'You two are all right in the tent, aren't you?' David says with the hint of a smile. He thinks the flush on Josie's cheek isn't just about the firelight.

The youngsters scurry about then, embarrassed, wanting to disappear together as quickly as possible. But before they go, Josie comes to David and interrupts him in his preparations. He straightens as she leans up to kiss him on the cheek.

'Thanks, Pa,' she says. 'Thanks for everything.'

XXVI

The forest looks brooding in the smoky light as another day begins to fade. There's no rain, but plenty of cloud and the temperature is dropping quickly. David sits in front of the camp fire, warming his hands around a cup of tea. He watches Josie and Dylan scavenging for wood at the edge of the trees. They work close together but exchange no words, a pattern he's observed since he arrived. They seem to communicate by small gestures and minimal sounds, their companionship endearing and mysterious.

They've spent the day fishing and beachcombing, but now David is worrying about the evening round the camp fire to come and the pressure on him to find further words of advice and encouragement for the two runaways. He peels some onions, ginger and garlic. They've had no luck with fishing again, so David has promised some improvised culinary delight: a veggie curry. At least he's confident of his cooking skills. It's the counselling role that perturbs him. He isn't qualified.

Josie and Dylan make their way back to the fire bearing armfuls of wood. They sit and watch while David heats some oil in a big pot over the camp stove and begins to sauté onions, garlic, and ginger—the base ingredients for his dish. He peels and chops spuds, carrots, a sweet potato, some red and yellow capsicum. He adds them to the pot as he goes, and when the veg are softened adds some curry powder, then a can of tomatoes. Soon the air is fragrant with the promise of food, but David warns the kids it will take some time before it's ready to eat.

It's dark by now, and a sickle moon can be glimpsed occasionally between the scudding clouds. David opens a bottle of wine and pours a small measure for himself. He suggests the kids have Coke for now and join him in a glass of wine later on. They seem happy with that. He's relieved. He thought such advice might be taken amiss, but there's no problem. It's almost as if they're grateful to have a break from their self-imposed regime of independence. They are nearly adults, David thinks to himself, but not quite.

When it's ready, David keeps the curry warm by the camp fire while he cooks rice over the camp stove. As he dishes up, there are murmurs of appreciation from both Josie and Dylan. All three of them get stuck in, and for a while there's only the sound of forks on plates and the kids refilling their cups with water from the plastic container in the mistaken belief that it will cool the spicy heat on their tongues.

After a second helping, Dyl wipes his plate clean with a piece of bread. 'I never knew veggies could taste that good,' he says.

'You should taste Pa's homegrown veg. They're the best.'

David enjoys the note of pride in Josie's voice.

'I still like meat, but,' Dyl adds.

'Same here,' says Josie. 'Kat's always going on about animal rights and that and I can see what she means, but,' she giggles, 'I really, really like roast lamb.'

'Lara's a vegetarian,' David offers.

Josie compresses her lips and gives him a sharp look. He realises maybe he's said the wrong thing. She looks for a moment as if she's going to say something to him, but then reconsiders. Instead, Josie turns to Dyl and explains that Lara is her dad's 'girlfriend.'

David ploughs on, trying not to sound too self-conscious. 'Lara reckons that if we learned to treat animals better, we might be kinder to each other as well. I reckon she might have something there.'

His gambit is met with silence from the kids. Josie takes the plates and rinses them while Dyl considers his boots. David thinks about the yippee shoot in Vietnam, the careless violence and cruelty towards the water buffalo. It makes him feel sick. But he doesn't want to be a hypocrite. He's eaten meat all his life. It's about respect for the creatures, he thinks. An attitude of mind. Not taking the animal's life and death for granted.

Josie and Dyl come back to their seats, but the mention of Lara has changed the atmosphere. Everything is tenser than it was before. David offers the wine and pours a slug into the empty mugs proffered by the kids. No one speaks.

The breeze has blown the clouds away and the sky is a rash of stars. The night is going to be cold and clear. The roar and suck of the waves on the beach provide a restless nocturne, while David considers how to broach the difficult matters that are on his mind. He finds no inspiration in the dancing flames that figure the elemental process of creation and destruction. At this moment, art is of no use to him. He needs the eloquence of the diplomat or politician and finds his tongue restrained and dumb.

The stretching silence seems vast as the night and makes David think of long horizons. He is conscious of his own smallness and doubts his ability to help the two young people who clasp their mugs and stare into the fire, occasionally glancing at each other, occasionally looking at him.

Though he's been trying not to smoke too much in front of the kids, David takes the makings from his jacket pocket and begins to roll one. He lights up, takes a drag, exhales. It's clear the kids aren't going to help him. He's going to have to take the initiative.

'Look,' he begins, 'I don't want to tell you what to do or persuade you to do things you don't want to do, but I would like to hear your plans, you know?'

Josie says, 'We haven't got a plan. We both felt trapped. That's why we came down here. We had to get away. What happened with Joel was just, like, the last straw, somehow.' Josie looks to Dylan for confirmation. He doesn't say anything. He stares into his cup, his mouth a grim line, morose and resentful. David senses the anger in him and doesn't know how to extinguish the blaze. He ploughs on regardless.

'I can see how being here is a good break, but what happens when the money runs out?'

'That's just it,' Dylan seethes. 'That's the trap. It's like go to college, get your HSC, go to uni, get your degree. All the time you're living at home: no freedom, no independence. Then after the degree, it's like get a boring job and buy a boring house in the boring suburbs and spend the rest of your boring life washing the car and mowing the boring lawn. It's all *futile*.'

It's only Dylan's passionate tone that prevents David from laughing. Instead, he says, 'Maybe you don't have to do any of that. It's not compulsory.'

Josie pipes up. 'But if you don't do all that, all that's left are the shit jobs.'

'I can see where you're coming from,' David says, 'but maybe it's not as simple as that. Maybe there are options. I reckon the most important thing is to go your own way. Find out what you're passionate about. Try and make your passion into your job. If you can't do that, make your job a means to finance and follow your passion. It's hard, maybe, but there are ways to make a space for yourself without having to conform completely.'

David's best shot is met with silence. Maybe he's overplayed his hand. After a minute or two, Josie says, 'What if you don't know what you're passionate about?'

'I guess you use the time at college or uni to find out. Or if you don't want to go to uni, maybe get one of those shit jobs you mentioned, use the experience to explore what you'd really like to do. Maybe you could save up and go travelling. Have a look at the world. Maybe that would help.'

There's another silence. David scratches with a stick on the ground, thinking of anything else he might say. He's not sure he's got much else to offer.

Dylan looks at Josie. 'I know you don't get this,' he says, 'but joining the army seems like a way to avoid all the meaningless stuff. I could apply to Duntroon or the Defence Force Academy. At least it wouldn't be boring. It'd be more of an adventure, a test, and I'd be doing something for Australia.'

Josie glances at David as if to say, *you tell him*.

David's stomach clenches. He thinks of his own experiences as a boy, his decisions as a young man. He remembers watching his father's rituals before the Anzac Day parade. The polishing of medals, the telling of tales. How thrilling it was when, as a ten-year-old, his mother took him to watch the march. The uniforms, the flags, the bands and bugles, the old blokes with their chests puffed out, their rows of gongs glinting in the autumn sun. Then, when he was a young man, the way being an infantry soldier had seemed more exciting, more meaningful than his job in an office. His father's disapproval. How he came to resent his father's silence about combat and its aftermath.

David is snared. Silence won't do in response to Dylan's words. But speech seems impossible.

David's reverie is broken by Dylan. 'I'd been talking to the cadets when it all kicked off in the nightclub. They have this confidence about them. They seem bigger and better than the guys at school who are calling me a wuss for not joining in with their stupid fight.'

Dylan's distress forces David to focus. 'Some of the soldier boys got involved though, didn't they? They weren't slow to throw some punches.'

'Yeah, but they knew how to handle themselves. They weren't going to kick anyone in the head. They didn't need to.'

David takes a breath. Considers what to say. He can hear Dylan. He knows what the boy is saying and feeling.

'For God's sake, Dad,' Josie says. 'Tell him. Say something. I've not put him up to this. It's not like with Michael. It's not about me either. It's about Dylan.'

David recalls the rage he and his comrades experienced all those years ago. Rage that they had to walk down narrow jungle paths carrying eighty pounds of equipment; rage that their mates got shot and blown apart; rage that they were scared; rage that they had to kill; rage that they had to dispose of damaged corpses. David has had to deal with the residue of that fury ever since.

He thinks of Dylan, this tall, slender boy under the brutal tutelage of a drill sergeant. Imagines him facing combat. Imagines him losing his best mate. Imagines him at the yippee shoot.

'Dad!' Josie says again, looking at him, her eyes pleading.

The sight of her brings David back to the present. The necessity of speech. The obligation to put his trauma to good use. He thinks of Donna, her calming voice. He takes deep inhalations. He has to be measured, rational, adult. Before he begins, he thinks of Zak as well as Dylan. Remembers Lara saying, 'Not Zak.'

He takes a few more moments to compose himself. He's aware it's now or never. Once he starts he won't be able to stop. And he knows he won't be able to say any of it again.

'Look, mate,' David begins at last, glancing first at Josie, then regarding Dylan, who has his eyes on the ground. 'I don't know. I don't want to tell you what to do. Maybe the army *is* the career for you. I thought it was right for me. It's an easy mistake to make. But there are things you need to think about before you start signing your life away. First off, if you sign on, you do as you're told. There's a chain of command, an institutionalised class system. Yes, sir; no, sir; three bags full, sir.

'And the army does what *it's* told. The pollies say go to war, off you go. If you're an infantry soldier at the pointy end, you go and fight, whether you like it or not, whether you believe in it or not. You can't suddenly say, "I don't agree, I'm not going." And if you're in a support role, you support the war, whether you like it or not. You forfeit the freedom to protest.

'Second. A paradox. Most jobs in the army are about supporting the pointy end. The numbers of fighting troops are a tiny percentage of the whole organisation. The others are doing management, logistics, signals, intelligence, communications, transport, training and all the rest. But you can do most of that other stuff in civvy street with better pay and conditions and more freedom. So, I think the only reason to join is to be a warrior, part of the pointy end, and that takes us back to the possibility of fighting, and fighting for a cause you don't believe in. In other words, you have to have faith in the pollies to do the right thing.

'Third. The business of fighting. When I was a young bloke, I didn't mind the training. I liked the fitness stuff and the various challenges. It was a way to feel good about yourself, get some muscle, and yeah, if I'm honest, to feel a kind of masculine pride. It gave me confidence. But you can get that from doing martial arts. In the army, the thing is, no matter how good the training, it's nothing like war because the reality of killing and being killed, of wounding and being wounded, isn't there. Unless you've seen it, no one can really imagine what a 7.62 mm bullet or an anti-personnel mine can do to human flesh. And unless you've been there, you can't imagine what it's like to lose your best mate, or to kill another human being. And it's that stuff that's terrible beyond words. Particularly if you end up fighting for something you can't, in the end, believe in.'

David pauses to throw his cigarette butt into the fire. He takes another swig of wine. His hands are shaking, his stomach churning. Images of ragged flesh and bone, the smell of blood, the putrid colours of viscera, the screams of the wounded assault his mind.

He breathes deeply again, trying to comfort himself, takes in the ozone and eucalypt scented air. He remembers the mouldy musty smell of the jungle at night, the heat and humidity, the sound of insect rustle, the hoots and cries of jungle creatures, the terror of picquet duty. How staring into the darkness he'd imagined the clear air and white sand of Australian beaches to keep him going. How he planted his bayonet point upwards beneath his chin to stop him dropping to sleep from exhaustion behind the big gun.

The memory pricks him back to the present.

Neither Josie nor Dyl are looking happy. David's not surprised. But he's going to finish what he's started. He's determined not to shirk in giving advice to Dylan. He'll deal with Josie's curiosity while he's about it. It's a necessity now. Like a man nauseous and dizzy from drink who needs to purge himself, David needs to have his say. He rolls another smoke before he begins.

'I'm not going to be in the business of telling warries. I've said the same to Josie often enough.' He looks at his daughter, who nods in confirmation. 'If I asked you two what you'd been up to in that tent for the last few nights, you wouldn't want to tell me, and quite right too. Because it's private and intimate. And even if you wanted to tell, it would be very difficult to put into words. A lot of what happened to me in Vietnam was like that. So I've nothing to say about it.

'What I can tell you is what everybody knows but chooses not to think about, or to ignore when it suits them. My dad told me before I went to Vietnam, but I chose not to hear him. My head was full of the Anzac tradition and all the rest of it. But the truth is that war is a dirty business, whatever the cause. It's about fear and it's about violence. It may sound obvious, but war is about killing each other. It's as straightforward as that. In war, ordinary people do appalling things. On both sides.

'People talk about service, discipline, and self-sacrifice. That's the fancy language they use to dress-up killing. It's just like the dress uniforms on parade, the gleaming brass and the knife-edge creases. They're images of order, control, cleanliness. War is the opposite: disorder, chaos, dirt. The rest is rhetoric. When people talk about serving the nation, it's best to ask whose *idea* of the nation and whose power interests are being served. And when you hear talk about the army and discipline, you should ask if a soldier is taught the ability to discipline himself or is it imposed upon him. Is the discipline more than being brainwashed to obey orders? Is it more than propaganda to enable men to kill each other?

'As for 'sacrifice' and 'self-sacrifice', war isn't about offering yourself to be killed. Oh no. That's only half the story. You might be risking your life, but you're trying your damnedest to kill the enemy before he kills you in order to save yourself from becoming a sacrificial victim. It's kill or be killed. And what drives you is fear.

'And when you've been through it and come out the other side, does it make you a man? It's just as likely to emasculate you. I ended up drunk in the gutter. Not much to be proud of there. Why should we define being a man by the ability to take and dish out pain? Why can't we celebrate masculinity as creativity?

'This is the best. Sitting here with you two having a yarn. Being a dad is the thing I'm most proud of —I wish I'd done it better, Jose, and I'm sorry I've not been great. But the point is I'm really proud of you. I want to do anything I can to help, to make things right.'

David stops, realising he's getting carried away with himself, moving beyond the scope of Dylan's question and maybe embarrassing his daughter. He flicks his cigarette butt into the fire, creating a scatter of sparks, and contemplates the dirt at his feet. He feels exposed, as if maybe he's said too much, let his guard down. He reaches for his tobacco pouch and prepares to roll another smoke.

But Josie prevents him. She stands and comes to him. She kneels and puts her arms round him, forcing him to hold her awkwardly, his tobacco still in one hand, cigarette paper in the other. She hugs him and kisses him on the cheek.

'I'm sorry if I've been a pain,' she says.

For a moment, David can't speak. He drops the tobacco and the cigarette paper and holds his daughter. 'You haven't, love,' he says. 'It's me that should be saying sorry. Sorry for all the times I was no good. Sorry not to have been there for you. Sorry I've not tried to talk to you more. Sorry I haven't been a better dad.'

Josie kisses his cheek again. 'You're the best,' she whispers. 'We'll always be friends from now on, yeah?'

David can feel her tears wet against his face. 'Too right,' he says.

They remain in their embrace for some moments, David with his eyes closed and his nose in his daughter's hair, smelling apple blossom and wood smoke, and feeling a miraculous communion: loving and beloved.

When he opens his eyes, he notices Dylan looking glum. He nudges Josie. 'You'd better go and give your young fella a hug. He looks as if he could use one after I've given him such a hard time.'

Josie takes her dad's advice. She goes to Dyl and kisses him. David watches as she murmurs something to her boy. They hold hands for a few minutes, before getting up together.

'We're going to turn in,' Josie says.

'I'll think about what you said, Mr Young,' Dylan says and raises his mug to David. 'But I still think it's a job someone has to do—the army, I mean.'

'Yeah, I guess. But it doesn't have to be you. Sleep well, kids,' he says. 'We're going to have to make some decisions about where we go from here soon. I can't stay down here indefinitely.'

'Everything's going to be okay,' Josie replies. 'Night, Pa.'

'No worries,' says Dyl.

They disappear into the tent, leaving David to retrieve the makings and roll a smoke. He sips the dregs of wine, luxuriating in the tobacco, wondering if he's said the right thing, but also feeling a curious lightening, as if he's shed a burden he's been carrying for years as heavy as his army pack.

XXVII

Forty-eight hours later, David is lying on his side, propped up on one elbow, looking at Lara in the warm amber light cast by the bedside lamp covered with one of her scarves. They have made love. It is more of a homecoming than anything he's experienced for years. David's right hand rests on the lovely smooth skin of Lara's belly, while he looks down into the unnerving depths of her electric blue eyes. He's overawed by her beauty and the generosity of her lovemaking, the way she seems to give all of herself in the erotic exchange, which encourages him in turn to surrender himself completely. He can't believe his good fortune.

Their intimacy encourages David to share the story of his recent days—finding Josie and Dylan at Durras Lake, their return to Canberra with him, the conversations he's had with his mum, the meeting that ensued with Margaret and Barry, and the deal he thinks he's brokered.

Margaret was so relieved to see Josie, she even wept a little. Barry was inclined to remain stern and huffy, but David wasn't about to be blown off course by BB. David was on a mission, an approach he'd agreed with Josie before they left the coast.

He figured there was no point delaying negotiations. He didn't want Margaret to have time to recover her equanimity and start making her own plans in conjunction with Barry. David felt for once he had a small advantage: he'd found Josie and brought her home. Now, for his daughter's sake, he wanted to outline a position.

Rather than speaking for Josie, in the first instance he encouraged her to reiterate to Margaret and Barry her unhappiness at the thought of moving to Red Hill and her objections to being grounded, etc. David then took up the reins and said he thought there were a couple of ways to resolve these problems. One was that Margaret and Barry should consider putting their real estate plans on hold until Josie had finished her HSC. If they agreed to this, Josie was willing to be more compliant with rules and regs concerning drinking, telephone use and nights out. If Margaret and Barry insisted on going ahead with the Red Hill move, David suggested that Josie might live with her grandma for a year while she finished college. David had checked out this idea with his mother, who thought it might work out well.

Margaret and Barry agreed to think about these propositions. David was hopeful they would climb down on the Red Hill move because Margaret would want to keep Josie with her.

'It sounds as if you've done a great job,' Lara says.

'I hope so. Whatever happens, I think I'm on the way to healing things with Josie.'

Lara leans up and kisses him. 'I think you're a good man, David Young,' she says.

David shakes his head. He's quiet for a moment. 'There's one more thing,' he says. 'It's Josie's birthday next week. I want to do something special. I've got this idea. We could all spend Saturday working at the allotment—Josie, Dylan, you, me and Zak—and then come back here for dinner. I reckon working together would be a good icebreaker between you and Jo-Jo, and then maybe we could have a good evening together. What do you say?'

Lara kisses him again. 'It scares me to death, but yes, why not? I'm frightened Josie won't like me. She might resent me. But I'll give it my best shot.'

'Once you get to know each other, it'll be fine. I've a good feeling about this. Camping with Josie and Dylan ... I dunno ... somehow, being out in the open, away from domestic spaces, it seemed easier to talk. I don't know why. It was as if being closer to the natural world made it easier for us to be natural with each other. I dunno. I can't explain it. Anyway, I reckon it might be the same at the allotment. It won't be like sitting around staring at each other over cups of tea. There will be work to do. We'll have to be a team.'

Lara is smiling at David's enthusiasm. 'I'm not sure what kind of a gardener I'll make, but I'm in. I mean, if gardening was good enough for Adam and Eve, it's good enough for me.'

'You mean you'll be sporting a fig leaf? Bring it on.'

Lara slaps him lightly on the arm before she switches out the light. They curl into each other. Soon, David hears Lara's breathing become regular. He lies awake, too excited to sleep. The future suddenly seems rich with promise. And tomorrow, he will have his painting again. In his mind's eye, he sees the picture of the water buffalo he wants to make, the image shining like a gift.

¢

In the following days, David works in a strange mood of exalted intensity. His journey in search of Josie, his burgeoning love for Lara and Zak, seem to coalesce into a fierce energy. He works from old instamatic photographs he took in Vietnam. He's rifled through boxes of old possessions to find them. In his struggle with the picture, he's seen again the beauty and nobility of the beasts he helped to slaughter all those years ago. Every brushstroke has been made with the sound of the wounded, defenceless creatures reverberating in his memory, their agonised bellows in the early hours of that Anzac Day morning somehow coming to symbolise and embody for him all the pain of the war.

As with the other paintings in the series, David has worked predominantly with black and red and umber, but in this picture the black impasto gives way to horizontal bands of lighter grey at the top of the canvas against which a streak of angry orange suggests the dawn. In the centre right foreground the water buffalo depicted in umber emerges from the blackness. Behind him, David has tried to suggest the paddies are scattered with literal blood and bone. He wonders now if the composition works.

He puts his brush and palette down. Sits and rolls a smoke. It's three in the afternoon and he's been working since early morning. The day began cold, the light diamond bright, the sky a luminous blue, but now those early grandeurs are beginning to fade and the sunshine through the window has an overripe quality presaging the slow fade towards dusk. He hopes the weather will remain fine for the weekend and Josie's birthday.

Now the five paintings of this Vietnam series are nearly finished, David is riven by doubts about the quality of his work. He doesn't know if any of them are good enough to offer as gifts to Josie and Lara. In the back of his mind, too, is the ultimate ambition of exhibiting and selling some canvases. As he sits and takes comfort from the tobacco, that goal seems impossibly distant.

He stands and prowls the room. The three paintings that constitute the *Redemption* triptych are propped against the long wall opposite the window, and the picture of the soldier carrying his comrade, *Bearing the Weight,* is on its own against the far short wall. He regards them in turn, trying to see them with detached eyes, trying to be critical.

The impossibility of accurately judging his own work frustrates him. He remembers Donna's advice to 'please himself'. There's no question he's had pleasure in the process of creating the work; but the product leaves him restless and dissatisfied, wishing for greater mastery to achieve his vision.

Bearing the Weight and the buffalo painting seem to him superior to the triptych. The complexities of the *Redemption* paintings have made for more interesting but less realised pictures. David also wonders whether Lara and Josie will understand the impulse behind the images of disjointed women, whether the dead girl on the track and the partial reflections of the bar girls—their legs, breasts, torsos, head—will seem too confronting. The final painting of the triptych, based on his sketches of Lara kneeling, might also seem too idealised placed against the other images.

On its own, though, at least it shares the simplicity of *Bearing the Weight*. The nude female figure reclines propped on an arm, her feet tucked to the side, her head in profile. Her right arm is decorated from the shoulder by a rose tattoo, the stem weaving from the elbow to a cerise bloom at the shoulder. As with the other paintings, the figure is placed against a black ground, which has abstract patterns down the right-hand margin in red and umber, which in this case are designed to suggest the anatomical beauty of bones and flesh. The woman is the light emerging from darkness.

David's reverie concerning his work is brought to an abrupt end by a vigorous pounding on his front door. He knows immediately it's Zak. The boy's small fists create a recognisable drumming. Since David's return from the coast, Zak has been a daily afternoon visitor, and when David hasn't been working, the routine of cartoon-watching has been resumed. On the occasions when David hasn't immediately wished to relinquish his brush, he's managed to set up Zak with some paper and crayons and persuaded the boy to have fun with drawing. In this way, their friendship has been consolidated and David has learned that he doesn't always have to be a solitary worker.

David opens the door and Zak walks in. 'Look at this, Dawid.' The boy opens his fist in which he's holding a small plastic model.

'Aha,' says David, 'it's Dino the dinosaur.'

'His name is Lawrence.'

'Why?'

'I do not know.'

'Right. Hot chocolate?'

'Yes please, yes please, yes please! With marshy mallows.'

In the cold weather, David has taken to concocting this treat for them both. It was something he did occasionally when Josie was young. He'd come home early from house painting and before going to the pub would lounge around at home. When Josie came in he'd make the chocolate and launch marshmallows on the frothy top. They'd drink it watching *Happy Days* together. He'd only done this once or twice with her, but somehow the memory is precious to him. Now, he's more conscious of the fleeting nature of such pleasures and is determined to make the most of his time with Zak.

David puts on a pan of milk to boil and waits ready to stir in the drinking chocolate. Zak stands next to him, chattering about Polly, his teacher, who has been telling the kids about dinosaurs.

'And do you know, Dawid,' Zak says, 'some of these dinosaurs was very big. As big as buildings, and their necks stretched all the way into the sky?'

'Mate, I'd heard they could be quite large.'

'They was 'normous.'

David spoons in the powder and stirs. This is his favourite

part, watching the transformation of colour and texture, before pouring the chocolate into mugs as the liquid comes to the boil.

Zak stands by his side, fiddling with his plastic dinosaur. He looks up and says in his most serious tones, 'What do you think would happen if you climbed up a dinosaur's neck?'

'I'm not sure the dinosaur would like it very much. He might be annoyed.'

'But it would be all right if he was a friendly dinosaur like Lawrence. And you could climb his neck right into the sky, past the buildings and past the moon and the stars and you could keep going up and up, past heaven and into Nowhere Land.'

David's eyes widen. Zak is on tiptoes, arms reaching skyward, following the path of his story.

'Blimey, Zak. Who told you about Nowhere Land?'

'Nobody.'

'You mean you made it up.'

'It's where you get to if you climb a dino-saur's neck.'

'Right. That's astonishing.'

David means what he says. He carries the mugs of hot chocolate over to the coffee table in front of the sofa. He switches the TV on. 'What do you reckon is in Nowhere Land, then?' he asks.

'You is silly, Dawid. Nothing is in Nowhere Land.'

Zak settles down to watch the cartoons, obviously confident in the promptings of his imagination.

David sits beside him and thinks about Nowhere Land.

¶

Later, Lara calls round and takes Zak home for his tea. She asks David if he'll be round later on. 'Too right,' David says, meeting the smile in her eyes.

When they've gone, David pours himself a whisky and returns to his painting room. He looks again at his work, still entranced by Zak's story of climbing the dinosaur's neck. What strikes David is the absolute conviction of the child's narration, the certainty that makes the impossible real. Thinking about this, he sees there's no point in trying to judge what he's done; other people will have to do that. The important thing is to keep working and to be true to his imagination. The work will then at least have integrity, if nothing else.

He leaves the room, whisky still in hand, and goes into his bedroom. Propping his glass on the little three-legged stool that serves as his bedside table, David gets on his knees and pulls from under the camp stretcher a wooden ammunition box. In it he keeps his memorabilia. He knows exactly what he's looking for. His time with Zak and Zak's story of Nowhere Land have taken David back to thoughts of his father and daughter. The gift of Zak's story has reminded him of something he must give Josie.

David removes from the box his medals, his discharge papers and the bundle of love letters that Margaret wrote to him while he was in Vietnam. His heart seems to take a heavier beat as he sees what he's looking for—an envelope with his name written in his father's hand. He puts the other stuff back in the box and takes the letter and his drink back to the table in the living room.

He takes the letter from the envelope. It's dated 3rd October 1987, the date of the Sydney Welcome Home march for Vietnam veterans, and approaching the 45th anniversary of the battles on the Kokoda track. But the old man had kept the letter back; it was given to David by his mother after his father died.

My dear son,

By the time you read this I will be gone. I hope you're not grieving for me and that this letter won't make you sad. I write it on this day to say how proud I am of you and what you did in serving your country. I wish you'd felt able to march today with the other veterans in Sydney. I think it would have been good for you. War is a ghastly business. I wish I could help you in your struggle to come to terms with it, but I honestly believe nothing I can say will help you. You have to find your own way to move on. I remember how long it took me after I came home from New Guinea.

I think perhaps you feel I should have said more to you about my experience of the war before you left for Vietnam. There was nothing I could say. I wasn't much of a soldier, and I couldn't bear for you to think badly of me. I don't remember the battle clearly. The terrain was terrible and we saw sights beyond description, the remains of the previous fighting, as we advanced across the track. When we engaged the Japs we were under fire and bombardment for days. I became what was known as 'bomb happy'. I have lived ever since with the fear that I was a coward and that I let down my mate, Lofty Dawson. He was as straight and true a man as you'd ever hope to meet. I'm told he died running to help someone who was wounded. He leapt forward under fire and was hit by a mortar round. I didn't go with him. I don't know why. I can't remember any of it. When I try to remember, it's like trying to bring back a dream or a nightmare. All I have are fragments and impressions, nothing clear or substantial.

I know we disagree about Anzac Day and parades like today's. For me, Anzac Day is a memorial and a penance. I go to remember and honour the dead, to mourn and to ask forgiveness. There's a sense with the other blokes, however little is said, that they understand how deep the feelings are. But your refusal to march has made me think a lot about things and I reckon I understand.

For some of us who fought, and for the bereaved relatives of those who didn't come back, Anzac Day becomes part of mourning. In recognising the dead, it gives meaning and comfort to the living. But for those who haven't been to war and have suffered no loss, the ritual can become the path to easy and spurious emotions. I know it's this you object to—the way that war can be made to seem glamorous, heroic and glorious—an incitement to the young to follow in their fathers' footsteps, as you have done.

I can see no answer to this puzzle. If you had a son, I'd

say be sure to show him the pleasures of peace. As it is, you're lucky enough to be blessed with a beautiful daughter. I hope you'll learn to look after her and Margaret. You and your mother are the best part of my life. Perhaps you will be able to interest Josie in gardening. After your mum, you two and Lofty, I loved my garden best.

I hope you will be able to remember and think kindly of me sometimes. I'm sorry I've left things unspoken between us. There was so much I couldn't find words for. Not least how much I love you. Be a better man than me, son. Look after your mum and Margaret and Josie. Go well in the world,

With much love,

Dad

David takes another slug of whisky and wipes the moisture from his eyes. He determines to photocopy his father's words. The time has come, he thinks, for Josie to see them. The letter speaks out of the silence of Nowhere Land and now he sees he must give it to Josie with the painting *Bearing the Weight*.

The two go together, part of the same legacy.

XXVIII

The first few moments when they are all together at the community gardens are awkward. They've seen each other before, but Josie and Lara have never been formally introduced. David does the honours, but it's clear neither Josie nor Lara know how to react. Should they hug? Shake hands? Kiss? Lara takes a step towards Josie as if to offer an embrace, but something in Josie's stiff manner and forced smile stops her. Dylan sketches a half-hearted wave when David announces him. Zak stands and stares, uncertain who all these people are and what they mean.

David hurries to get things moving. 'Come on,' he says. 'There's no time to stand staring. There's work to be done.' He indicates the beds that need weeding. Once weed free, the soil needs turning over and spreading with straw and manure, ready for planting.

He dishes out the tools. With a grin, he suggests Lara and Josie work together on one bed, while he and Dylan tackle the other. Zak is free to roam or help. He's armed with his own miniature spade and trowel. Dressed in his blue wellington boots and red anorak he's ready for action.

David knows he's taking a chance pairing Lara and Josie, but he has faith in them both. If they learn to relax with each other, give each other a chance, he knows it will be okay.

As they begin work there's not much chatter, everyone concentrating on their allotted tasks. David keeps an eye on Lara, Josie and Zak. He overhears Zak say to Josie, 'Is Dawid your dad?' When Josie says *yes* the little boy is assertive. 'Well, Dawid's my mate,' he says, before asking Josie if she likes dinosaurs. The little boy embarks on a long monologue concerning Lawrence the Dinosaur and his long neck which leads into the sky and Nowhere Land.

'I'd like to do that, sometime,' Josie replies. 'Climb into Nowhere Land.'

For a moment David thinks her sentiment is uttered with too much heartfelt seriousness. But then he sees she's smiling. Maybe she's just playing the game. He hopes so.

After an hour or so, everyone has warmed up. It's a blustery day with mild sunshine and lots of sheep's fleece clouds unravelling across the sky. It's easy to work up a sweat, but if you stand too long the chill invades and reminds that spring is still a couple of months away yet.

David watches Lara and Josie leaning on their spades, taking a breather. Lara is asking Josie about college and her plans for the future. Josie talks about not knowing what to do and the difficulty of deciding on a career at the age of sixteen. Lara sympathises, talks about the problems of balancing work with looking after Zak. By the time they go back to work, it seems some of the strangeness between them has dissipated.

Dylan remains uncommunicative. David wonders if he should bite the bullet and initiate another conversation about the army. But he decides he's said enough. If the lad asks, he'll answer. But it doesn't seem right to interfere any further. David doesn't want to set himself up as some kind of font of wisdom. He doesn't have the confidence for that.

Lara and David have brought food and coffee for lunch. They spread a blanket close by the hut in which David keeps his gear. They eat hard boiled eggs and tomatoes, cheese and bread rolls.

'Why is it,' Josie asks, 'food tastes extra good outside? It's like when we were camping. I love being outdoors like this.'

They all agree with Josie. Even Dylan is enthusiastic. 'I never want to work in an office,' he declares. 'I couldn't stand being cooped up all day.'

Josie agrees with him.

'You'll have to be gardeners.' David smiles.

'Or park rangers,' Lara offers.

'Or vintners,' David says. '*In a high hunger and heavenly thirst, the good men made the wine.*' He can't remember where he's dredged that from. It's a poem his father was fond of.

The kids look at each other. They don't say anything.

After lunch, once the veggie beds are prepared, David organises the planting of leeks, potatoes, cauliflower, onions, garlic and broccoli. Dylan helps him put up a trellis for peas. Around the borders of the beds, David distributes herb seedlings for planting: sage and thyme, marjoram and coriander. He gives

Zak a watering can so the little boy can have fun watering in the plants and seeds. He sprays water all over the place.

By the time their work is done, the afternoon is well advanced, the sun dropping from the sky and the beginning of evening chill apparent on the breeze. David is pleased with the day's work and the way everyone seemed to enjoy it. A relaxed camaraderie has been achieved. Now it's time to go back to the flats for hot showers and dinner.

¢

Lara takes Zak for a bath while David hosts Josie and Dylan. Josie says she'll go last in the shower because she wants to wash her hair. When Dylan and David are out of the bathroom, David sticks the footy on TV and liberates a couple of beers from the fridge. It's a luxurious feeling after the day's work, glowing from a hot shower, to sit and kick-back with a cold VB. Dylan certainly seems to enjoy it.

The beer seems to loosen Dylan a little. He's more inclined to chat, even though his knee has a manic bounce. He says, 'I've been thinking about what you said, you know, about the army and that. I'm still kind of interested in it—I mean, it's not like working in an office or in industry, is it? It seems more active, more worthwhile. It *is* service. And there might not be a war. I mean, there's peacekeeping, isn't there? It's not necessarily about violence.'

'Look, mate,' David says. 'Like I said before, I don't want to tell you what to do. I'm glad you're giving it some thought. If you're going in, go in with your eyes open. The trouble is there's always a war to go to. Look what's happening in the Middle East right now with this stand-off between Iraq and Kuwait. It's brewing up nicely. It'll kick-off sooner or later and the story's always the same. It will be in Australia's national interest to support the Yanks and fight. It's worth bearing in mind that the 'national interest' doesn't necessarily equate to an ethical decision. If it's raining, it might be in my interest to steal your umbrella, but it doesn't make it right.'

David shuts up. He realises he's mounted a hobbyhorse and ridden it hard. Dylan looks a bit glazed.

'Sorry,' David says. 'You can tell this stuff gets to me. I don't believe in patriotism, my country right or wrong and all that. I think it's bullshit. But I shouldn't be shoving my ideas down your throat. You have to think it through for yourself.'

Dylan nods. 'It's good to talk about it, but,' he says. 'My dad's not interested. He says I should do whatever I like.'

David doesn't want to take that remark much further. He says, 'Well, I suppose there's something to that as well.'

He's relieved when Josie walks into the room with a towel turban wrapped round her hair. She's discarded the green dungarees worn for gardening in favour of a powder-blue jumper worn over a red plaid miniskirt with black tights and black block-heel shoes. Both outfits today have gladdened David. He hopes she's learning the colours of her happiness. She looks a picture.

It brings David's conversation with Dylan to an end when she says with a smile that it's good to see them bonding.

Once Josie has given her hair another rub and combed it out, the three of them troop next door. David initiates the cook-a-thon. In memory of the Durras Lake camp, he's devised a menu of veggie curries: potato and pea, eggplant masala, pumpkin curry, and daal. He gets the kids peeling and chopping, while Lara sorts the music. She chooses Hunters and Collectors rocking it out. Zak is busy showing Josie his robot and Mr Robinson. She takes time out from veggie prep to build Lego with the little boy.

Soon, David has the onion, ginger, garlic and chilli frying, filling the kitchen with fragrant fumes. Lara passes round the cold beers. The atmosphere is just what David had hoped for: relaxed and festive, unconstrained, informal. A happy time.

Zak is allowed to stay up for dinner. Everyone crowds round the table and hoes into the feast. There's rice with the curries as well as pickles and pappadams, ice-cold water and beers. Zak says the curries are ''isgusting' but still manages to eat some of the milder ones—the daal and the potato. When everyone has finished eating, David on a high because the day's gone so well, decides he must make a toast. He wishes Josie a happy birthday and proposes raising a glass to 'winter sowing and new beginnings.'

Lara enters into the spirit with a toast to new friendships. David quickly follows with 'Here's to romance: Josie and Dylan.' The boy blushes bright scarlet.

Zak says, 'What about me?'

Josie reacts immediately and proposes a toast to Zak and Lawrence the Dinosaur and Mr Robinson.

The bright and bubbly atmosphere can't last. It's way past Zak's bedtime. Lara apologises for breaking up the party, but she's sure Zak needs to be settled down for the night.

Zak isn't so sure. 'I'm sorry, I cannot do that,' he says.

'*I'm sorry,* but you'll have to do that,' his mum replies.

This is David's cue. So far, he's been carried along on a tide of elation, but now he registers a tightening, a weight on his chest, a slightly breathless quality. Addressing himself to the room, he says, 'I need to borrow Josie for a few minutes, if that's all right?' He looks first to Dylan, then meets Lara's eyes. She knows what he's up to and gives him a small nod of encouragement. Dylan shrugs, looking perplexed and not entirely happy to be left alone.

'Won't be long,' David offers. 'Come on, Jo-Jo, I want to show you something.'

Josie frowns a little. She realises something serious is coming. She looks as if she doesn't know whether to be nervous or excited. David leads her next door.

'What's this about, Pa? What's the big mystery?'

'Wait on a minute,' he says. 'You'll see soon enough.' He goes into the kitchen and pours himself a small whisky, while Josie stands watchful and uncertain.

'Righto,' David says. 'Here we go. Step this way.' He leads her into his painting room and switches on the light. On the easel, is *Bearing the Weight*. On the wall opposite the windows, he's hung the *Redemption* triptych. On the far wall is the water buffalo painting he's entitled *Totem*. The glossy black, red, and umber of the paintings shine in the light. There are whites as well. David enjoys the drama of his work, has a momentary flutter of pride.

Josie stops in the centre of the room gazing around. 'Oh, my God,' she whispers.

David sips his drink. He doesn't know what more to expect from her, if anything. Josie stares at each of the paintings in turn. Still, she says nothing. David is aware of a heightening tension. Maybe she doesn't like them. Maybe she thinks they're too weird.

After another long look at each canvas, Josie says, 'These are ... amazing. I'm not sure I understand them, but they look *fantastic*.'

'You don't need to *understand* them,' David says. It's enough to look at them. I mean really *look* at them. See how you respond.'

'I love them,' Josie says. 'They're such a surprise. They don't, like, depict war at all, but I can see how they relate.'

'That's the point,' David says. 'I don't want to explain them to you. Except to say they're about transformation. No art can depict the reality of war. War is brutal, ugly, chaotic. Art is about beauty, order, significance. I've tried to make something meaningful out of the awfulness. That's all there is to it.'

He pauses for a moment. Josie is still looking at the pictures, moving from one to another. 'They're wonderful,' she says. 'Awesome.'

'I want you to have this one.' David points to *Bearing the Weight*. 'For your birthday. I painted it with your granddad in mind. I'd like to think it might be a token between you and me. It's the only way I have of saying something to you about Vietnam. And Jo-Jo, I'd like you to forgive me for all the bad times when you were little and all the sad times I've caused you. I want to do better from now on. Less booze and smokes, too.' He takes a breath, smiles and drains his whisky.

'I also want you to have this.' David picks up the envelope he's left on the chair, ready. 'It's a copy of a letter my dad wrote to me. I think you're old enough to understand it now. It explains a lot about Granddad and the war. And me, I guess.'

Josie moves to open the envelope, but David puts a restraining hand on her arm.

'No need to read it here and now. Save it for later, when you have a quiet moment.'

Josie comes to him and walks into his arms. David can feel the tears on his cheek as he kisses her.

They stand in the middle of the room holding each other for a long time.

XXIX

There are no short cuts. It's about dredging images out of the dark.

It's 4.00 am in the morning, it's cold and clear outside, the sky purple and splashed with stars. David is in his painting room, under the garish yellow of the unshaded electric light, contemplating the beginning of another Vietnam painting. His trip to the coast has given him the idea. Round the camp fire with Josie and Dylan he found words he didn't know he possessed. Now, he's making sketches for a composition he's already titled *Telling the Story.*

In the left foreground he has the fire, the focus of light, illuminating the spectral figures seated around its margin. Beyond, David hopes to figure the forest in different shades of coal. The more difficult part of the work, with which he's now struggling, is to suggest unnatural creatures in and amongst the trees. He thinks of them as the dancing devils of the dark, gargoyles and goblins, but somehow he has to make them subtle, blended shapes so that an observer will see them as they might with night eyes, uncertain as to their veracity or meaning.

As he works, he thinks about the demons that drive his insomnia and the way that he's learned to carry his war in different ways. 'It's about transformation.' That's what he told Josie. That's what he believes. Grief and anger and shame never go away—they just change shape. If you're lucky they become lighter to bear, easier to heft. But you have to take them with you. No one else can carry the burden.

Lara and Zak, Josie and Dylan are the companions of his work. He trusts they are peacefully asleep. He's determined from now on to be more involved with Josie's life. He doesn't want to impose on her or stifle her with concern, but he's intent on fostering their newfound relationship. He reckons sharing the garden with her and Dyl is going to be part of that.

David smiles to himself, thinking how pleased his dad would be with the kids' interest.

There's not much more he can do or say if Dylan insists on pursuing his interest in joining the army. Josie is worried about it, too. But maybe like so many young men before him, Dylan has to go his own way and find out for himself the cost of surrendering to the romance of military service. Josie might mount her own campaign against it. David hopes so.

As for Lara and Zak, David hardly dares hope that the blessing of this second chance might last. In the long run, he wonders if Lara will understand and cope with his need for solitary hours, the demands of his wakeful nights, the oppression of his violent dreams. But he recognises there's no point in trying to foretell the future.

For now, things are working out fine.

They've agreed to maintain their two separate households and to spend some nights apart. The combination of space and proximity suits them both. Zak, they figure, has the best of both worlds. While they are happy with their arrangement, why change it?

David lays down the charcoal with which he's been mapping the new canvas. He sits in his battered chair and rolls a smoke. He's both tired and exhilarated. In a minute, he'll brew some coffee to keep him going until dawn. Then, he has a plan. He'll walk out early to the city markets and buy some fruit and croissants and a small bunch of flowers and surprise Lara and Zak for breakfast. It's a way of thanking them for enabling his night of work.

Back at the easel, David labours on. He tries not to analyse but to follow his intuition, allowing the ambiguity of his drifting thoughts and feelings to fuel his vision. He's aware that round the camp fire at Durras Lake, somehow he said enough to satisfy Josie.

At least, for now.

To keep the darkness and the devils at bay.

He hopes she will never ask him for more. Like all stories, his depend on what's left unsaid. He knows there are things he will never learn to speak—the death of his mate by friendly fire, the dead Vietnamese girl on the track, the massacre of the buffalo—the brutal particularities of his war will remain only his. There will be no sharing of atrocities. For better or worse, there are things Josie will never find out. The communion around the fire depends on silences. David wants his painting to embody and deliver this paradox: the truth of the truth never told.

In the absorption of his pursuit time goes quickly, and soon David is aware of the light changing. The sound of vehicles on the road outside begins to intensify. The day is beginning and the solitary hours of creative effort are nearly done. He's made a good start on a work he knows will keep him obsessively interested in the days to come—a source of energy and hope.

It's no hardship to stop now. David leaves his painting room and switches out the light. In the bathroom with the heater on he quickly discards the layers of his clothes, realising that he's let himself get cold while he was drawing. The hot shower feels as if he's rinsing clear the dark places where his art has taken him, making him ready for another day in the life. He shaves, too, deciding to present his best face next door when he turns up with the treats.

Dressed again, David puts on his jacket and boots, grabs his wallet and ventures out into the fresh early morning. The light provides a fine glaze; the day is beginning to sparkle. He strides along the concrete walkway. There's no sign of life at Lara's yet. He hopes to be back just as they're stirring.

Full of purpose, he's down the steps and onto the street. As he turns into Limestone Avenue and walks towards the city, his breath making clouds, he knows he is a lucky man.

Acknowledgements

A Winter Sowing is a work of fiction. No attempt has been made to recreate precise historical events relating to specific units serving in Vietnam. My appreciation of the Australian military experience in Vietnam has, however, been enhanced by several works of non-fiction, in particular: Robert A. Hall, *Combat Battalion,* Allen and Unwin, 2000; Gary McKay, *In Good Company,* Allen and Unwin, 1987 and *Delta Four,* Allen and Unwin, 1996; Brian Hennessy, *The Sharp End,* Allen and Unwin, 1997. The many unpublished letters, diaries and memoirs recording experiences in Vietnam held by the Australian War Memorial in Canberra also proved invaluable.

Since the novel is set some years ago, various locations in Canberra and Bateman's Bay have been described through the filter of memory and imagination. For the sake of David Young's journey, I have also taken some liberties with the geography, roads and trails through Murramarang National Park.

The 'someone famous' David Young quotes on p.62 is, of course, Leonardo Da Vinci. And the lines he remembers on p.208 are from John Shaw Neilson's wonderful poem, *The Good*

Men and the Wine. David's *Bearing the Weight* was inspired by my friend Stephen Harrison's painting, *Angel Cradling Pilot*. I'm also indebted to Stephen for sharing with me some of his methods, which David emulates. (Stephen is not a Vietnam Veteran). David Young's other paintings are the product of his imagination. My thanks to another friend, Russell Smith, and his son, Isaac, for the gift of 'Nowhere Land.' I'm grateful to Jude Barlow for her generous response to my questions about Indigenous culture.

Jane Novak has been a source of wise advice about the publishing industry for several years. Rebecca Wylie's editing and copy-editing of the manuscript has been exemplary. I'm very grateful for her astute interventions which pushed me to improve the book. Likewise, my gratitude goes to Luke Harris for his care and expertise with typesetting and design. Many thanks to Nick Walker and the team at ASP/Arcadia for publishing my work.

Friends and family have lent their support to me and my writing through challenging times. In particular, I'd like to thank Richard Caesar, Lottie Ladbury and Jane Campbell. My biggest debt of gratitude is to Claire, who lived through the tough times with me and whose belief in me and my work has never wavered. Without her this book would not have come into being. It goes without saying that any deficiencies in the work are all mine.

Further information about Adrian Caesar and his work may be found at www.adriancaesar.com

Printed in Australia
AUHW021219130122
358187AU00002B/2

9 781922 454997